WINTER MOON

The Paha Sapa Saga Book Two

Robin Deeter

Can a passionate romance survive in a land fraught with danger and turmoil?

Handsome French fur trader, Ames Duchamp, and beautiful Kiowa warrior, Willow, have been secretly engaged in a fiery, all-consuming love affair. When tragedy brings their relationship to light, can they withstand the heartache and hold onto their love or will feelings of inadequacy and pride tear their happiness to shreds?

Continue the adventure set in mid-eighteenth century North America, which is a hotbed of unrest between many Native American tribes, who are feuding over territory. Follow the exploits of our newly allied Kiowa and Lakota tribes as they settle in a new land and face danger and uncertainty.

Table of Contents

Dedication

This book is dedicated to all you brave readers who continue to accompany me on this adventure. We still have new characters to meet, exciting events to share, and new places to explore together. I hope you enjoy reading this story as much as I enjoyed writing it. As always, your faith, friendship, and kindness are so very appreciated. Happy reading!

A Special Thank You

To my Essie, you are my rock and my biggest fan. You're always there to cheer me on and give me a kick in the caboose when I need it. I treasure your love and loyalty and I couldn't do this without you.

There are people who leave indelible marks on your life and I'm blessed to have an incredible group of people who support me and help me with my endeavors. There are several people I must thank for being there for me when I first struck out on my own. Christy Urquiola Stetson, Rebecca Edwards, Barbara Ainley Wright, and Crystal Lynn Kirby held my hand, so to speak, and helped me navigate the tricky waters of becoming an Indie author. I'll always be grateful to them for supporting me during that rocky period and for their friendship.

I'm also sending a huge thank you to my fantastic beta readers, the Deeter Streeters: Sheila Davis, Avyona Cripps, John P. George, Angie Mitchell, Rachel Donegan Hart, Harriet Renaud, Jessica Miller, Mary Wiles, Jennifer Church, Kathie Hamilton, Sydnee Walsh, Janet M. Smith, and Anne Rollin. They provide valuable insights into my stories and catch my booboos. They're also fun to work with and I'm incredibly grateful to them for making my books better.

Other books by Robin Deeter

**Chance City Beginnings
(Prequels to Chance City Series)**

Part One
Part Two

Chance City Series

Mail Order Mystery
Mail Order Mystery Audio Book
Mail Order Mystery Print Book
On the Fence
Crossroads
Gray Justice
When the Thunder Rolls
And the Lightning Strikes

The Paha Sapa Saga

Sacrifice and Reward
Sacrifice and Reward Audio Book
Sacrifice and Reward Print Book
Winter Moon
The Bear, Part One
The Bear, Part Two
The Phantom Horse Bridge Series

Phantom Origins Book 0
Phantom Heat

Wolf Junction Series

Silver Bell Shifter

Chapter One

Traveling through the snow didn't bother Ames Duchamp at all. In fact, he loved the cold season when the drifts were deep and the world was still. There was a peace about winter that suited him perfectly. However, since it was only early October, the couple of snowstorms they'd had hadn't amounted to very much. Therefore, they'd made good time.

As he trekked southward along the Mississippi River, he was accompanied by fifteen pack dogs, three mules, and two Indian friends. Firebrand was a former Mohawk captive of the Fox Indians, whom Ames had won gambling three years prior. Ames had immediately freed him, saying that he could return home if he so desired.

However, Firebrand had stayed with Ames to repay him for giving him his freedom by helping with Ames' fur trading business. He hadn't been treated kindly by the Fox and he was extremely grateful to Ames for rescuing him. Firebrand's ancestors harkened back to the mighty Susquehannock Indians, the vast majority of which had been absorbed by the Iroquois Nation almost a century earlier.

After their numbers had been greatly depleted by diseases brought by the white man, the Susquehannocks had been defeated by the Iroquois around 1676. Some of Firebrand's relatives had kept their oral stories alive, telling him tales of their ancestors' great battles and about their strongholds in the East.

Having been very impressed by all of this, Firebrand had decided to honor his ancestors by altering his appearance to look like them. He was a fairly large fellow and wore his hair in the old Susquehannock manner; shaved on the right side, cocks comb in the middle, and grown long on the left side.

Ames' other friend, Panther, was a member of the Kiowa tribe that Ames now considered his family. Panther was shorter in stature, perhaps five ten or thereabouts, and wore his hair in the Kiowa style, with bangs and his hair cut short over his right ear.

At six-four, Ames was taller than either of his companions and broad with his height. His own pack weighed close to eighty pounds, yet he carried it with ease. Although he was a Frenchman by birth, there were Swedes on his mother's side, big blond men, whom he took after physically.

Although in his heart he would always be part French, he'd become Indian, too. He'd had run-ins with many different tribes, but he got along with most of them. His father, François, had brought him and his mother to the New World, where Ames had quickly began making friends with various Indians who traded with the English, French, Dutch, and Swedes.

His father had seen nothing wrong with this, in fact, Ames' ability to quickly learn languages had come in handy, and he'd begun taking Ames with him on his trade runs when he'd been a boy of just eleven years old. Ames had been in the fur trading business ever since, taking over for François when he'd passed on.

His mother, Marie, had remarried and moved to Boston, away from the vast wilderness that she'd never embraced. Ames had been twenty years old at the time. Marie had wanted him to go with her, but the fur trade was in his blood and the Indians were in his soul, and he wouldn't leave either. Eight years later, here he was making his way south to spend the winter with the people he loved most in the world—and the woman who held his heart.

Although he walked silently as he led one of the mules, in his head, Ames sang a bawdy French song about a buxom, lusty tavern wench who was very generous with her attentions. Yet, he was still acutely aware of their surroundings, his companions, and their pack animals.

The surefooted mules followed easily and the dogs were largely silent as they'd been trained to be. The big, wolfish beasts trotted along, keeping their trace lines straight. Their lead and heel dogs made sure they did so. Tangled trace lines could get caught on brush or other obstacles and cause all sorts of problems.

Ames smiled as they neared his village, but when he let out his wild cat screech, there was no answering signal from the sentries. He stopped, as did Firebrand and Panther. He let out another screech, but still silence reigned in the snowy forest.

He signed, "I do not like this. There are no sentries. This is not good."

Panther shook his head a little while Firebrand signed, "We will stay with the animals while you find out what is happening." It would be better to have two guards with all the animals and cargo.

Ames nodded and took off his pack, laying it beside his mule, which he tied to a sapling. He was already wearing a pistol and a quiver of arrows. He untied his bow from where it was lashed to his mule. Setting out for Chief Growling Wolf's village, Ames moved as silently as possible, keeping a sharp eye out for any movement. Presently, he came to a spot that overlooked the camp and kept hidden as he peered through the foliage at the village. People moved about the camp, but they weren't *his* people.

Ojibwa. Ames' heart sank to his feet as he recognized their garb. *Where is my family? What have you done to them?* He fought back his apprehension as he remembered the hiding place and his instructions to his little friend, Moonbeam, to leave him a message if need be. Hope rose in his breast as he left the edge of the village.

He couldn't go through the camp to the secret cave as he normally would have. Instead, he backtracked and used an alternate route to reach it. His bow at the ready, he proceeded cautiously, making sure that there were no guards posted near it.

When he was able to reach the little clearing at the mouth of the cave, Ames saw that no one had been there. The snow was too pristine, indicating that the Ojibwa hadn't discovered the cave. Taking out his strike-a-light, he made his way into the narrow passageway, feeling his way along until he entered the large anteroom within the mountain.

Creating a series of sparks, he was able to make it to the hidden crevasse in the wall on his left side. Reaching inside it, he felt a parfleche and smiled. *Ah, my little Moonbeam! What a good girl you are to have remembered.* He took heart from the presence of the small package. It meant that at least some of his family still lived.

Back outside in the daylight, Ames opened the parfleche and took out a piece of paper. Unfolding it, he saw a dark mountain range drawn on it, along with a note telling him that his family had gone there and that he should go to them. His heart raced with elation and he grinned as he tucked the paper back into the parfleche and stuffed it inside his thick, wolf-skin coat.

Greatly heartened, he quickly made his way back to his party.

Quietly, he said, "They have gone west, to the place of a dark mountain. We must alter our course."

Firebrand's eyebrows rose. "That is all the information they left? Dark mountains?"

Ames grinned. "That is all the information we need, no? We will find them."

Panther and Firebrand nodded. Ames' uncanny ability to find people when it seemed they'd disappeared had stood him well over the years. They had no doubt that he'd find their family.

Turning to the west, they set out at a good clip, determined to make as much progress as possible before nightfall.

The next day, they followed the route that the Kiowas most likely would have taken. They looked closely for clues left for them and were rewarded.

Mid-afternoon, Panther stopped and pointed to a tree. "Ames, look."

Ames almost shouted with joy, but caught himself at the last minute. The loud noise could potentially alert their location to enemies who might be traveling nearby. Ames hurried over to the elm tree and traced the A on its trunk with his mitten-clad hand.

"We are on the right track, *mes freres.*"

Firebrand smiled at his calling him and Panther his brothers because he knew that Ames genuinely thought of himself as such.

They resumed their steady pace. Four days later, they saw the black mountain range in the distance. It took them another couple of days before they began seeing signs of civilization. They came across some footprints and a scalp hung on a nearby tree.

Panther examined it. "It is not cut in the Kiowa manner. I cannot tell which tribe it is otherwise, but it is a warning to stay away."

Ames blue eyes took on a fierce light. "Perhaps it is a sign from our family. We will soon find out."

They came upon the camp suddenly, a vast village that was much too large to be their family's.

"Lakota," Firebrand said. "They are the ones who left the scalp."

Ames looked at the village and then up at the mountains beyond it. Although dangerous to take a chance, especially given the precious cargo they carried, Ames decided to risk approaching the Lakota. He'd had dealings with them in the past, but most likely not this particular band.

Calculating their valuables, he mentally went through what he could afford to trade and what he was reserving for their family.

Grimly, he said, "There is nothing to do but to go meet them."

And so, they started towards the village, apprehensive about what kind of reception awaited them.

Lakota brave, Rushing Bull, stood sentry in a small stand of pine trees near the eastern edge of his village. The line of dogs, mules, and men walking across the landscape near their camp had captured his attention when they'd come over a rise and stopped. After a few moments of conferring, they'd changed direction and had started towards the camp.

Although still somewhat suspicious, he was almost certain that these were the friends that his tribe's Kiowa kin were expecting. During their travels together and their time as neighbors, Growling Wolf's tribe had told them much about Ames Duchamp and his friends, Firebrand and Panther.

The pack dogs and mules were a dead giveaway because most of their people didn't travel with dogs anymore since horses were plentiful now. However, someone like Ames would still be dependent on those modes of transporting goods. Dog sleds and wagons were cumbersome in snowy, wooded areas, but pack dogs and mules could easily traverse such terrain.

As they neared, Rushing Bull stepped from his hiding spot, his bow at the ready. "Stop! This is Lakota land!"

The dogs started growling and the hair along their backs rose in response to his threatening manner. One of the men spoke quietly to them and they all laid down. Another man, one wearing a wolf-skin coat raised a hand.

"*Hau*, we are peaceful. We only seek information," he said in Lakota.

Rushing Bull smiled at his strange accent, now even more sure that this was Ames Duchamp. He lowered his bow and walked towards them.

"Perhaps you would like to know where those filthy Kiowa are?"

Anger glinted in the man's blue eyes, but his lips curved in a smile. "I would be careful about insulting my family."

Rushing Bull grinned. "Why? They speak just as badly of us. They have been waiting for you, Ames Duchamp."

Ames' eyes widened. "How did you know who I was?" His tribe would never give up his name for any reason.

"We are kin now, you and I," Rushing Bull said to allay his worry. "My good friend, Dark Horse, married one of your women, Sky Dancer. We are now allies and kin. Your medicine man is betrothed to one of our maidens."

Ames shook his head a little. "Why would Singing Water be taking another wife?"

A look of sadness settled on Rushing Bull's face. "The one you speak of finished his journey along the Red Road. I am afraid that he is not the only one."

Ames, a temperamental man by nature, had trouble containing his grief. "How many?"

Rushing Bull shrugged, which meant too many for him to count.

"Shit! Shit! Shit!" Ames swore in French.

Rushing Bull stepped back from him, surprised by the outburst. He wasn't used to such behavior, nor did he know the French word Ames had practically shouted. While Ames stomped back and forth, swearing and acting like a crazy man, Rushing Bull looked over the two Indians with him.

He was surprised by the one's hair style, a kind he'd never seen before. He had no idea what tribe the man might come from, but the other man he recognized as Kiowa. By this time, Ames had whipped off his beaver pelt hat and thrown it on the ground, whereupon he stomped on it a couple of times.

Rushing Bull cocked an eyebrow, truly beginning to wonder if Ames was possessed of some sort of spirit. He'd seen men angry before, but never had he witnessed such histrionics.

Ames finally stopped and took out his knife, a fine specimen, Rushing Bull noted. Ames yanked his long hair out from under his coat. He cut off the sun-colored mass, leaving the rest of it not quite shoulder-length. The Indians with him did the same. In this way, Rushing Bull realized that they also considered themselves family with the Kiowas.

Unabashedly, Ames brushed away his tears and said, "What do they call you, brother?"

"Rushing Bull."

Ames brushed his hat off and put it back on. "This is Firebrand and Panther." He motioned to each man in turn. "They speak Lakota. There is no need for sign."

Rushing Bull nodded. "Welcome. Come meet our chief. Soaring Falcon is anxious to make your acquaintance. We will give you food and you can rest."

"How far are we from our tribe?" Ames asked.

Sensing Ames' impatience, Rushing Bull replied, "Not quite a day's travel, but the hour grows late. You would be better to stay the night and leave at first light. You can visit with Cricket."

Ames gave him a sharp look. "Do you mean Chirping Cricket?"

"He was Chirping Cricket, but he was renamed simply Cricket by the Spirit of Bison. It is a long story, one that he should tell you," Rushing Bull said.

"Why is he here?" Panther asked.

"He is your medicine man now and comes to learn healing from our medicine men. He is the one betrothed to our chief's granddaughter. Although a good healer and very powerful in other ways, he still has much to learn and there is no one else to teach him." Rushing Bull shook his head. "He has had much to endure, but he is strong despite being as skinny as a stick."

Ames couldn't make further inquiries because they'd now entered the camp. He and his friends knew better than to speak to the women, but they did nod in a friendly way as they followed Rushing Bull. People began following them, something that the trio was used to when they peddled their wares.

The dogs took exception to this and growled whenever people came too close. They'd been trained to guard their loads and did their job well. They came to a large lodge that Ames realized must belong to the Lakota chief.

Suddenly, Ames' lead dog, a furry, gray brute, yipped excitedly and bowed down playfully. He jumped up and let out a howl, which was echoed by the other dogs. Ames and his companions had to forcefully restrain the canines from entering the tipi.

"What is wrong with them?" Rushing Bull asked.

Ames laughed. "There is someone in there that they know."

Rushing Bull said, "Most likely Cricket. As far as I know, none of your other family is here."

As if summoned, a figure emerged from the tipi and Ames grinned. "Chirping Cricket!" He grabbed the surprised young man, hugging him and switching to Kiowa. "I have missed you! Your sister did exactly as I told her. Between that and your clues, we were able to find you. How are you?" He pulled back, taking the boy's face in his hands, and looking into his eyes.

Cricket laughed. "Much better now that I know you are all safe and sound."

Ames grinned and then kissed each of Cricket's cheeks in the way of the French. "Did you doubt us? What have I always told you?"

Cricket's grin widened. "That you are Ames Duchamp, able to find anyone, anywhere."

"Right!"

Panther and Firebrand also fondly greeted the young man, grasping arms with him and inquiring after his family.

Immediately, Cricket sobered. "This fall was a terrible time. We were attacked by the Ojibwa and forced from our homelands. Many of us no longer walk this life, including my father and my mentor. Nor Sky Dancer's father."

Having vented some of his initial grief earlier, Ames was able to contain himself now. He didn't want to embarrass Cricket in front of the Lakota. He also wanted to support the boy and he couldn't do that if he was ranting and raving like a lunatic. However, his eyes stung and his chest felt tight with sadness. Fear that the woman of his heart also walked the next life filled him with dread.

Putting a hand on Cricket's shoulder, he said, "I am greatly grieved by all of this news. Rushing Bull told us that there were losses, but he could not name them all."

Cricket swallowed back tears. "It is a long, sad story, I am afraid."

Another person emerged from the lodge.

Rushing Bull said, "Chief Soaring Falcon, this is the famed Ames Duchamp and his friends, Firebrand and Panther."

Ames smiled at the man who stood proudly before him. "It is good to meet more kin," he said, holding out his hand.

Soaring Falcon took his measure, noting that he was about Rushing Bull's size. It had been a while since he'd seen any of the Iron Makers, as the older generations had called the whites. His keen eyes took in Ames' vivid blue eyes, golden hair, and darker gold beard. He saw that Ames had cut his hair, a sign that he grieved. "It is good to meet such a famous man." Soaring Falcon grasped arms with Ames as he returned his smile. "Please come inside out of the cold. My wife and granddaughter will fix you something to eat." He caught sight of Firebrand. "A *Gandastogue*?"

Firebrand recognized the old tribal name of his ancestors and was surprised that Soaring Falcon knew it or that those were the people from whom he came. He asked, "Do you know my ancestor's language?"

Soaring Falcon replied, "Only a few words. I have not heard about any of your people in a long time. I thought they were all dead."

Firebrand shook his head. "Most were absorbed by the Mohawks and other Iroquois, but there are still a few old ones who remember our original people."

Soaring Falcon nodded his understanding as his eyes noted the dogs and mules. He was curious as to what kinds of goods the trio of men had brought. "Rushing Bull, show our guests to the council lodge. They can leave all of their packs there." To Ames, he said, "Nothing will happen to your things. You have my word."

Cricket smiled. "He speaks the truth. Come. I will help you."

He and Rushing Bull led the way to the council lodge. The dogs wouldn't allow Rushing Bull to approach them, so he just stood out of the way. Cricket played with the dogs as he helped remove packs and harnesses. They stored all the packs inside the lodge and tethered the dogs outside of it.

Ames sorted through his own pack, pulled several sacks made from duffle cloth from it and put it inside the lodge. Firebrand and Panther did the same with their packs.

"Do not worry," Rushing Bull said. "Your things will be safe."

"Thank you," Ames said.

Cricket took them back the way they'd come.

Ames said, "Rushing Bull tells us that you are betrothed. Is that true?"

Cricket smiled bashfully. "Yes. Her name is Hummingbird and she is Soaring Falcon's granddaughter."

"You look happy about this."

Cricket nodded. "Yes. She will be a good wife and she is very pretty."

Ames was highly amused by Cricket's shyness. "When is the wedding? I am glad that I did not miss it."

"Oh, it will not be for three years," Cricket replied. "I cannot support a wife yet."

"It is wise of you to wait," Ames said as they arrived at Soaring Falcon's tipi.

The three travelers went inside with Cricket, were introduced around, and given a meal. When it concluded, Cricket began his sad tale.

Chapter Two

Cricket's arrival with their three returning family members created much excitement among the Kiowa band. Between the dogs greeting their human family with barks and yips and all the human crosstalk, it was a noisy time.

As was his custom, Ames embraced most of his kin, expressing both joy at seeing them and grief over their lost loved ones. Soaring Falcon had also accompanied them and he watched their interaction with great interest.

Ames spotted Moonbeam, who'd been standing politely a short distance away. "There she is!" he said, moving through the throng of people to get to her. He picked her up and swung her around. "You're even more beautiful than when I left!" he said in French.

Moonbeam hugged him tightly as she responded in kind. "You found us. We were worried that you wouldn't."

"I will always find you," Ames said. "Especially when a very smart young lady leaves such good clues."

Moonbeam pulled back and smiled at him. "I did well then?"

"Well? You did wonderful, my pet," he told her and kissed her cheek. "Come. I've brought you something."

He put her down and Moonbeam followed him over to the pack mules. From a saddlebag, he pulled out two leather bound journals and several graphite pencils, which he handed to Moonbeam.

"We will continue our lessons this winter, yes? You can write down the story of your journey here," he said.

Moonbeam nodded, but lowered her eyes.

Ames knelt on one knee and made Moonbeam look at him as he now spoke in Kiowa. "I know that this has been an awful time. Chirp—Cricket told me about your father and my heart weeps, little one."

Moonbeam tried to hold back her tears, but she couldn't. "I miss him so much, Ames. I want him back."

Enfolding her in his embrace, Ames said, "Me, too, Moonbeam." He sighed. "But we must honor him by going on as he would want us to. We will be strong together, you and I, eh?"

Next to her father and brother, Ames was the man Moonbeam loved most and his return gave her such happiness and courage. "*Oui, je vais être forte.*"

Her agreement to be strong made Ames smile. "I am glad that you haven't forgotten what I taught you, *mademoiselle.*"

He rose and was struck by a jolt of desire and joy as he met the gaze of the woman of his heart. She stood tall, strong, and proud as she looked at him. For the briefest of moments, he saw his love returned before Willow strode over to him and held out her arm. Now her smile only contained fondness.

"It is good to see you, Ames. I am running out of people to beat at knuckles."

He grinned as he grasped arms with her. "Then it is a good thing that Firebrand is here now. You will not best me."

Giving him a teasing look, she said, "We will see about that."

Neither of them wanted to let go, but they had to. They released each other and stepped back. The group took the dogs and mules to the council lodge and relieved the animals of their burdens, storing their goods inside the lodge. Then the three travelers were shepherded to the central fire, where a feast had already started to be prepared in their honor.

As they all situated themselves around the large bonfire that had been built up, Soaring Falcon sat with Growling Wolf.

"I see why everyone likes Ames so much," he said in Kiowa.

Over the last couple of months, both chiefs had worked on learning the other's language and they were fairly proficient now.

Growling Wolf chuckled as he watched Ames tease one of their Dog Soldiers, Lightning Strike, about something. A celebratory air prevailed as many people came to visit with the new arrivals.

"He has genuine love in his heart for us and that is what draws us to him. Unlike most of the trappers who only make marriages to create alliances for trading, Ames comes because he has adopted us and cares about us." Growling Wolf smiled. "It is the same with Firebrand and Panther. Panther is Fang's cousin." He spoke of their war leader. "When Ames was leaving the first time, Panther wanted to go with him. He has always been curious about other cultures and sought excitement and knowledge. He has traveled with Ames ever since."

Soaring Falcon nodded. "And what of the *Gandastogue*? How did he come to you?"

"He was an Fox captive from the Mohawks. Ames won him in a gambling game and set him free, but Firebrand stayed with Ames out of gratitude. Now, the three of them are very close friends. Much like brothers," Growling Wolf said.

"Interesting. Do you think they brought it?"

Growling Wolf chuckled. "I am certain that they did. We will find out tomorrow. Tonight is for celebrating."

Soaring Falcon asked, "Ames has never taken a wife among other tribes?"

"No. I asked him when he first came to us."

"He has no wife anywhere?"

"No. No white wife, no Indian wife."

"I find it odd that he has not taken a wife among you since he keeps returning," Soaring Falcon said.

Growling Wolf smiled. "You are suspicious. I understand why, but there is nothing to worry about."

"Why are you so sure of him?"

"Have you heard of François Duchamp?"

Soaring Falcon nodded. "Yes, but I have not seen him or heard anything of him for some time."

"François was Ames' father."

Soaring Falcon's surprise was great. "Why did you not tell me Ames' identity?"

Growling Wolf met his gaze. "It was not important until now. Now you understand why we trust him and why we have accepted him as one of us."

"Yes. I can see why counting him as family would be advantageous."

"Very. But, it is more than that. Ames has fought with us side-by-side. He has proven himself as a warrior and a friend," Growling Wolf said. "He is not someone we just trade with. He has saved lives and killed in our honor. As far as we are concerned, he is Kiowa."

Soaring Falcon nodded as his gaze settled on Willow. She laughed and nudged Cricket, obviously teasing him about something. From the bashful look on his face, Soaring Falcon surmised that it had something to do with his granddaughter.

He was pleased with the way he and Hummingbird were getting along. Cricket had never done anything improper around Hummingbird and Soaring Falcon had every confidence that he never would. Both the young medicine man and Hummingbird had too much integrity.

As the meal progressed, the gaiety continued as Ames, Firebrand, and Panther related amusing and exciting stories of their exploits. Then drums were brought out and some of the men performed a hunting dance, including the three travelers. Ames wasn't the most graceful dancer, but he knew the steps well enough.

Taking off his bulky coat, he then dropped it on top of Moonbeam, who giggled and wrapped it around her. He wore a pair of heavy tan woolen French fly breeches, high moccasin boots with bands of white and blue at the top of his calves, and a buckskin shirt with blue bead work on it. Although he didn't wear earrings, he did wear a dog's tooth necklace made from the teeth of one of his most beloved canines who'd passed on a couple of years ago.

Soaring Falcon was surprised to see him dance. He'd known of white men who'd taken up with Indians before, but he'd never seen one participate in a dance before.

With difficulty, Ames kept his eyes away from Willow as he performed the dance steps. If he looked at her, he was sure to become mesmerized by her and make mistakes. He didn't want to be embarrassed his first night home and he didn't want to make anyone aware of his attraction to her.

Instead, he concentrated on the dance, raising his voice with his brothers and moving in time with the drums. Being back among his people restored his soul and he danced with great thanksgiving to Sendeh for bringing him safely back to them.

Although she would've like to have, Willow never participated in the men's dances. It was the one male thing that she refrained from doing. Despite being a warrior, she was still female and the mixing of a female spirit in what was only meant for males could taint the magic of the dance. If she'd been two-spirit, it wouldn't have mattered who she danced with, but despite her more masculine interests and skills, she was still very much a woman.

She enjoyed watching the dancers, especially the golden-haired man with piercing blue eyes, who made her heart beat faster. Careful not to pay more attention to him than the others, she smiled at Cricket, who played a hand drum and sang, or conversed with a couple of other women who sat by her. But she watched him as much as she could without raising suspicion.

When the dancing ended and things began winding down for the night, she made sure to grasp arms with him, as he did with the other warriors. She smiled and gave him the briefest of winks while no one else was looking. His smile broadened and her heart expanded before she turned away.

Ames turned to Lightning Strike. "Where have you set up my tipi?"

"Follow me," Lightning Strike replied.

Saying goodnight to people as he went, Ames walked with Lightning Strike through the new camp, feeling out of place. It was only because of the new locale, not the people. They stopped by the council lodge so that he could get his pack, and then continued to the northernmost side of the camp.

Ames tipi was always situated a little further away from the other tipis since his snoring was very loud at times. He'd requested for it to be placed there so that he didn't disturb others.

Lightning Strike pointed it out to him. "We couldn't salvage any of the hides from your old one."

"Do not worry. It does not matter. All that does is that I am home again," Ames said.

"Yes. It is good to have you home, brother. Sleep well and try not to snore too much," Lightning Strike said.

Ames chuckled as his friend walked away. He ducked inside the tipi and deposited his pack on the soft hide floor. Just as he laid his coat on top of his pack, he heard someone slip into the tipi. It was just a whisper of sound, but his keen hearing picked it up nonetheless.

"Ah, there you are, *mon amour*. I knew that you would come," he whispered, smiling.

Willow stepped around in front of him and into his waiting arms. "Did you think that I would be able to stay away?"

"No more than I from you," he said, holding her tightly. "I was petrified when Rushing Bull said that there had been losses to our tribe. I was afraid that you would be among them. I wept with grief over those who have gone to the next life, but also with joy when Cricket said that you still lived."

"And I could have wept when I saw you this afternoon," she said. "I prayed for you to safely return to us, to me. I was so worried about you. You would not have known that the Ojibwa had taken over our land and you—"

"Shh." He cupped her face. "We knew right away that something was amiss. It took us longer to get here because we went well out around them to make sure we were not detected. But now I am here and everything is all right." He kissed her softly. "I have missed you so much."

Willow rarely cried, even when she was in great pain, but seeing Ames again made her heart sing and being held by him stirred her feelings as nothing else did. When his lips claimed hers, tears leaked out from under her closed eyelids. Winding her arms around his neck, she sank into his embrace, glorifying in the way he leisurely plundered her mouth.

She'd yearned for him all summer, had counted the days until they'd be reunited. Need for him quickly grew and she became impatient. Breaking the kiss, she backed away from him and let the bison robe she was wearing around her shoulders drop to the floor.

"Wait, *mon petit oiseau.*" Ames knelt and took out his fire starter from a pouch at his waist. "I wish to see you and it is chilly."

Willow smiled. "If anyone else called me their little bird, I would hit them."

Ames chuckled as he started a small fire. "But I am not just anyone, no?"

"No. You are not."

As the flames dimly lit the interior of the tipi, Ames stood back up and stripped off his tunic. He moved to begin undoing the buttons of his breeches, but Willow stopped him. Stepping up to him, she ran her hands over his broad shoulders, enjoying the firm muscles she encountered.

At a little over six feet tall, Willow didn't have to look up to very many men, but she had to tilt her head up to meet Ames' eyes. The heat in their silvery-blue depths made her melt inside. His proud, aquiline nose led down to a sensual male mouth and strong jaw.

So much about Ames was so different and fascinating to her. She stroked his beard, something that the men in her culture didn't grow. He would most likely shave it the next day, as he usually did once he'd come for the winter. Its rough texture pleased her and she liked the way it felt when he kissed her. Lowering her gaze, she caressed his powerful chest, playing with the fine, golden curls that covered it.

A line of short, blond hair made a trail down over his taut, defined stomach and disappeared into the waist of his breeches. Playfully, she hooked a finger in them and tugged before undoing the first button.

"No, no," Ames said. "You know the rule."

Her smile matched his as she raised her arms. Anticipation grew as he lifted her buckskin shirt from her.

"Mmm. You are the most beautiful thing I have ever seen," he said, pulling her to him.

Willow gasped as he filled one of his palms with her breast and kissed her throat. "Please, Ames, I need you. Now."

With a deep growl, Ames released the thongs holding up her leggings. The tie holding her breechcloth on her slim hips quickly followed. Their first coupling when he returned to her was never gentle. Their mutual desire was too intense to hold back for very long.

Ames kissed her urgently, their tongues meeting in a fiery, velvet clash as she unbuttoned his breeches the rest of the way and shoved them down. His rapidly hardening member jutted out from his body under his drawers. Willow made quick work of the undergarments and pushed them down along with his breeches.

Their hands were suddenly everywhere, teasing, kneading, and stroking as their carnal need mounted. Ames pulled her down to the sleeping pallet and pinned her on her back with a knee between her legs. Thrusting a hand into her hair, he bent her neck back a little to give him better access to it.

He kissed and bit his way down to her breasts. They were in proportion to her elegant, long-limbed body: not overly large, but certainly enough to indicate her gender. In his eyes, they were perfect and he took his first taste of one dusky nipple.

Willow gasped and arched her back a little just as someone scratched on the tipi flap. Her and Ames' eyes met in a look of panic.

As quickly as he could, given his aroused state, Ames scrambled off Willow, who grabbed her clothing and ducked behind one of the privacy panels since she was slim enough to fit into the narrow space.

"One moment," Ames said, putting his breeches on without bothering with the underwear.

Thankfully, his arousal had started to deflate, so it wouldn't be too painful. Sitting down, he threw a deerskin robe around his shoulders, which was also long enough to hid his lap.

"Come in," he said.

A jolt of surprise went through Ames when Growling Wolf stepped into the tipi. *I hope he will not stay long. Poor Willow will freeze.*

"Chief, to what do I owe the pleasure?"

Growling Wolf lowered himself stiffly down to the floor. His knees cracked loudly as they protested the movement and the chief grimaced. "This gets harder all the time."

Ames felt badly for the elderly man. "I am glad that Chir— Cricket was able to make a poultice that helps."

"As am I. I will not keep you, but I must know: were you able to secure ammunition?" Growling Wolf asked.

Ames smiled. "Have I ever let you down?"

The chief chuckled. "No."

"We started out with two hundred weight of lead sheets. At night around the fire, we made musket balls with the molds I purchased. They are ready for use. We also brought plenty of cartridge paper and powder. Where are the guns?" Ames asked. "Were you able to salvage them?"

"They were one of the first things we packed," Growling Wolf replied. "If it were not for our new Lakota family, we would have been wiped out. As much as I hate to admit it, the Ojibwa were too great in number for us to defeat on our own."

"It is good then that we have such a wise chief. You have always been skillful in creating alliances," Ames said.

Growling Wolf grunted. "It was Cricket who set it all in motion by calling the bison to us. Therefore, most of the credit goes to him. I should not have doubted his mentor in choosing him to join the medicine men."

"True on all counts, but you still played a large part in it." Ames faked a yawn. "It is good to not have to travel for a couple of days. Willow said that they have scouted out some good areas for trapping."

"Yes. We knew how important it would be." Growling Wolf rubbed one of his knees. "You will need to lay your traps right away since you are getting a little later start. But we can talk about this tomorrow. You are no doubt exhausted."

Ames nodded. "I will sleep like a rock."

Growling Wolf sighed. "Will you help me up? Depending on others this way is very humbling and no one will let me do what I should do."

Ames rose and assisted him in rising. "I am glad they will not. You are still needed too much and your mind is as sharp as ever." He made sure that Growling Wolf was steady before letting go of him.

"Humph. I suppose so."

Ames chuckled at his grumpy response. "Do you want me to walk with you?"

Growling Wolf frowned at him. "No. I got here on my own and I will get to my tipi on my own, too. Allow me *some* dignity."

Ames held up his hands in surrender. "I did not mean to offend you with my concern."

With a little smile, Growling Wolf said, "I bid you goodnight, my friend."

"Goodnight, Chief."

Chapter Three

When Growling Wolf left, Willow came out from behind the privacy panel. She'd been able to get her tunic on and she'd sat on her leggings and breeches, but it had still been cold. However, her training had come in handy and she'd been able to deal with it. Her tunic barely covered her nakedness.

She loved the way Ames' gaze devoured her and her body warmed as he looked at her. She knelt on the sleeping robes and took off her tunic again.

Ames arched a brow at her. "You are not leaving?"

She shook her head and lay down. "I cannot go until you have made love to me at least once. I have waited too long."

Looking over her lovely, tawny form, Ames wanted nothing more than to make love with her, but something told him that Growling Wolf wouldn't be the last visitor he had that night.

His voice was full of regret. "Willow, you—"

She rose gracefully to her feet and started dressing without speaking. Words weren't necessary. Her anger showed in her flashing eyes.

Ames signed, "Do not be cross with me. I am not happy, either, but I am sure that others will be along. We would not have to sneak around if you would just marry me."

Willow finished dressing. "We have talked about this."

"Yes, we have and you are being stubborn when there is no reason to be," Ames said.

"You do not understand."

Ames blocked her path to the door. "Because you will not explain it to me."

"I just do not wish to be married." Willow tried to get around him, but he grabbed her by the upper arms.

"I cannot keep living half a life with you. It is bad enough that I am away from you so much," Ames said. "When I am here, I want to be with you all the time, but I cannot because you will not marry me. And if they knew that I took your virginity and did not marry you, there would be a lot of trouble."

Willow shook her head. "They will not know. Neither one of us are telling anyone."

"There is always the chance that they will find out," Ames said.

"Then we will keep being as cautious as possible so that does not happen."

Ames drew in a deep breath. "No. I cannot, will not keep living a lie."

Willow's eyes widened. "What are you saying?"

His grip loosened and he rubbed her arms. "I am saying that I love you more than anything, but that I cannot keep up this pretense. I want to marry you, have children with you. I want everyone to know about our love. Hiding it feels so wrong. I cannot be with you unless you agree to marry me, Willow. Do you not love me enough to marry me?"

Her nostrils flared and her eyes stung with tears. "I love you as much as you love me, but I cannot marry you."

Ames' heart cracked as she spoke. Clenching his jaw, he stepped back from her. "Then I guess that we are at an impasse."

Willow stared at him for a moment and then ducked through the doorway and walked away before she changed her mind. She wandered blindly through camp, and then on to the river they now camped near. Sitting down by the bank, she pulled her robe around her shoulders.

Tears of misery and frustration trickled from her eyes. *Why did Growling Wolf have to show up? I would be making love with Ames right now if he had not. We would not have argued.* A quiet sob rose from her.

Someone put a hand on her shoulder. Surprised, she whirled around and struck out, knocking their legs out from under them. They landed heavily, letting out a loud "ooff!" She was on them in an instant, straddling them with her knife at the ready.

"Willow! It is just me, Cricket! Do not kill me!"

His black eyes were wide, showing his fear.

Willow sheathed her knife and moved off him. "I am sorry if I hurt you. You startled me."

Cricket sat up and rubbed his left shoulder. It had been injured during a clash with an Ojibwa brave and still bothered him sometimes, especially when it was jarred.

Willow noticed. "Are you all right?"

Cricket smiled. "I am fine. I did not mean to sneak up on you. I was not aware you were here until I heard you crying. What is wrong?"

"Nothing. I am fine," Willow said, sitting back down.

Cricket sat down by her. "You did not sound fine."

Willow pounded the ground. "I am fine. I will be fine. Everything is fine."

"Are you trying to convince me or yourself?"

"I do not have a choice but to be fine," Willow responded.

Cricket sighed. "Even warriors are allowed to have feelings."

"You do not understand. It is different for me. I have to constantly prove myself, even more so than a man does," Willow said.

"I do not know about that." Cricket pulled his robe tighter around him. "I think everyone knows what you are capable of. How brave and deadly."

"Perhaps, but if I do not keep performing up to those standards, I will be found lacking," Willow said. "I could not stand that."

"Is that what is bothering you? Has someone said something to you? Is Growling Wolf unhappy with you?"

"No. Not him."

"Fang?"

"No one has said anything critical to me." *At least not about that.* "I will be fine."

Cricket was silent for a moment before saying, "As a medicine man, it is my duty to keep conversations confidential if a person so wishes. You are obviously troubled by something. If you need to talk to someone, you can always talk to me. I would never betray your confidence."

In a rare show of affection, Willow took Cricket's hand and squeezed it. "You are a good friend, Cricket, but this is something that I must deal with on my own."

Cricket tightened his hand around hers. "You may think you do, but you really do not. But I will respect your wishes."

"Thank you. I am going to bed. Goodnight."

Cricket was very concerned about his friend. He'd never seen Willow cry before. Whatever was bothering her must be very painful to have made her weep. *Sendeh, please help Willow with what is weighing on her heart and if she should come to me about it, give me the wisdom to help her.*

It was cold the next morning when Willow awoke just after dawn. She had her morning tea and a breakfast of leftover venison stew and fry bread. Unlike other unmarried warriors, who either lived with their mothers or sisters, Willow lived alone and had for several years. Her parents were gone, as were her aunt and uncle who had finished raising her.

Outside of Lightning Strike and his sister, Tulip, she had no blood family. Therefore, she lived alone and preferred it that way. She came and went as she pleased without having to account to anyone for her whereabouts. That didn't mean that she didn't like to entertain, though. She was a competent cook and homemaker and sometimes had her friends over for the evening meal.

Living alone also made it easier to see Ames. Or at least it had. She couldn't believe that things had gone so wrong the first night he'd returned. He'd asked her to marry him the first season he'd come to their tribe. Their attraction had been immediate, but she'd been shy at first, which was very unlike her.

As a woman warrior, Willow was used to attention from men. She fascinated them and she wasn't unaware that she was beautiful. However, outside of a little flirting, she'd never had anything to do with a man romantically. That had all changed when Ames had shown up out of the blue.

He'd captivated her with his sky-colored eyes and beautiful, sun-like hair. His size and power had enthralled her and his flirting had the power to make her blush. Unused to feeling such things, she'd been unsure of what to do. She wasn't like other women who gazed at their men with longing in their eyes—or so she'd thought.

From the first moment Ames had kissed her, she'd been his. She shouldn't have let him take her virginity, but she'd never regret it. Neither of them had been able to resist temptation. He'd wanted to marry her before he left at the end of winter, but she'd refused. And had kept refusing.

Sighing as she finished her breakfast, Willow set her bowl aside and put on her buffalo hide coat. Gathering her weapons, she stepped out into the chilly day.

"Willow!"

She froze at hearing Ames' voice. Turning, she watched him walk towards her with long strides and a determined expression on his clean-shaven face. *Oh, no. I know that look.*

He smiled, but his eyes held a hard light. "Come, show me this new trapping run."

Her status as a warrior enabled her to be alone with men, so it was not unusual for her to travel with them unchaperoned. She narrowed her eyes at him for a moment, but then smiled because a couple of people were watching them.

"Very well," she said and began walking.

Falling into step with her, Ames thumped her on the shoulder, just as he would've any of the braves. "I am eager to see this new territory."

"I think that you will harvest many good pelts from it this year," she said, playing along even though her temper simmered.

Once they were out of earshot of the others, Ames asked, "Did you sleep well?"

She met his gaze head on. "No. Did you?"

"No."

They headed toward the rising sun. It glinted off the frost on the tree branches and made the sparse snow sparkle. They walked in silence for about fifteen minutes. Then Ames took Willow by the arm and yanked her off the deer trail they were walking along, pulling her into a densely wooded area.

"What are you doing?"

She shoved at him, but he pinned her against an elm tree, using his muscular bulk to keep her in place while he held her wrists so she couldn't hit him. He kicked one of her legs out to the side and stepped further into the V of her legs.

Their gazes locked and they didn't move for several moments until Ames' face relaxed into a smile. Chuckling, he leaned his forehead against hers. "I can't stay angry with you, my love," he said in French. "And I can't stay away from you, either, even though I should."

She grinned. "That's because I have bewitched you."

Ames ground his hips against hers. "Yes, you have. Do you feel how much you've bewitched me?"

"Yes. I'm just as bewitched by you. Please make love to me now. Please." Ames was the only man who could reduce Willow to pleading. "I need you, to be one with you."

His eyes darkened with desire before he kissed her with all the passion of a summer storm. She met his hungry mouth, opening to him as he cupped the back of her head with one hand and slightly loosened the waist thong of her breechcloth. He tugged the front of it loose, baring her to the morning air. Laying a large hand on her stomach, he caressed his way downward until he found her mound.

Willow couldn't hold still as he gently teased her. She moaned into his mouth and hooked a leg over his hip.

Ames released her lips. "I want you so much. You drive me mad with need."

"Good. I want you to burn for me the way you make me burn for you," Willow told him, quickly undoing his fly. "I think you are very much on fire."

Ames growled quietly as she took his hard length in hand and caressed him. His loins tightened. "Yes. On fire."

He drew her hand away, grasped her buttocks, and lifted her up. Willow wrapped her legs around his waist and moaned as he slowly filled her. She encircled his neck with her arms and kissed him as he began moving. They danced their tongues together as he set an even pace.

Breaking the kiss, Ames said, "Marry me."

"No."

"Marry me."

"No."

It became a litany that was timed with every thrust. His tempo increased and a sweet tension built within Willow as she held on to his powerful shoulders. She whimpered, a sound that only Ames could ever elicit from her. As one, they sought the ultimate pleasure, their muscles straining and their breath coming in short pants.

"Marry me. I love you so much."

"Ames, please. I love you, but I can't," she rasped out between breaths.

He growled in frustration and pleasure. "I'll beg, if that's what it takes."

"No. It won't work. Please, Ames."

Ames couldn't resist her plea, nor the heavenly sensations surging through his body. He gave in for the moment, both to ceasing their conversation and to their mutual quest for fulfillment. Getting a better grip on her derrière, he thrust his hips forward hard.

"Yes, yes." Willow closed her eyes and leaned her head back against the tree.

Ames increased the tempo and Willow trembled around and against him. Again and again, he drove her against the tree, seeking to give her as much pleasure as she could take. She dug her fingers into his coat as she suddenly went rigid against him, her face caught in an expression of utter bliss. Her climax held her so tightly that she couldn't breathe for a moment.

Ames kept moving, mesmerized by the look of rapture on her gorgeous face and the pulsing heat around his rigid shaft. Her lungs began working once more and a she let out a shuddering moan that conveyed her pleasure.

"We are not through quite yet. Hang on, my pet."

Willow had been without him for so long and she still needed him. "Yes, love me more."

With power and precision, he took them higher. Together they strove towards the summit, their bodies colliding over and over. Willow buried her face against his shoulder to muffle her gasping cry of pleasure as an even stronger release flowed through her.

Ames shot into a climax with such intensity that it created a roaring in his head. He gripped her toned, shapely flesh tighter as he froze, a very willing captive of searing ecstasy. Gradually, the roaring faded and the bliss ebbed away. A very pleasant state of satiation took hold of them and Ames locked his knees to stay upright as their bodies relaxed.

Lowering her feet to the ground, Willow gave him a slightly dazed smile as she caught her breath. "I cannot think when I am with you like this." She caressed his now-smooth jaw. "I do not want to think. I just want to feel."

Embracing her, Ames said, "You are not the only one. You drive away all my reason. I need you as I have never needed another."

They now spoke in Kiowa.

A frown of uncertainty appeared between her eyebrows. "When you go away, do you lay with other women?"

"Willow, how could you ask me that?" Kindness and a little irritation shone in his eyes. "Since our very first kiss, I have never touched another woman. I have no desire for anyone but you." He arched a dark gold brow. "And what of you? Have you been with any braves while I was gone?"

"Of course not." She smoothed hair back from his temple. "I have given myself only to you and you are the only man I will ever love with either my body or my heart."

He kissed her and then moved away. "Tell me why you will not marry me."

Willow refastened her breechcloth around her hips with angry movements.

"Have I not proven myself to you?" Ames asked. "Why can you not be honest with me? We share such intimate pleasure, but you will not let me completely into your heart."

Willow shook her head as tears burned behind her eyes. "I cannot...you will hate me."

Coming back to her, Ames took her in his arms. "I could never hate you, my sweet. Please talk to me."

"Ames, I never expected to fall in love. I never thought I would. I knew that one day I would give myself to a man, but it would only be for physical pleasure." She rested her forearms on his shoulders. "But I fell in love with you the moment we grasped arms and you looked at me with your beautiful eyes."

He smiled and her heart flooded with love. "It was the same for me. I knew that I must have you."

"I am a warrior, Ames."

"Yes, and a very mighty one. I am aware of this."

Willow played with the fringes on the bottom of her tunic. "I cannot be a warrior if I am pregnant."

Understanding dawned on him. "Ah, I see. You are worried that if we marry, that I will expect you to give up your position. I would never do that. Yes, you could not do battle once you are pregnant, but otherwise..."

She shook her head. "I cannot have children right now. Our number of fighters are low and I am one of the most highly skilled. I must continue to be available to fight. If we marry, I will be expected to bear children. It is one of a woman's most important duties."

"Do you not want children?" He gave her a mischievous smile. "Perhaps little blue-eyed Indians running all over camp? I must confess that I have secretly been hoping that you would become pregnant. Then you would *have* to marry me."

Willow decided to be completely honest. "I will not become pregnant."

Ames cupped her face and tilted her chin up. "Why not?"

"Because I take a purging tea every morning to make sure that does not happen. So that your seed does not take hold," she whispered.

This wasn't unusual. Many women did the same thing, especially at certain times of the year when having a child during a different season wouldn't be convenient. This was also done during lean times, when a tribe couldn't support more mouths to feed. To lessen the chances of conception even more, couples would limit their lovemaking or refrain from actual intercourse for a time.

Ames' eyebrows rose. "This is why you would not marry me? Because you were afraid that I would be angry that you do not wish to have children right now?" He kissed her forehead. "Children belong to women and if it is your choice not to have them for a while, so be it. As long as you have them within a few years, this does not bother me. I am twenty-eight winters old. Do not make me wait too much longer to be a father."

Light suffused Willow's soul. "You truly are not angry that I have prevented a child?"

Although a part of him was disappointed, Ames knew that she'd done the right thing for her tribe. She was also right about being needed to protect their people, something she couldn't do if she was heavy with child.

"No. I am not angry," Ames said. "Is this the only thing holding you back from becoming my wife?"

"Yes."

"Then since I have removed that obstacle, Willow, the woman of my heart and my reason for living, will you please honor me by marrying me?"

His romantic proposal and the love shining in his eyes touched her heart. Knowing how honest and straightforward Ames was, Willow believed him about being willing to wait for children.

"Yes! I will marry you."

Ames embraced her tightly, capturing her lips in a tender kiss. When they parted, he chuckled a little. "Finally, I have captured my little bird. I promise to make you happy."

"You already do."

He frowned. "Who do I ask permission to court you?"

Willow hadn't thought about that, either. "I guess you will have to ask Lightning Strike. He is my only living male relative."

"Then I will do it tonight. I do not want a long courtship. I have plenty of bride price gifts," he said.

"Such as?"

"No, no. You will see," he teased.

"Very well. We must go. There is a stream not far from here where we can bathe. Then we will have to hurry through the rest of the trap line so that we do not raise suspicion by being gone for so long," she said.

He took her hand and kissed it. "Soon we will not have to worry about that and we will be able to be together whenever we want to."

Willow smiled. "I cannot wait."

They set off along the deer trail, happiness flowing between them. They shared a new closeness, looking forward with great anticipation to their lives being joined.

Chapter Four

Lightning Strike looked at the vast array of bride price gifts that lay around him on the floor of his sister's tipi. Two fine flintlocks, ammunition, a sack of high quality glass beads, several iron arrowheads, a sack of coffee, and ten beaver pelts lay before him. Ames had also bought a horse from Rushing Bull and given it to Lightning Strike.

"These are all very fine gifts," Lightning Strike said. "But I am confused."

"What about?"

Lighting Strike shifted his position a little. "I did not know that you were interested in Willow. She has never said anything. Have you spoken to her about this?"

"Yes, we have talked about it. It has taken a while to convince her to marry me, but I finally wore her down," Ames said.

Lighting Strike's expression grew serious. "Are you sure that you can handle being married to a warrior?"

Ames understood Lighting Strike's concern. He knew that Willow was an oddity who fascinated men, but they would only want her casually, just to see what making love to her would be like. They wouldn't love her warrior's heart the way he did. They wouldn't see past her tough exterior to the caring, loving, and passionate woman within.

"Willow is unique, but it is that uniqueness that draws me to her. She is beautiful, strong, and intelligent. She knows how to take care of a home, but that is not all that important to me. She has great trapping instincts and is a great help to me, but more than that, I believe that we will be happy together," Ames said. "I care for her very much and I promise to treat her with respect."

Lighting Strike nodded sagely. "I will speak with Willow and let you know my answer tomorrow." It wouldn't be wise to appear too eager.

Ames wasn't offended about being put off. He'd expected it. "Very well. I have a few things to do before I go to sleep. Have a pleasant night."

Lighting Strike bid him goodnight and he ducked out of the tipi. Inhaling the cold night air, Ames smiled up at the stars, confident that all would be well between him and his lady warrior.

"Open your eyes, Cricket."

Slowly, Cricket woke up and stretched. Cool grass pressed against his bare back and he realized that this was a spirit dream. It was always summertime whenever Bison visited him. The seasons sometimes changed once their time together began, but it always started out during the warmer months.

Getting to his feet, Cricket smiled. "Greetings, Mighty Bison. It is good to see you."

"As it is you, Cricket." Bison pawed the ground a little. "I have good news."

Cricket patted his shoulder. "I am glad to hear that."

"And I have bad news."

Cricket dropped his head. "Somehow I knew that you would say that. Is it very bad news? Are we going to be attacked again?"

Bison just said, "Walk with me."

Looking around, Cricket realized that they were on the path to their new camp. "I miss our old home. Things feel so strange here. It does not have the same energy. The energy that is here often disturbs me."

Bison nudged Cricket playfully. "How so?"

Birds twittered in the trees as they passed and a squirrel chattered on the path up ahead. "There are times when I feel it inside me like a second heartbeat. A couple of times, I almost passed out because it was so strong," Cricket replied.

They entered the camp, but it was empty and the central fire was completely out. No smoke rose from the tipis and no dogs ran through the camp. All birdsong and other wilderness noises had ceased. A chill ran through Cricket as the silence hummed around him.

"Where is everyone?"

There was no answer. Cricket found himself alone. Bison had left him.

"I hate it when he does that," he muttered. "What is it that I am supposed to see in this deserted place?"

A child's laughter pierced the quiet, making Cricket smile. He saw a small figure dart between a couple of tipis. The glimpse was too quick for him to tell the child's identity. Cricket jogged to where he'd seen the little one vanish. More laughter came from behind him and he whirled around.

The child was almost completely translucent, making it difficult to see its exact age or whether it was a boy or a girl. However, he was able to make out that it had very light hair and smiling blue eyes.

"A spirit child." Cricket crouched in front of the little one. "Hello. I am Cricket. What is your name?"

The child shrugged. "I do not know."

Cricket nodded. "I see. You have not been born yet."

"No, but I must be. Sendeh says that no matter what, I must be born."

With that the child backed away and faded from sight.

Cricket rose and felt Bison's presence behind him. "Is that the good news or the bad new?"

"Both."

"Whose child is it?"

The loud silence returned and then the hum began growing louder until it swelled around Cricket. He put his hands over his ears, but it didn't help. He fell to the ground and just as his body collided with the earth, he woke up with a start.

His heart thundered as he lay on his sleeping pallet. Raising his head, he saw in the dim light from the low flames in the fire pit that his mother slept soundly. But Moonbeam lay staring at him. Had he been talking in his sleep and woken her?

He gave her a half smile and rested his head back down to indicate that all was well, but was it? His mind returned to the spirit child. Why must it be born and why was it both good and bad news? Gooseflesh broke out over his body, a sign that usually meant that he would find out before long.

Willow had just finished her breakfast the next morning when Lighting Strike came to see her.

"Good morning, cousin," she said. "Please sit. I still have some tea left."

Sitting down, Lighting Strike's gaze rested on his cousin's face. Now that he was looking for it, he saw a difference in her. A happiness that he hadn't noticed before and he knew that it must be because of Ames.

He accepted a cup of tea. "Thank you. I had an interesting visit last night."

A smile played around her mouth as she poured herself another cup and took a sip. "Oh?"

Lighting Strike chuckled. "I think you already know who the visitor was."

"Perhaps."

"When did Ames first express his interest in you?"

Willow said, "A while ago, but I would not agree to marry him because I was worried that he would expect me to give up being a warrior."

Lighting Strike raised an eyebrow. "You would deny yourself a husband to retain your status?"

Willow sobered. "My duty to this tribe comes first, even if that means denying myself happiness. Protecting our people makes me happy. Being a warrior makes me happy."

Lightning Strike watched her closely. "What about children?"

Prepared for this question, Willow said, "They will come whenever the time is right."

Meeting Willow's eyes, Lightning Strike understood what she meant. As a man, it was impolite of him to question her further about such a thing, so he merely asked, "Are you sure that Ames is agreeable to that?"

Her expression tightened. "It is not for him to decide, but yes, we have discussed it and he completely understands."

With a slight nod, Lightning Strike said, "He has offered many fine gifts for you. Would you like to come see them?"

Willow grinned. "Yes."

"You love him."

His statement didn't surprise Willow. Lightning Strike was a perceptive man and he knew her well. "Yes. Very much."

"You both hid it very well," Lightning Strike said. "I had no idea. Everyone will be very surprised."

Willow rose to her feet when he did. "It took me by surprise, too. I never thought I would fall in love, and certainly not with a white man, but Ames is special in many ways."

"Yes, he is. Come so that we may look at these gifts together. If they meet with your approval, we will make the announcement and begin planning the wedding," Lighting Strike said.

Willow followed him out into the gray daylight. The scent of snow hung in the air and she smiled as she thought how happy Ames would be that a storm was imminent. How many times had they made love during a nighttime storm with the sound of sleet or a driving snow falling on his tipi?

With difficulty, Willow stopped smiling, knowing that if she kept grinning like a fool that it would make people curious. Reaching Lightning Strike's sister, Tulip's tipi, she ducked inside and greeted her other cousin.

Tulip smiled. "You have been holding out on us, cousin."

"I wanted to keep it private," Willow said as she sat down. "There was no sense talking about it until something definite had been decided."

Lightning Strike began unwrapping Ames' gifts. "You were successful."

As the arrowheads, knife, and other presents were revealed to her, Willow's eyes widened. "He has given all of this for me?"

"And the horse outside, too."

Tears stung Willow's eyes and she had to clear her throat to speak. "These are such expensive gifts. I cannot believe that he would give so much for me."

Tulip took her hand. "He must love you very much."

Blinking rapidly, Willow nodded. "Yes. And I love him." Admitting that out loud to her family felt so freeing, so right, and she was glad that she'd finally talked to Ames about her fears. It had been stupid of her to have thought that his reaction would've been any different than it had been.

"Then these gifts meet your approval?" Lightning Strike asked.

Willow nodded. "Yes."

"Then we will announce your betrothal," Lightning Strike said.

Excitement and happiness flooded Willow's being and she couldn't contain her grin. "Please do not wait long. I want to marry him as soon as possible."

Tulip rose. "Let us go speak with Cricket right away in that case."

Lightning Strike went outside with them. "I will tell Ames that his gifts are acceptable." He touched Willow's arm. "I am very happy for you."

"Thank you."

Then she followed Tulip to the medicine lodge where they were sure to find Cricket. A thrill ran through her as she thought that soon she would be able to be with her beloved all the time. Building a life with Ames would be such a joy and she couldn't wait to begin it.

Chapter Five

The news of Ames' and Willow's betrothal was met with great surprise and happiness. They were congratulated and all approved of their union. It further solidified Ames' place in the tribe and increased their love of him even more.

Now that it was out in the open, their feelings for each other were very apparent. Willow was teased about it, but she didn't mind and took the ribbing good naturedly. Ames was likewise teased that Willow would soon train him. He replied by telling them that he was happy to be trained by his beautiful bride-to-be.

Growling Wolf called Willow to his tipi a couple of days after their announcement.

"Sit with me," he requested.

Willow complied and waited for him to speak.

"I have invited our Lakota kin to attend the wedding of one of our most celebrated warriors and that of our good friend and ally."

Willow's eyes widened. "Why would you do this? I do not want them here."

Growling Wolf's eyebrows rose. "Is it not apparent why I would do this? We were invited to Dark Horse and Sky Dancer's wedding."

She'd intended to only ask Sky Dancer and Dark Horse to come. If the Lakota were coming that meant that Soaring Falcon would attend. She didn't want the man she hated so much to be present at her joyful occasion.

Growling Wolf's expression turned stony. "They are our kin, so they will attend. I know that you do not like Soaring Falcon, but I cannot figure out why."

Anger ran hot through her veins, but Willow kept it in check. "He and his people are mainly responsible for the reason we had to leave our homeland. They killed many of our men and hunted in our territory, making it hard to find game. Is that not reason enough?"

"I am well aware of our history with them, but the time has come to put that aside and to embrace our alliance and new friendship," Growling Wolf said.

Willow knew that once her chief made up his mind that there would be no changing it. "Very well. You are my chief and I will obey you, but I do not like it." She gave him a rare direct stare and left the tipi before anger loosened her tongue.

Growling Wolf sighed. *She can be as prickly as a porcupine. May Sendeh give Ames plenty of patience in dealing with her.*

The first heavy snow of the season fell all that day and night. It didn't deter Cricket from sitting outside for a while, however. He sat on a thick, furry bison robe with a couple more draped over him. He needed to see the stars while he prayed. Ames' lead dog, Gray, lay curled up against Cricket's back under the robes, lending his body heat to keep Cricket warm.

He meditated more on the vision about the spirit child. It was now obvious to him that it was Ames' and Willow's child, but what was its significance and what might keep it from being born? Should he speak to Willow about it? Ames? It was a delicate matter and he wasn't sure that it was his place to say anything.

"My mentor, I wish that you were here to help me decide what to do," he whispered. "There is so much that I do not know and, while I am grateful to Smoking Fire for teaching me, I feel that it is somehow wrong to be learning Lakota medicine when I am Kiowa." He shook his head.

"Chirping Cricket?"

He sighed when he recognized Moonbeam's voice. "Yes, sister."

"Why are you out here in the snow? Come home. You will become sick. I will make you some tea." Her face appeared before him when she crouched in front of him.

"I am praying," he said sternly. "What have I told you about disturbing me when I am out here?"

Gray's tail thumped the ground and he squirmed around until he could reach Moonbeam. She giggled and scratched his ears. "I see you have company."

Cricket smiled. "Yes, but unlike you, he does not bother me while I am praying."

Moonbeam smirked at him. "I will leave you, but do not sit out here too much longer."

Gray followed her, leaving Cricket completely alone. He pulled the robes tighter around him and tried to concentrate again, but it was no use. Aggravated, he rose from his spot and picked up the robe he'd been sitting on. He started walking to the medicine lodge, intending to crush up some of the willow bark he'd collected the day before so it was ready to make tea.

His mind strayed to his betrothed and he smiled as he ducked inside the lodge. Hummingbird was much wiser than many people knew and she had a pleasant disposition. She made delicious food and behaved very wifely towards him sometimes. One day when he'd gone to visit her, she'd noticed a small tear in his leggings and had made him give them to her to repair.

She often did things like that for him. In return, he had his mother make Moonbeam jewelry and sometimes he gave Hummingbird pretty stones he found. He'd purchased a few white man's needles from Ames and planned to give them to Hummingbird when he saw her in a couple of days.

Ames hadn't wanted to charge him anything, but Cricket had informed him that he was no longer a boy who had to be given things. He now had currency in the form of medicines and potions and he could pay for the needles. They'd agreed on a fair price; a jar of bear grease salve and a pouch of dried eucalyptus for ten good needles.

Cricket couldn't wait to see Hummingbird's eyes shine when he gave them to her. It made him feel warm when he thought about the few brief kisses they'd stolen. He wondered what it would be like to really kiss her, but it wouldn't be proper for him to actually do it. Still, he couldn't help thinking about it.

His musings were interrupted when someone scratched on the lodge flap. "Come."

He was surprised to see Growling Wolf come inside. "*Há:cho,* Cricket."

"*Há:cho,* Chief. Would you like some coffee?"

Growling Wolf's eyes lit up. Ames always brought coffee with him and the chief greatly enjoyed it. "I will not refuse some."

Cricket put it on to brew while Growling Wolf shook off his robe near the tipi entrance and then sat down.

"I am glad to see you, Chief, but you should be careful walking around in the snow," Cricket said.

"Stop mothering me." His chuckle took the bite out of his words. "What are you doing?"

"Grinding up dried plants for either tea or poultices."

Growling Wolf's lips curved in a knowing smile. "One day you will have a pretty wife to help you."

Cricket's cheeks heated as he smiled. "Yes. I look forward to that time. Oh! There is another reason I am glad you came. I want to try something I think may help your knees."

He took a big pot outside and scooped and packed snow into it. Going back inside, he hung the pot over the fire. "There are many things the white men make that I do not like, but these metal containers are very handy."

Growling Wolf grunted. "Yes, but I fear that one day, we will depend too much on these things and that our old ways will be lost."

"I pray that does not happen."

"As do I." Growling Wolf watched Cricket grind up willow bark. "Have you had any great revelations lately?"

Cricket met his eyes. "I am not sure. A few things, but they do not seem very big right now. I will keep meditating on them."

The chief nodded. "It is growing closer to the time when I must go away." He raised a hand. "Do not disagree with me. You know that it is true. If we had not been close enough to the Hidatsa this fall, I would have slowed us down too much."

Cricket couldn't meet his eyes, but he nodded. "Yes. It pains me greatly to say it, but you are right. But, before you decide to do anything, I would like you to think about something."

"Very well."

Sitting back, Cricket said, "You are one of our few elders left to tell the ancient stories. I would ask that you tell as many as you can remember before you leave us to go to the next life. I say this because our other Kiowa brothers and sisters have gone further west and I do not know when we will meet up with them again.

"Our small numbers mean that there will be fewer choices of mates. Our ban on marrying blood kin will mean that we will be forced to do one of two things; we must go find the other Kiowa or..." He swallowed hard. "Be absorbed by our Lakota kin. Already Sky Dancer and She Sings have gone to live with them. Hummingbird will come live with me once we marry, but our children will still be half-Lakota."

Growling Wolf sighed. "I have also thought of this, but I do not have a solution right now. I will do as you ask and keep our oral traditions alive."

"Thank you."

He handed Growling Wolf his coffee and checked the water in the pot. It was just beginning to simmer. Carefully, he filled two water containers made from soft doe stomachs and tied them off tightly. He sat them off to the side and poured some coffee for himself.

They spoke of Willow and Ames' upcoming wedding and various things concerning the camp. Cricket tested the filled water containers and found them to be the right temperature now.

"Lie down and straighten your legs," he directed Growling Wolf.

Growling Wolf slowly complied and watched with curiosity when Cricket placed a water skin on each of his knees. Warmth seeped through his leggings to the joints and it felt very pleasant.

"Let me know when they are cool and we will see how your knees feel then," Cricket said.

"All right. Shall I tell you a story?" Growling Wolf offered.

Cricket smiled. "Yes. I would enjoy that."

Growling Wolf thought for a moment and then began, "When I was a brave of about your age..."

As Cricket listened, he tried to commit to memory everything the chief told him. Perhaps he could have Moonbeam write the story in one of the journals that Ames' had given her. In fact, maybe she could write down many of their stories.

By the time Growling Wolf had finished, the water containers were cool and Cricket took them away. "How do your knees feel now?"

Growling Wolf flexed one and the pain wasn't as bad as usual. "Much better." He sat up. "Thank you."

"You are welcome. I do not know how long it will last, but you can do that as often as you like. The bags are yours," Cricket said.

"I will bring payment tomorrow," Growling Wolf said, rising. His knees didn't crackle quite as loudly and he didn't need assistance. "I am very grateful to you, Cricket."

"I am always happy to help." Cricket said.

Growling Wolf wrapped his robe around him, nodded, and went out into the night. Cricket would've walked him home, but he knew that Growling Wolf would've been offended by the offer. As he went back to making medicine, Cricket's eyelids began to droop. He shook his head and yawned, but soon found himself nodding off again.

Knowing that it wouldn't be good to continue when he was so tired, Cricket put away his supplies and equipment. He finished and dowsed the fire. No sooner had he stepped outside than he was greeted by the spirit child from his vision. The fine hair on his arms stood up and his shoulders prickled with gooseflesh.

The blue eyes glowed in the night and its long, flaxen hair flowed around it, as though blown around by a strong wind. Again, Cricket couldn't tell if it was a boy or a girl.

"What is it, little one?" he asked.

The spirit giggled and backed away. Cricket started following the child, but it faded away into the snowy night.

"No! Do not go! What are you trying to tell me?" Cricket waited for a few moments, but the spirit didn't come back. His shoulders sagged and he turned towards his mother's tipi. "Bison, can you please show me what this means?" All the way home, he prayed for his spirit guide to pay him a visit and provide the answers he sought.

Chapter Six

Willow sat in the women's lodge, utterly bored. She hated her moon time because it interfered with her usual activities. She couldn't hunt or repair weapons because she could taint the hunt or the power of her weapons. Repairing and beading clothing or making jewelry was tedious work that didn't hold her attention very long. This moon time had lasted longer than usual.

Even though her flow had stopped, Willow would wait until the next day to leave the lodge, just to make sure. So, she was stuck there until morning.

The tipi flap opened and Green Leaf, Moonbeam's mother, entered. Willow was surprised when Moonbeam followed her. The young girl kept her eyes averted, obviously embarrassed and Willow surmised that this must be her first time staying in the women's lodge.

Willow exchanged pleasantries with the new arrivals. Green Leaf made sure that Moonbeam was settled before leaving.

Moonbeam took a tunic that she was working on out of the bag she'd brought. "I had other things to do today."

A smile curved Willow's lips. Moonbeam had just echoed her thoughts. "Me, too. Some women enjoy their time in here, but I do not."

"I am happy that I am now a woman, but I was going to scrape hides and make squirrel stew for Chirping Cricket."

"You can make him some when you leave the lodge."

"Yes, but I had just started making it when my moon time started. I had to throw it out. All of it went to waste."

Women were not allowed to prepare food during their moon time because if men accidentally ate it, it could adversely affect their hunting and fighting abilities.

"I see. That is too bad." Willow watched Moonbeam hold up the tunic. "That is too big for Cricket."

The wiry young medicine man hadn't grown much over the last year.

"I am giving it to Ames for Christmas."

It amazed Willow that Ames had talked their tribe into celebrating his white man's holiday. "He loves it and it is very fun. I guess if he can believe in Sendeh, we can believe in Jesus, at least a little bit. You are very skillful. Ames will appreciate such a fine tunic."

Moonbeam smiled. "You are very lucky to be marrying him."

After refusing him for so long, knowing that she would soon marry Ames felt a little surreal. Willow's heart swelled with love for her handsome trapper.

She was about to reply when a bad cramp hit her. Remaining silent, she wondered why she would have one when her moon time was over. It passed and she started asking Moonbeam about the tunic in French. They often did this so that they stayed in practice.

Ames and Firebrand were going to continue teaching them English, too. They knew some of the language, but he was proficient in it. They all felt that it was to their advantage to know other tongues. Even though they might not ever have any use for it, it was better to be prepared.

Another woman entered the lodge and all three of them worked on their French to pass the time.

His breathing came in loud pants as he struggled against his opponent. Although he fought hard, it didn't get him anywhere. Cricket lay on his stomach with his face pressed into the snow. "I give up."

The weight on his back lifted and he yelped when he was bodily lifted and set on his feet like a small child. Fang frowned at him. "Never say that in battle. Ever. A warrior does not give up."

Cricket glared at him. "In case you did not notice, this is not battle. This is just you torturing me."

"You are the man of your tipi now and must defend your women," Fang said. "We need every man of fighting age available, including you."

"That is not who I am. I am not a warrior," Cricket said. "I am a scrawny medicine man."

The corners of Fang's mouth lifted. "But you are the scrawny medicine man who fought an Ojibwa warrior and saved his sister's life. You saved many lives that day, Cricket. You put your life on the line for your people. That makes you a warrior. You may not think so, but you have a warrior's heart."

Pride filled Cricket as he thought about that. "Do you think I will ever be a good fighter?"

Fang said, "You already are. You just fight differently."

Cricket brushed snow from his hair. "What do you mean?"

"I would not have thought to kill that horse the way you did," Fang said. "It was a good tactical move. A warrior does not always have to be among the strongest to fight well. Cunning is just as important as strength, and while you are not physically strong, your mind and heart are."

Bison had said something very similar to Cricket that fateful day. The day when his father had bravely fought and died defending their village. So many of their men had perished. Had it not been for Dark Horse's warriors showing up, their small band would've been wiped out.

"I need to become stronger, though. I want to be able to defend my people." Cricket's voice held determination.

"Then you must practice. Sitting in a medicine lodge all day will not build your muscles," Fang said. "I will teach you and Lightning Strike will, too. There are many of us who will help you learn."

Cricket inhaled deeply. "All right."

"Good. Let us try it again."

Fang came at Cricket, who feinted to the left and ducked when Fang swung at him. Cricket meant to kick out to catch Fang's unguarded side as he'd been taught, but he slipped in the fresh snow and went down.

Fang laughed as he turned around with a smile on his face. "You would have gotten me if not for the snow. You must..."

His smile fled at the sight of Cricket lying on his back, his eyes wide open. The boy's chest rose and fell, so Fang knew that Cricket wasn't dead. He was having a vision. Slowly, Fang backed away, careful to make no noise lest he disturb Cricket. He knelt nearby so that he could warn others to stay away.

Cricket lifted his head from the snow and looked around for Fang. "Where did you go?" Rising, he saw that the camp was empty and realized that he was in the spirit world again.

A child laughed and Cricket turned around quickly. The spirit child stood a short distance from him.

"What is it that you wish to tell me, little one?"

Its bright blue eyes shimmered with tears. "Not this time. It will not happen this time."

"What will not happen?" Moving closer to the child, Cricket crouched. "I will not hurt you. What is not going to happen?"

Slowly the spirit child shook its head. "She does not know." It turned as if hearing a noise.

"I do not understand," Cricket said. "Who does not know what?"

Tears spilled from the child's eyes and disappeared. "She does not want me, but I must be born. You must tell her." Again, the child looked around and then faded from sight.

Frustration rose hot in Cricket's chest as he stood again. "Now what?" he called out. "What else am I supposed to see?"

The whiteness of the snow filled his vision, filled his mind, and he felt himself falling. He didn't fight it, instead just let his body freefall, knowing that he was about to wake up.

When he did, his eyes burned from being open without blinking for so long. Pressing the heels of his hands to his eyes, he sat up. For several moments, he stayed there, trying to process what he'd been told. Lowering his hands, he blinked and his eyes no longer felt as though someone had thrown sand in them.

"Cricket?"

"I am all right, Fang."

Several other people had gathered around, including his mother. Her concern showed plainly in her eyes, but she said nothing.

Rising to his feet, he asked, "How long have I been here?"

"Perhaps two hours," Fang replied.

A chill ran through Cricket and his leggings felt damp. "No wonder I am cold. I must go warm up and pray."

Green Leaf said, "I will bring you some soup and bread."

With a meaningful look, Cricket said, "Make sure that Moonbeam has not touched it." It was slightly embarrassing to mention this, but he couldn't allow anything to weaken his power.

"I will." Green Leaf gave him a small smile and left.

Cricket rolled his shoulders. "I am sorry that our lesson was cut short, Fang, but this is important. I just have to figure out why."

"Do not worry about it," Fang said. "We can practice tomorrow."

His thoughts already turned inward, Cricket made his way to the medicine lodge and ducked inside.

Early the next morning, Willow emerged from the women's lodge and went to her tipi, where she started a fire. Then she took her bag of clean clothing and jogged to a private spot along the river and quickly bathed. Feeling refreshed, she hurried back to her tipi and warmed herself by the fire.

Since she'd been in the women's lodge, she didn't have any food on hand outside of some tubers. Smiling, she picked up her bow and quiver and changed knives. As she stood, what felt like a menstrual cramp hit her. It was strong enough to make her put a hand on her stomach and wince.

Nausea suddenly washed over her as the pain became more intense. Dropping to her knees, Willow panted for breath as a hundred knives sliced through her abdomen. As she knelt there, she felt a gush of warm liquid between her legs and something more solid slide from her body.

Terror paralyzed her as the pain started to subside. Her chest heaved as she tried to comprehend what had just happened. She was scared to look, but she had to. With shaking hands, she untied her breechcloth and slowly lowered it. An involuntary cry burst from her at the sight that met her eyes.

No, no, no! It cannot be! But the proof was there. She'd been pregnant and had miscarried. Had lost her and Ames' baby. Shock set in and she didn't know what to do. *How could I have been pregnant? I have had a moon time each month and I did not feel any different. When did I conceive? It must have been right before Ames left. He did not want to leave me and waited until late in the season to go north.*

She couldn't stay there like that. Drawing on her mother's teachings, Willow wrapped the evidence of her and Ames' love in her breechcloth and set it aside. She separated her emotions from her actions as she cleaned herself. Her stomach still cramped, but she was able to bear it.

Ignoring the painful twinges, Willow tied on a new breechcloth and leggings. She needed to bury her baby and wash again. She would also have one of the midwives tend to her. Her blood froze as she realized that she couldn't do that without exposing the fact that she and Ames had been intimate.

But she was still bleeding and couldn't be around men, either. She would have to go back to the women's lodge, but how would she explain why? Willow was not given to lying. None of her people were. Fighting her rising panic, she forced herself to deal with one thing at a time.

First, she had to bury her baby. Tears flooded her eyes as she thought how disappointed Ames would be. There was no way to get around telling him, she knew. She put her bloody clothing in her bag and picked up the precious bundle, laying it gently on top of her clothing.

Brushing away her tears, she rose despite her pain. She picked up the pelvic bone of a deer she used to dig with and tucked it into her bag. Gaining control of her emotions, she left her tipi, relieved when no one approached her. Keeping her head as high as she could, she put one foot in front of the other, intent on completing her heartrending task.

Dry-eyed, Willow walked upstream along the river, looking for an appropriate place to bury the baby. Nausea plagued her and pain stabbed at her, but she marched onward. Up ahead on the right, she saw a formation of three large rocks of various heights, the tallest one being about even with her shoulders. Something about it appealed to her and that was where she decided her baby should rest.

Gently sitting her bag down, she took out her shovel and cleared away the snow from the spot between the rocks. She was relieved that although the ground was cold, it hadn't frozen yet. It made digging the grave easier. The hole needed to be deep enough so that animals wouldn't disturb the little grave.

When it was about three feet deep, Willow cradled the small bundle, saying prayers for a safe journey back to the spirit world. She held her sorrow at bay even though it made her chest ache. Tenderly, she lay it in the grave and started covering it up. Fatigue and pain clawed at her, but she refused to give in to it. Nothing would keep her from finishing.

Once all the earth was back in place and firmly packed down, Willow scooped clean snow over the grave. As she stood up, the world tilted and she had to lean against one of the stones to keep her balance. It took a couple of minutes for the dizziness to pass enough so that she could start out for the village.

She didn't make it very far before pain tore through her. It brought her to her knees and she felt blood soaking the absorbent cloths she wore. Knowing that she would die if she didn't make it back to camp, Willow started crawling, thinking that if she got close enough, she could scream for help. With her indomitable will, she continued, refusing to admit defeat.

Chapter Seven

Green Leaf was busy cutting up meat to make wasna from when Cricket stirred on his sleeping pallet. She smiled, thinking that it would be at least a couple of hours before he rose. Her son didn't sleep much at night, so he wasn't an early riser. And when he did finally wake, it took him a little while to become fully alert.

Therefore, she was surprised when he raised his head and sleepily looked around.

"Whose baby is crying? Is someone visiting?" he asked.

"There is no one here, Cricket. You must have been dreaming."

"Oh."

He laid his head back down, but in a couple of minutes, he was awake again when the baby cried once more. This time, he sat up and rubbed his eyes. His mother was the only one in the tipi with him.

"Was there someone close by with a baby?" he asked.

"No."

Cricket frowned. He'd heard a baby crying as plain as day. "You did not hear it?"

Green Leaf's brow furrowed. "No. Did you have a vision?"

"I do not know. I do not think so, but I keep hearing a baby cry," he said.

He moved to the fire and dipped out of cup of coffee from the pot that sat near it. "I am so glad that Ames was able to bring us more coffee. I missed it."

"He spoils us," Green Leaf remarked. "We are fortunate to have him."

This time the baby didn't merely cry, it screamed. The sound reverberated painfully in Cricket's head and he dropped his coffee to grab his ears. "Mother! Do you not hear that?" he shouted.

Green Leaf's heart lurched at the pain in his eyes and the anger in his voice. "No, Cricket. I do not. What is it?"

Cricket took his hands away and shook his head. "I do not know, but something is very wrong. I think it is the spirit child I have been seeing. It said that..."

She does not know. She does not want me. Not this time.

Cricket sat dumbfounded as he understood what the spirit child had been trying to tell him. "Oh, no."

Green Leaf was alarmed when her son rushed from their tipi.

Cricket sped through the camp, unmindful of the surprised looks on the faces of those he passed. He came to a skidding halt outside of Willow's tipi and scratched on the flap. "Willow? Are you there?"

Receiving no answer, he ducked his head inside. A small fire burned in the pit, but the tipi was empty. Turning around, he saw footprints leading away from the tipi. He started following them and was glad that not too many people had gone the way to the river that Willow had taken.

Dread lent his feet wings and he churned through the snow at breakneck speed. All the while, the baby screamed in his head, making it throb. What he thought was an animal appeared in the distance, but when he drew nearer to it, he saw that it was Willow crawling on her hands and knees in the snow.

"Willow!" He stopped her. "What happened?"

She didn't speak as she looked up at him. The pain and sadness in her eyes froze his blood. Then he looked behind her and saw a trail of blood drops in the snow.

"Oh, Willow," he said softly as sympathy brought tears to his eyes. "I am so sorry."

Willow's widened eyes revealed her shock. "You know?" Her voice was raspy.

"Yes, but do not worry about that right now. We must get you home. Can you walk at all?" he asked.

Willow shook her head.

Cricket knew that he couldn't carry her. Filling his lungs with air, he let out the loudest distress cry he could. He kept repeating it, hoping that his trills would reach the camp and guide someone to them. Just when it seemed as though he was going to have to run back to the village for help, several men came on the run, including Ames.

Upon seeing her, Ames rushed to her. "Willow, where are you hurt?" He'd seen the blood in the snow and assumed that she'd been hurt hunting.

Fear sent his pulse racing when tears welled in her eyes. "I am sorry. So sorry," she whispered.

Cricket cut in. "We need to get her back to camp. She is very sick."

Something in his eyes told Ames not to ask any further questions. "Do not worry, *mon amour*. I will get you home."

He helped her to her feet just long enough for him to scoop her into his arms and started for the village. When she wound her arms around his neck and wept against his chest, Ames became even more worried. He'd never known Willow to cry like that and it scared the hell out of him.

Repeatedly, she apologized to him, but he didn't know what for. When her grip on him relaxed, he looked at her, noticing that her eyes had closed. Her arms dropped and hung loosely.

"Willow! Stay with me," he said. "Stay awake."

He shook her a little, but she didn't rouse. Shifting her in his arms, he glanced down at her and noticed that her breechcloth was soaked with blood. Where was she injured? Ames started running at that point, knowing that if they didn't get to camp, she was going to die. He would move heaven and hell to prevent that from happening.

Cricket kept pace with him. "You must take her to her tipi. I cannot have her in the medicine lodge. Just do as I say and do not question me."

Unaccustomed to Cricket issuing orders, Ames was about to do just that. However, the quiet authority in Cricket's eyes once again kept him silent.

Upon reaching Willow's tipi, Ames took her inside and laid her down on her sleeping pallet. Cricket followed them inside.

"I sent Lighting Strike to get Mother," he said.

Ames asked, "Why are you not going to treat Willow? She needs you."

Cricket took a deep breath. "Ames, I cannot treat her because what is wrong with her is of a womanly nature. I am so sorry to have to tell you this, but I am almost certain that Willow has had a miscarriage."

Shock made Ames' chest constrict. "What?"

"This will go no further. Have you been intimate? Do not lie," Cricket said.

Ames met Cricket's eyes even as guilt ran through him. "Yes."

"When was the last time?"

"The other day, but we were together the night before I left at the end of June."

Cricket nodded. "She must have conceived around that time."

"But she takes a purging tea every morning."

Although these delicate matters embarrassed Cricket, it was his responsibility to deal with them. "Nothing is foolproof when it comes to preventing a child."

Green Leaf came into the tipi, interrupting them. "What has happened?"

Briefly, Cricket explained the situation. Green Leaf tried to hide her shock, but she couldn't quite manage it. She understood why Cricket couldn't treat Willow. She gave him a list of things to bring her and then made him and Ames leave.

As they went outside, Tulip came to help and ducked into the tipi.

"I cannot leave her," Ames said. "Why did she not tell me?"

Drawing him farther from the tipi, Cricket said, "She did not know. Your child's spirit came to me several times. It told me that it must be born, but not why. It also said that Willow did not know, but I could not figure out what it meant. Not until the baby kept crying and woke me up this morning."

Ames rubbed his chin, wondering if what Cricket said was true. He'd heard the stories about Cricket's visions and his negotiating skills from several people, but he hadn't witnessed anything like that.

"Why would she not have known? She did not mention missing her moon time," Ames said.

Cricket said, "Most likely the purging tea made her bleed, but it did not kill the fetus. She did not seem to feel sick in the mornings, either. I remember hearing one time that she had gone to the women's lodge. I truly believe that she did not know."

Ames thrust a hand through his hair. "Ah, my poor Willow. How scared she must have been out there all alone. Was she hunting?"

"I did not see any weapons, but I was more concerned with her," Cricket said.

"This is my fault." Ames rubbed the back of his neck. "I kept trying to convince her to marry me." He met Cricket's gaze. "I know that you must be angry, but until you fall in love and desire a woman so much that it steals your sanity, do not judge me—or Willow."

Cricket pursed his lips, but he didn't pursue that topic. "This is very serious, Ames. Do you understand that? Even if Willow had not miscarried, her baby would have come much too soon after the wedding. Everyone would have known that you had been together before then."

Ames didn't care about his own reputation, but he was very concerned for Willow's. "It is no one's business. No one needs to know that she was pregnant. Only that this is a womanly issue. Nothing more."

Cricket nodded. "I agree. I will instruct my mother and Tulip to say no more than that about the nature of her illness."

Ames put a hand on Cricket's shoulder. "It is not for my sake that I say this. You know how important Willow is to our tribe. I do not want her position or status affected by this. I do not want anyone to think badly about her."

"I understand and I do not want that to happen, either." Cricket closed his eyes for a moment. "I am going to go make a tincture that will help build Willow's blood again and fight infection."

"I need to know how she is," Ames said. "I need to see her."

He moved towards Willow's tipi, but Cricket grabbed his arm. "Let them work. Mother will come out when she has news."

Clenching his jaw to keep his angry words in check, Ames nodded. "All right. I love her so much, Cricket. She is my heart. I need her."

The raw emotion in Ames' voice made tears start behind Cricket's eyes. "We all do. I will be back."

Without regard for himself, Ames sat in the snow outside Willow's tipi. He couldn't bear to leave without knowing how she was. With every beat of his heart, he willed her to live. Prayer upon prayer did he lift up to God, asking Him to help her survive. Eventually, he ran out of prayers and simply tried to send his love to Willow, tried to lend her his strength.

Ames couldn't sit still any longer. He rose from where he sat and paced as Lightning Strike watched him. The anxiety twisting his stomach needed an outlet. He wanted to hit something and he kept berating himself for being weak in not being able to resist Willow's charms.

However, there was also a part of him that didn't regret their moments of passion. He'd meant it when he'd told Willow that he'd been hoping that she'd conceive. Not only because they would've had to marry, but because he badly wanted children with her.

Ames practically pounced on Green Leaf when she emerged from Willow's tipi. "How is she?"

Deep concern was etched on her face. "She is very weak, but I believe she will recover."

The force of Ames' relief made him feel faint. "Thank you, Green Leaf. I am very grateful to you. I need to see her."

She blocked the tipi entrance. "She needs rest."

Ames hid his irritation. "I will not stay long. I must see her. Please."

"She still bleeds."

There were many Kiowa beliefs that Ames had adopted, but a woman's moon time affecting a man's virility in any way wasn't one of them. In his lifetime, he'd been around many women at that time of the month and he'd never suffered any adverse effects from it.

"I do not care about that. I will purify myself once I have seen her."

Seeing that Ames wouldn't be deterred, Green Leaf let him pass.

He stepped into the tipi and Tulip looked up at him in surprise.

"Green Leaf said that I could see her for a few minutes. May we have some privacy?"

Tulip didn't bother hiding her disapproval, but she acquiesced and exited the tipi.

Ames knelt beside Willow, alarmed by the sickly pallor under her usually bronze skin. He took her hand, kissed it and held it against his cheek. "I am so sorry, my love. So very sorry."

Willow heard his voice and opened her eyes despite her deep fatigue. "Ames."

Needing to be close to her, he lay down beside her. "I am here." A tear rolled down his cheek. "You must rest."

Her grip tightened on his hand. "I swear that I did not know I was pregnant. If I had, I would have stopped drinking the purging tea. I would never have killed our baby, no matter the consequences."

She reached for him and Ames gently gathered her in his arms. "I know, Willow. I believe you."

"Our baby, Ames…"

Willow hadn't wanted to become pregnant before, but losing the little life that she'd created with the man she loved devastated her.

She clung to Ames as sobs wracked her body and he tightened his embrace. His strength comforted her.

"Shh, my love. I am not angry with you. I am very sad, but I am not angry, nor do I blame you. I love you more than ever and I am so happy that you will be all right."

Stroking her sweaty hair, Ames rocked her and murmured soothing words to her. After a time, her tears started to slow and he wiped them from her face with one of the soft cloths that lay nearby.

"There. That's better," he said in French. "You need to rest now."

Willow rallied herself a little. "Ames, I buried our baby at the place of three stones. My trail will lead you there."

Startled, Ames jerked slightly. "Is that what you were doing out there?"

Exhaustion weighed on Willow and nodding sapped the last of her strength. She stopped fighting the force that pulled her down into black oblivion.

Her hand went slack in his and Ames kissed it before laying it down beside her. Then he tenderly covered her with a blanket and kissed her forehead. "I'll be back in a little while. Sleep well." He kissed her one last time and left the tipi.

Tulip had been waiting outside and she went back into the tipi to be with her cousin.

Cricket had returned and stared at him with wide eyes. "You should not be in there."

Anger and grief made Ames' tongue sharp. "Am I not a strong warrior? Have I not found anyone, anywhere? Have I not helped on bison hunts and am I not the best trapper you have ever known?"

Cricket's eyebrows rose. "Yes."

Others, including Growling Wolf had gathered around.

"And do I not make excellent trades and keep coming back every year despite the danger?"

"Yes, you do."

"Perhaps I have a special power. I raised around women who were having their moon time all my life and it has never once caused me to falter!" he bellowed and then lapsed into French as his temper burned hotter. "I've never shot worse, lost a fight, ran slower, or was made weaker by being near a woman who—"

He broke off and took a huge breath. Yelling wasn't going to help the situation. He held it for a few moments before slowly expelling it. "I will purify myself every time I come out of there, but I will not be kept from Willow. She needs me and I *will* be there for her."

Giving everyone a wide berth, he walked to his tipi. He made a cedar and sage grass fire and stripped down to his drawers. When the fire was high enough, he bathed well in the smoke and dressed again. Putting on his coat, he went outside and was met by Firebrand.

"I have something I have to go do," he said.

Firebrand nodded. "Do you want company?"

"Thank you, but no. This is something I must do on my own."

"You do not need me to tell you how strong Willow is. She will be fine."

Ames smiled tightly at him before he strode away.

Chapter Eight

He kept his head down as he jogged through the village, not wanting to speak with anyone. A light crust covered the snow and his boots broke through it as he ran. The exercise felt good and helped to calm him—until he saw the spot where they'd found Willow.

Blood stained the snow in spots. Her trail was easy to follow and it didn't take him long to find the three rocks she'd described to him. Going to them, he saw the way the snow was disturbed and knew he'd found the right place.

Our baby is here. It's not supposed to be. Our baby should be safe in her mother's womb, not here in this cold place. Ames leaned against one of the stones as a wave of grief broke over him. He'd wanted a child with Willow for almost four years and now, just when they were about to be married, she'd miscarried.

Thinking about the loss of the precious little life and how ill Willow was crushed Ames and he sank to his knees. "Why now when we were so happy?" he asked, looking up to the sky. "I don't understand."

Rocking forward, he gave into his misery. Even while he cried, Ames prayed for their baby's spirit to be delivered safely to Heaven. He also prayed for Willow, the woman who'd captured his heart the first time he'd looked into her lovely dark eyes...

Three Years Earlier...

As he slogged through the deep, slushy snow, Ames readjusted his pack and hummed under his breath. He'd been following a tributary of the mighty Mississippi River south for two weeks. On a lark, he'd decided to go exploring to see if he could find a location where the game was more plentiful. Beaver and mink were becoming scarce up north.

Accompanying him was Firebrand, a former Mohawk captive of the Fox. Upon seeing some recent deer tracks, they veered away from the large stream, intending to track down the animal. They hadn't had any fresh meat for a couple of days and the venison would taste good. They'd trailed the deer for about a quarter of a mile when they were suddenly surrounded by four warriors.

The travelers held up their arms to show that they meant no harm. Ames identified their captors as Kiowa and spoke to them in their language.

"We are peaceful and have no wish to fight you," he said.

One of them, a tall, well-built brave stepped forward. "You know our tongue, yet you speak with a strange accent."

Ames gave him a friendly smile. "I have met a great many Indians since I was eleven winters old, Kiowa among them. I am called Ames Duchamp and I am a French fur trader. This is my good friend, Firebrand."

"A trader?" The brave's eyes settled on Ames' pack. "What do you have to trade?"

Ames lowered his arms, but kept his hands in plain sight. "Perhaps we could go somewhere more hospitable than this to do our trading? You know our names. Might we know yours?"

The brave didn't smile, but his eyes glittered with good humor as he extended an arm. "I am Fang, our war leader."

The two men grasped arms.

"It is an honor to meet you," Ames said.

"This is my brother-in-law, Lightning Strike. This is Badger and Willow."

Ames grasped arms with the first two braves, but he was startled to see that Willow was in fact a woman. The most beautiful woman he'd ever had the pleasure of looking upon. She was as tall as Lightning Strike and Badger and had a stern air about her.

As she frowned at him, her delicate eyebrows puckered. The white snow on the ground was reflected in her black eyes, adding to their luminous beauty and her pretty lips looked supple and soft. Her curiosity matched his and Ames wondered if she'd ever seen a white person before. Their eyes met and Ames' heart leapt into a faster rhythm. Since she'd been introduced to him as a warrior, Ames held out his arm to her.

She hesitated a moment before taking it. Her grip was as strong as any man's, but her long-fingered hand was more delicate. Beautiful.

He gave her a flirtatious grin. "I have not had the pleasure of meeting such a beautiful warrior before. I hope your husband appreciates you."

She smiled back at him and Ames was completely enchanted by her. "He would if I had one, but I do not. Nor do I want one."

Ames laughed. "You are a smart woman."

With the introductions made, Fang motioned for them to follow him and Lightning Strike. Willow and Badger brought up the rear, keeping Ames and Firebrand between them. As they walked Ames had a difficult time not turning around to look at Willow. He had no idea, but she couldn't take her eyes from him.

He is a beautiful man. I have never seen yellow hair or blue eyes before. He is big, strong. I wonder where he comes from? Where does he call home? *More questions crowded her mind, but she remained silent as they walked to their village.*

Presently, the trees gave way to a large camp. A group of children ran to greet them.

"Fang, who are they?" a little girl asked.

"They are traders, Moonbeam," he said.

Ames smiled at her and she smiled shyly back at him. "Your hair is like the sun."

The skinniest boy Ames had ever seen put a hand on her shoulder. "Moonbeam, you are being impolite. Wait to be spoken to."

A group of people began to form around them and Fang raised a hand for silence so he could introduce them. An elderly man cut through the crowd and Ames surmised that this was their chief. He carried himself with pride even though he was a little stooped, and everyone treated him deferentially.

"I am Chief Growling Wolf. Did I hear that your name is Duchamp?" he asked.

"Yes. Ames Duchamp."

As they grasped arms, Growling Wolf looked him over. "Are you related to François Duchamp?"

Ames' eyebrows rose. "Yes. He was my father. Did you know him?"

Growling Wolf nodded. "I met him several times when we lived farther north. I do not recall that you were with him, though. You would have been just a boy. He was a good friend of ours before we had to move. Only a couple of our younger people ever met him, though. Unlike many trappers, he treated us fairly and never tried to cheat us."

"I remember him mentioning a Growling Wolf, but I did not make the connection. He spoke well of you," Ames said. "He was just starting out and I did not travel with him for the first few years. I took over for him when he passed away several years ago."

Growling Wolf sobered and sadness shone in his eyes. "I am sorry. We wondered why he did not come back to the trading post the season before we left. I had hoped that it was not because something bad had happened to him."

Ames said, "He was killed by men who robbed him on the trail one day. I was not with him at the time, but I tracked them down and made them pay for his murder. There was no need for them to kill him. He would have given them his wares without any trouble."

Willow listened with sympathy and admiration. She would do the same thing if she could find the people responsible for killing her parents. It also impressed her that Growling Wolf had known Ames' father and thought highly of him.

"Your father was well-liked by most people and preferred not to fight if possible. It was what made him such a success. He was able to move freely between warring tribes because he genuinely liked them all and did not take sides," Growling Wolf said. "Come. I will have my wife, Sleek Doe, make you something to eat."

Willow would've liked to go with them and hear more about Ames, but she had to go back to sentry duty. Although she remained alert as always that day, a separate part of her mind lingered on Ames. She'd seen appreciation in men's eyes before, but the way he'd looked at her had been different.

It was as though he'd looked inside her somehow. Or maybe it was just his piercing blue eyes that made it seem that way. Either way, he'd captivated her, something that no man had ever done before. Shaking off those thoughts, she signed back and forth with Badger about his wife and her best friend, Sky Dancer, who was expecting in a couple of months.

Over the next week, Ames and Firebrand traded the small number of goods they had with them. Ames wished they had more, but he'd left his stash up north because he hadn't known what they might encounter during their travels. Their trek had been exploratory in nature, so traveling with all their cargo wouldn't have been smart. Ames was impressed by the abundance of ermine, beaver, and minx in the area, not to mention bigger game.

He worked out a deal with Growling Wolf that would benefit them both. In exchange for him and Firebrand being allowed to stay the winter and collect pelts, he would return the next fall with whatever goods the tribe most wanted. Due to his relationship with François, Growling Wolf extended the same trust to Ames.

"Where are the best trapping places?" he asked the chief.

Growling Wolf said, "Willow is our best small game hunter. She can show you the best places to trap."

Ames was surprised by this, but he didn't let on. "All right. I will ask her to show me."

Their conversation then shifted to the types of goods Growling Wolf wanted Ames to purchase when he went north to the trading posts in the early spring.

The next day, Ames and Firebrand followed Willow as she led them to a small lake. A huge beaver dam was situated along the far side. When they'd started out, Ames had expected another brave to chaperone Willow so that she wasn't alone with them.

However, none had, which didn't bother Ames in the least.

"This beaver family is so large that some of them moved further downstream to a big pond," she said.

"Then there are plenty for the taking, but I will be selective and not wipe them all out. That would be foolish. I will leave enough to mate and then when I come back next year, there will be more to harvest. They will keep replenishing themselves," Ames told her.

Firebrand had started circling the pond, looking for the best places to lay the traps.

Willow tried not to stare at Ames, but it was hard. He was so handsome and she liked his sense of humor. Any time he'd been around her, he treated her like a woman without being condescending or disapproving of her unusual status.

She'd never encountered a man who made her pulse race or who created a fluttery feeling in her stomach. From the time she'd become a woman, she'd heard about the way women in love felt about their men, but she'd never experienced anything like that until now.

Ames made her feel all of that and more, but she didn't know what to do about it. She shouldn't do anything about it. He was only there for the winter and then he'd be gone in spring.

When Ames turned his gaze on her, Willow couldn't look away from him. An intense expression crossed his face. She didn't know what it meant, but her heart beat inside her chest like a drum and her breathing quickened.

He glanced over at Firebrand and his jaw clenched before he looked back into her eyes. "This is improper, but I am not known for following propriety." His voice was huskier than normal. "You are incredibly beautiful and if we were alone, I would kiss you if you let me."

Willow gasped, but she wasn't offended at all. She'd never been told outright that she was beautiful and hearing it from such a virile man excited her. Everything about Ames attracted her to him.

"I would let you."

His mouth curved in a delighted smile and his eyes danced with mischief. "Then we will have to make that happen."

Willow's heart thundered in her chest. "I will come to you tonight."

His eyebrows lifted at her bold statement. He knew that Willow lived in her own tipi, which meant that it was easy for her to move about unnoticed since she had no one to answer to. Knowing Indian customs as well as he did, he knew that they were treading in dangerous territory.

He should tell her no, refuse her offer, but he'd never wanted a woman so intensely. "I will be waiting."

Willow forced herself to sober and step away from him. She nodded once and he did something odd. He blinked only one eye as he gave her a conspiratorial smile.

"What does that mean? What you did with your eye?" she asked.

Ames laughed. "Do you not..." He trailed off when he realized that there was no Kiowa word for winking. "The French people call it cligner de l'œil and the English call it winking."

"What does it mean?"

"It can mean two different things. Sometimes it is used between two people who have a secret with each other. Other times, it means that you are teasing someone and that you mean no offense," Ames explained.

Willow tried it and did it correctly on the third try.

"Yes! Now you have it." Ames thumped her on the shoulder, much like he did the men. But unlike with them, he let his hand linger and squeezed her tricep a little.

Then he took his hand away and steered the conversation back to trapping.

Willow sharpened arrowheads and knives to occupy herself until she felt it was late enough to go to Ames' tipi. *I must be insane. I should not go, but I*

want to so badly. I have never wanted to kiss a man before. A few have stolen one, but I did not want them to kiss me. She smiled as she remembered punching a couple of braves who'd made passes at her.

She hadn't meant to blurt out that she'd let Ames kiss her, but he'd caught her completely by surprise with his honest compliments. Just thinking about kissing him made her feel warm. *What would it feel like? Would she like it?* She hoped so. *Would he like kissing her?* She almost panicked. *What if he didn't? Or, what if he did? What then?*

Unaccustomed to feeling so unsure of herself, Willow buried her face in her hands and groaned. Most women were married by the time they were twenty winters old, but most women weren't warriors, either.

Stop this! It is just a kiss. *She shook off her anxiety. I am a warrior and warriors do not show fear.* Back in control, she left her tipi and kept to the shadows as she made her way to Ames' tipi. She waited to make sure that no one else was around before going to it and scratching on the flap. He responded quietly and she slipped inside.

His blue eyes smiled as his sensual mouth lifted at the corners. "There you are. Come sit with me." He patted the spot next to him. "Would you like some coffee?"

Willow's heartbeat accelerated and her mouth went dry at the sight of his shirtless torso. Seeing men with very little covering them was something she was used to, of course, but Ames was built so differently than the men she knew.

His muscles were more rounded, heavier, and rolled as he moved. Fine golden hair covered his chiseled chest and his skin was much paler than hers. As she sat down beside him, she felt small next to his bulk, something she was unaccustomed to. Although her hands were large for a woman, his hands were twice as big as hers.

Ames took his time preparing their drinks, letting her look him over. Her perusal amused him, and he knew without a doubt that her scrutiny meant that she'd never seen a white man up close.

"Have you ever drank coffee before?"

His voice startled her. "What? No."

He handed her a steaming cup. "It is like tea, but different."

Willow took a whiff of the brew and found the aroma very pleasing. "It smells good." She blew on it and took a sip. It was a little more bitter than tea, but she liked the taste.

Ames held up a little pouch. "Sucre?"

"Sucre?" She repeated the French word for "sugar". "What is that?"

"It is sweet. Much like maple syrup. Do you want to try it?"

"Yes."

Ames put some sugar on a small spoon and stirred it into her coffee. "See what you think."

Willow thought that the sugar improved the taste of the coffee. "It is very good."

He smiled and took a drink of his own coffee.

"Where do you come from?" she asked.

"Well, my first home, France, is very far from here. Across the great water that we call an ocean. It takes several moons to get here, sometimes longer if there is bad weather," he said.

"Several moons? How do you travel? A canoe cannot stay in the water that long," she asked.

Ames told her of the huge sailing ships that European people built and sailed on to the New World.

"New World?" She shook her head. "It is not new. It has been here since time began. Thousands of years."

"True, but it is new to us. We came here when I was just a boy. Truthfully, I do not remember much about my life before we came to this continent. My father sought fortune in the fur trading business, and while he did quite well, he always said that the real treasure was in meeting so many kinds of people," Ames said.

"What sort of people?"

"Swedish, Dutch, more French people, and English. All of them are much like me. White men. But he loved all Indians, too. Iroquois, Ojibwa, Seneca, Lakota, Kiowa, Mandan, and many others. He taught me to love them, too."

"Do you speak all of their languages?" she asked.

"Oui. That is French for 'yes'. I speak some of them better than others, but I also know Indian sign," he said, demonstrating.

Willow smiled, impressed with his intelligence. "Will you teach me?"

"Mais oui, *which means, 'yes, of course'."*

Willow mimicked him, trying to replicate his pronunciation and intonation as closely as possible. "Mais oui."

"Tres bien. *Very good."*

Seeing her eagerness to learn, Ames thought that it would be the perfect way to spend time with her and also help her learn valuable skills. Knowing various languages had kept him and his father alive many times and was invaluable to him as a trapper.

Ames taught her some other simple phrases as they drank more coffee. He would've instructed her all night if it meant that he was able to watch her lovely lips form French words. However, he knew that there would be big trouble if someone discovered them.

"I have one more thing to teach you tonight," *he said.*

"Oui?"

She was catching on quicker than he'd anticipated. "Puis-je vous embrasser?"

"Puis-je vous embrasser? *What does that mean?"*

"It means, 'May I kiss you?'."

A jolt of surprise ran through Willow and her heart leapt. He was not only instructing her; he was asking her for permission. She'd told him that she'd let him, but now he was actually asking. He wasn't just taking it for granted that she would allow him to kiss her.

And she did want him to kiss her. For the first time, she wanted to know what it was like to be treated like a woman. "Yes. Oui."

Ames shifted closer to her and took one of her hands. His eyes held hers as he kissed the back of it. Her lips parted on a tiny gasp and desire stirred within him. While her palm was slightly calloused, the rest of her hand was soft-skinned and smooth under his lips. Her chest rose and fell a little more rapidly and her eyes had grown even darker.

He kissed her hand another time before tugging on it as he leaned towards her. When she moved closer, he gently put his fingers under her chin to tip it up a little. Slowly, he settled his mouth lightly over hers in a gentle, chaste kiss. Pulling back a little, he saw confusion in her eyes.

"What is wrong?"

Willow wasn't sure how to respond. The kiss had made her tingle a little, but she felt as though something were lacking.

"Are you all right?"

She nodded. "Yes. That was...nice."

His smile drew her eyes to his mouth and she reached out to touch it. He remained motionless as she ran a fingertip over his bottom lip and then over his cheek. His jaw was rough with stubble and she liked how it felt.

"Kiss me again."

Her soft request sent heat surging through him. "Say 'Embrasse-moi encore?'"

"Embrasse-moi encore?"

"Oui."

His kiss was firmer this time, more insistent and Willow's pulse rose. Then she felt his mouth open and the tip of his tongue touched her lips. He took her chin between his thumb and forefinger and exerted gentle pressure on it, encouraging her to open her mouth.

When she did, Ames slanted his mouth over hers and dipped his tongue inside to meet hers. She tried to pull back, but he slid his hand into her hair and cupped the back of her head to hold her in place. Hesitantly, she mimicked him, seeking his tongue with hers.

Deepening the kiss, he leaned closer, running his hand over her shoulder and down her arm. He tasted of coffee and smelled of snow and cedar. She let him pull her closer and her hand came to rest against his bare chest. His muscles flexed under her palm, fascinating her.

Moving her hand over his chest, she liked the texture of his chest hair. As they continued to kiss, the tingling in her body grew stronger and she felt very warm. He growled as she caressed his chest and played with the short curly hair. Instinctively, she knew that it was a sound of approval.

Ames pulled her harder against him, caught up in her taste and the way she touched him. He wanted more, so much more. Then suddenly, she wound her arms around his neck and kissed him back urgently. It seemed as though learning languages wasn't the only thing she caught onto quickly.

He'd been holding back, but he let her feel the full intensity of his desire for her now.

Willow felt herself spiraling out of control and loved it. The feelings Ames was evoking in her were beautiful and enthralling. She never wanted to stop kissing him. He was so strong and made her feel womanly.

Suddenly, he dragged his lips from hers and stared into her eyes.

"You are so beautiful and exciting, Willow, but we must stop," he said.

Her breathing had grown heavy as though she'd been running for a couple of miles. "I do not want to," she said, her voice slightly husky.

"Nor do I, but it would not be right to go further."

His eyes had turned to blue fire and she understood his meaning. He was right, of course, but she wanted him more than she'd ever wanted anything before. She wasn't sure what exactly that meant, but she wanted to find out.

"How do you say 'I want to make love with you' in French?"

Ames' eyes widened. "No. I will not tell you that."

"Why?" she asked, running a hand over his chest.

Because I will not be able to resist you if I hear you say it in my native tongue. *Her touch was driving him crazy. He'd been with many women, but Willow ignited his ardor in a way that no other woman had. He suspected that no other woman would ever excite him the way she did.*

She pressed a kiss to his lips. "Tell me. S'il vous plait?*"*

In that moment, Ames realized that refusing her was useless. "Je veux faire l'amour avec vous."

"Je veux faire l'amour avec vous."

Her pronunciation was a little awkward, but hearing her say those words drove all reason from his mind. He took her lips in a fierce kiss, helpless against the tide of passion she created in him. His body hardened even more as he kissed her and held her close.

She buried her hands in his long hair and moaned against his mouth. Ames' need to possess her was too strong. He had to have her now. Not since he'd been a young man had he lost control, but Willow did something to him that he couldn't define and really didn't care to.

Grasping the bottom of her tunic, he pulled it up over her head and flung it away. Her tawny skin glowed in the firelight as he gazed upon her. Although her breasts weren't overly large, they were perfectly formed. He kissed her neck as he palmed one of them.

"You are magnificent, chérie."

Willow shivered as he grazed her nipple and felt it tighten. As he trailed more kisses over her neck and throat, she vaguely wondered why she wasn't scared or nervous. She knew that many women were apprehensive their first time, but there was something about Ames that made her feel safe. She couldn't explain why, but she trusted him implicitly.

He gently pushed her onto her back and lay down beside her. Willow hooked a hand around his neck and drew him down so she could kiss him. Her senses were filled with him; the way he tasted, his man-smell, and his rough hand gently caressing her sent tremors of need through her.

She arched her back when he ran his thumb over her nipple. Ames broke their kiss and moved lower so he could take the tight bud in his mouth. As she gasped and buried her hand in his hair, she felt him untie her leggings and breechcloth, but she didn't care. The fire raged too hot inside for her to be shy.

Ames' voice was hushed and raspy. "You must not make noise, chérie. We cannot be found out or there will be dire consequence for both of us. Do you understand?"

His eyes blazed with passion. "Yes. I understand."

He sent her a rakish smile. "Very well, then."

Standing up, Ames rid himself of his blue French fly breeches, amused at the way her eyes widened as he stripped. His gaze roamed over her, taking in her long, toned legs, slim hips and pert breasts. Every inch of her strong, bronzed body was beautiful and his hunger grew stronger yet.

Kneeling between her knees, he kissed and nibbled his way up one of her shapely thighs until he could sample her taste. The sight of her biting her lower lip and her soft whimper was almost more than he could take. But he managed to hold himself in check so he could pleasure her. It was his way of making up for any discomfort he would cause her. He was thorough and savored her sweetness, knowing that he'd never get the memory of her taste out of his mind.

A shudder ran through Willow and she grabbed his forearms, which rested on her stomach. Never had she dreamt that such wondrous sensations existed. She couldn't hold still as tension mounted in her body. Her grip on his arms tightened as the tension broke and she was barely able to hold back a cry as bliss washed through her.

How long it lasted, she had no idea, but it faded slowly. However, she was about to find out that it was only the beginning. Slowly, he moved up, rising over her like a golden god, all muscle and beautifully male.

"You are the most stunning woman I have ever seen, Willow. I have never wanted a woman so much, but I want you to be absolutely sure. I could not bear it if you regretted making love with me," he said.

Reaching up, she cradled his face, stroking his jaw with her thumbs. "No matter what, I will never regret giving myself to you. Please, make me yours."

Ames didn't need to hear any more. Gradually, he made them one, moving into her with tender care. There were only a couple of times when her expression grew pained, but with a patience he hadn't known he possessed, he soothed away her discomfort with passionate kisses and caresses.

Holding on to Ames' broad back, Willow reveled in the way he possessed her. His movements were fluid and graceful. She ran her hands over his powerful muscles, urging him on as need intensified deep inside her again. Faster they moved, until their pace grew frenzied.

Swiftly, Willow reached the crest and teetered there for a moment before ecstasy unlike any she'd ever known swept her higher. In the heat of the moment, she forgot to be quiet until Ames' mouth covered hers, muffling her moan of pleasure. Just as she began drifting down, Ames wrapped his arms around her and froze. He whispered in French against her ear as he pressed into her hard.

She had no idea what he was saying, but she understood that he was experiencing the same sort of pleasure as her. It was a heady, magical experience to know that she had the power to make him feel such bliss. His back muscles bunched and held for several moments before he let out a low growl and grew slack. Their chests rose and fell with their labored breathing as he slowly sank down on top of her.

As they came down from the lofty, sensual peak, Ames lifted his head and met her gaze. Something so powerful passed between them that it made tears gather in his eyes. He'd never been so moved by lovemaking before. Words failed him right then. There was no way for him to convey all that he was feeling. He kissed her softly before carefully disentangling himself from her.

When he rolled over on his back, Willow went with him, rising up on her elbow to look down at him.

He smiled at her. "Do you have any idea what you have done?"

She shook her head slightly. "What have I done?"

His smile broadened. "You have ruined me for other women, Willow. There will never be another woman for me as long as I live."

Willow grinned and buried her face against him as she blushed. Quiet laughter rumbled in his chest.

"You think I am kidding, but I am serious," he said. "Look at me, Willow."

When she did, all traces of humor had gone from his expression.

"Perhaps I am crazy. You will most likely think I am, but what just happened between us is much more than physical pleasure. The expression 'two souls brushing' is how you might put it. I have never felt such a connection with a woman before," Ames said.

Willow pressed a kiss to his chest. "I do not think that you are crazy. I feel it, too. Until you came here, I never seriously thought about being with a man. I did not even know how to kiss. I cannot explain why, but I had no fear about making love with you. And I do not regret it at all."

Ames was relieved to hear it. "I am glad."

Willow sighed and sat up. "I must go before people start rising. I do not want to."

"I do not want you to, either, but yes, it is best." He stood up with her, pulling her into his embrace. "Get some rest. We will check traps later."

"Yes." She played with his hair as she gave him a teasing smile. "I think that you have caught me in your trap, Ames Duchamp."

"And you have caught me in yours." He kissed her and held her close for a few moments.

Then Willow reluctantly stepped back from him. They watched each other dress and by the time they were done, both hungered for each other again. Boldly, Willow stepped up to Ames and said, "Tomorrow night."

A roguish smile curved his lips. "What makes you think I can wait that long?"

She laughed and ducked out of his tipi, leaving him chuckling as he watched after her.

Chapter Nine

Firebrand watched with amusement over the next few days as the Kiowa band dealt with Ames. He confused them with his odd ways and actions. A demonstrative man, Ames often patted, hugged, and kissed people, even the men.

At first, the warriors especially had found it offensive when Ames sometimes kissed both of their cheeks when he greeted them. Firebrand had quickly stepped in and explained that this was a French custom and that it only meant respect and friendship. He also told them that he was not trying to steal anyone's wife or being disrespectful when he flirted or happened to lay a hand on a woman's shoulder.

He was also very talkative and loved telling stories. The children adored him and sometimes followed him around the village. Ames returned their affection and often gathered them around him so that he could have French and English lessons with them. Some of the adults participated in this as well. Ames enjoyed teaching them and was free with his praise whenever they mastered something.

Out of all the children, Moonbeam was his best student and Ames decided to also teach her how to write. Ames instructed anyone who wanted to learn, but Moonbeam's hunger for knowledge impressed him. He gave her a journal and had her practice every day, then checked it at night for her.

Ames' generous, outgoing nature soon endeared him to the tribe and their friendship was solidified over that winter. His and Willow's bond also grew stronger. It was incredibly difficult for them to stay away from each other, but they spent every moment they could together.

Their hunger for each other was unquenchable and they made love every chance they had. Firebrand had accidentally found them kissing one day in the woods, but he swore that he would never reveal their relationship. They'd also been afraid that he'd disapprove, but they needn't have worried.

"When I was a captive, I was tortured, beaten, and degraded all the time. I had little happiness until Ames rescued me. If you make each other happy,

then that is all that matters. You must hold onto happiness whenever possible because you never know what the future holds," he'd said.

And they did make each other happy. The winter passed much too quickly and the end of March came before the lovers knew it. They spent the night before Ames and Firebrand left in each other's arms.

"I do not want you to leave," Willow said, holding onto him tightly. "I love you so much. I am going to miss you terribly."

Ames sighed and kissed her. "It is the same for me, mon amour. My heart is yours and always will be. We must keep busy so that the time goes fast until it is time for me to return."

Willow gazed into his beautiful blue eyes. "Promise me that you will come back."

He cupped her cheek with his hand. "Of course, I will. Never doubt my love for you or that I will return. I want you to think about something over the summer. I want to marry you, to be your husband and share our lives. Do not answer now. Consider it and tell me your answer when I come back in the fall. Will you do that for me?"

Willow swallowed her tears of happiness and sorrow. "Yes. I will think about it."

"Thank you." His sensual smile set her heart and body on fire. "Now, let me love you one more time before we must part, chérie."

Their blissful journey was tinged with the need to brand each other on their souls. They drew it out as long as possible before collapsing together. As hard as she tried, Willow couldn't hold back the tears that streamed from her eyes. Ames held her, comforting her as best he could even while his own heart ached over being parted from her.

Finally, there was no avoiding their separation and they shared one last kiss goodbye before she left his tipi. Normally, Willow bathed every morning unless it was freezing outside. However, that morning, she didn't want to because she didn't want to wash Ames' scent from her body. But she reluctantly went to the stream and bathed before going to her tipi to make something to eat.

When the time came for Ames and Firebrand to leave, they were sent off with much fanfare and more than one person had tears in their eyes.

Moonbeam hugged him tightly and cried. His promises to return made her feel better and she let him go. One of their braves, Panther, was going with them to help them carry large number of pelts they'd harvested that winter.

One by one, Ames grasped arms with the men and then came to Willow. "Thank you for all of your help. My trapping would not have been such a success if not for your assistance."

Holding her emotions firmly in check, Willow smiled. "You are welcome. I am glad it all worked out so well. Have a safe journey."

"We will."

Not since her parents' deaths had Willow's heart hurt so badly. Watching Ames and his friends disappear into the trees was sheer torture. Once they were gone, it seemed as though all the color bled out of her world.

All day long, she faked smiles and forced herself to act happy and unaffected by Ames' departure. But when night fell and she was all alone in her tipi, she poured out her heartache, muffling her crying with a thick blanket. Her body shook with sobs...

The Present...

...just as Ames' shoulders shook as he mourned the loss of their child. Anger at the unjustness of it burned through him and he pounded on one of the rocks. Reining in his turbulent emotions, Ames dried his eyes and rose from the ground. When he reached the spots of blood in the snow, Ames kicked fresh snow over them. He couldn't stand seeing the evidence of Willow's pain and their loss.

He was met on the way back to camp by Lightning Strike. Anger glowed in the brave's eyes.

"How long have you been deceiving everyone? I know that you took something from Willow that was not rightfully yours, Ames. How long have you been having an affair? Did you only offer for Willow because of the baby?" Lightning Strike grabbed Ames' coat. "Tulip has miscarried twice and the last time was much like what Willow is going through. So, do not lie to me and try to say that there was no baby."

Ames said, "Neither of us knew that she was pregnant. I swear. The reason I asked for permission to marry Willow is because I love her. She is everything to me. I wanted to marry her before now, but she would not because she was afraid that I would make her give up being a warrior if we wed. With everything that happened, you needed every fighter and she did not want to let anyone down."

Lightning Strike let go of Ames' coat with a little shove. "You had no right to take what was not yours."

"No one takes anything from Willow that she does not want them to have. You know that. She is not like other maidens."

"She is still a woman. Only her husband has the right to claim that gift."

Ames' nostrils flared as his temper mounted. "I am her husband in all ways that count, Lightning Strike. If it would not have embarrassed her and caused discord in the tribe, I would have made our relationship public even though she objected. We have essentially eloped. I finally just convinced her to marry me. I love her too much to force her into a marriage she was not ready for. How many other people know?"

Lightning Strike crossed his arms over his chest. "I have no idea, but people are not stupid, Ames. Most women and a few men understand what kind of female illness would cause her to become so ill."

"As soon as she is better, we will have the wedding," Ames said. "I will not answer detailed questions about this. It is no one's business. Do you understand that both Willow and I have lost a child this day? It is as though our hearts have been ripped from our chests. So, you will have to forgive me if I do not care about what people think right now."

He brushed by Lightning Strike and strode quickly back to camp. Cricket sat on a blanket outside of Willow's tipi.

"How is she?" Ames asked.

"Still sleeping."

Ames motioned for Cricket to come with him and moved farther away from the tipi. When Cricket joined him, he said, "I know that you are disappointed in me, but there is something I need you to do."

Looking closely at Ames, Cricket noticed that his eyes were slightly puffy and red-rimmed. He'd been crying. Sympathy replaced Cricket's disapproval. "What is it? You know that I will help you."

Ames' brow furrowed as he looked down at the ground and cleared his throat. "Follow Willow's trail to the place of three stones. That is where she buried our baby."

The pain and tears in Ames' eyes pierced Cricket's heart, his soul and he grew a little dizzy. Cricket took a deep breath as an odd strength flooded his being. Sudden knowledge made him stand a little straighter. "Ames, do not feel guilty any longer, and if someone says something to you, tell them to talk to me. I will go pray over your baby."

He walked away, leaving Ames to watch after him in confusion.

Willow awoke with a start that evening. Tulip sat nearby, stirring something in a pot over the fire. She noticed that Willow was awake and smiled a little.

"How do you feel?"

When Willow spoke, it felt like dust was clogging her throat. "Thirsty." She rose up on an elbow and immediately felt dizzy.

Tulip moved closer and helped her drink some water. "You need to eat. I made blood soup and Cricket has made a tincture for you to drink."

Fighting the dizziness, Willow sat up despite the pain it caused. "I need to pass water."

"There is a basket here for you," Tulip said.

"No. I will go to the trench."

"You are not strong enough yet."

Willow wasn't about to lie around being taken care of. Taking a deep breath to clear her head, she got shakily to her feet. Tulip jumped up to help her.

"You are so stubborn. How is your pain?"

"I have some cramps, but otherwise I am fine."

Tulip nodded. "I am glad that you do not have a fever. Green Leaf and I made sure to clean you well. We believe that your miscarriage was complete, but you must tell us if you start feeling worse again or if you begin with a fever."

Agony tore at Willow's heart as the memory of the little bundle she'd buried struck her. Gritting her teeth against tears, she nodded and stepped towards the tipi flap. She stopped and turned back to Tulip. "I assume that everyone knows."

Tulip looked down. "They suspect, but only a few know for certain."

"I see. I am not ashamed of my relationship with Ames. He wanted to marry me, but I would not agree."

Tulip came to stand beside her. "If you love him, why would you refuse him? Is it because he is white?"

"Do not be stupid. Of course not. I am a warrior first and a woman second. My first duty is to our tribe. I cannot hunt or protect our people if I am heavy with child," Willow said. "If I marry, people will expect me to bear children. I could not do that while we have had so much turmoil over the last few years."

Shock widened Tulip's eyes. "Years? How long have you and Ames been together?"

Willow cursed her loose tongue and put it down to her fatigue. "Since the first winter he came here." She couldn't help smiling at the stunned expression on Tulip's face. "We took great pains to hide our love. It was not easy because what we feel for each other is so intense. I also took great care to prevent pregnancy. I drank a purging tea every day. I did not know I was with child. I had my cycle each moon. Although my cycle did start early this time and was heavier. I had more cramping, too." She put a hand to her mouth. "Was it starting then? Was I starting to lose our baby then?"

Tulip softly said, "It is possible. I am so sorry, Willow. I know what that kind of loss feels like."

Willow couldn't breathe. The tipi was suddenly stifling and she needed to get out of there. Ripping aside the tipi flap, she stumbled outside despite Tulip's protests and slipped as her bare feet hit the hard-packed snow right outside the entrance.

A large hand clamped around her arm and she found herself pulled against Ames' broad chest.

"What are you doing out here like that?" he asked, keeping her upright. "Why are you on your feet at all?" He lifted her into his arms. "You need to rest."

Willow put her arms around his neck and buried her face in his furry coat. "I have to pass water."

Tulip joined them. "She will not listen to me. She insists on going to the trench." She started putting moccasin boots on Willow. "She is as stubborn as your mules, Ames."

"Yes, I know," Ames said. "I will take you this one time, but you use a basket the rest of the night. Do you hear me, woman?"

Willow thought that where she urinated was a silly thing to argue over and it made her smile. "Yes. I can walk."

"Humor me, eh?"

"Fine."

Tulip finished with the boots and Ames started off, unmindful of the peculiar looks they drew from the tribe members they passed. It didn't matter to him anymore if everyone was now aware of their relationship.

"You're lucky that I was on my way inside just as you came out," he said in French. "Or you would've wound up on your beautiful backside."

"I had to get away," she said. "I don't want to lay around for days, Ames. I'll have too much time to think. You shouldn't touch me or be around me."

Ames arched an eyebrow and grunted. "Don't start with the whole bleeding issue. I've been around women all my life who were having their cycle. It's never affected me, nor will it now. Besides, nothing is going to keep me from you. You know that."

Willow toyed with his hair as he walked. "I miss your long hair."

"It'll grow back." They neared the women's trenches and Ames put Willow on her feet. "I can't go further with you. Will you be all right?"

The fresh air had helped Willow and she felt steadier. "Yes and you aren't carrying me back. I'll walk."

He cocked his head and smiled a little. "We'll see."

She narrowed her eyes at him before she left him. When she was through and returned to him, she was tired, but she wasn't experiencing much pain.

"I can walk."

Ames sighed resignedly at her firm tone. "Very well. I am staying with you tonight."

"You can't do that," Willow said. "We are not married."

Cupping her cheek, Ames met her gaze. "Does it really matter now? Can't you see that I need to be with you? To hold you and to keep you safe?"

"Keep me safe? I can do that on my own," Willow said.

He frowned. "Not physically, although you aren't at your strongest right now. I meant so that I can comfort you." He drew her against him. "And don't think that I'm not grieving, too, because I am."

Willow wrapped her arms around him. "I know. I'm so sorry, my love."

He kissed her forehead. "Me, too, but we will get through this together. I went to the grave and had Cricket pray over it."

Willow tightened her embrace. "Please don't talk about it anymore right now. Please?"

"Shh. All right. We won't speak of it again tonight. Let's get you back inside. You've had a walk. Now you need to eat and to rest."

Her strength was fast leaving her, but Willow made it back to her tipi on her own two feet.

Ames escorted her inside and helped her sit down. "Now, you must eat."

Tulip smiled as she watched Ames dip out a bowl of soup for Willow and hand it to her. Now that she knew about them, his love for Willow was very apparent. It was sweet to see him take care of her.

He put a blanket across her lap and made her some tea while she ate. Even though Tulip knew that his heart had to be broken, too, he told them a funny story about Firebrand and Panther and made sure that Willow finished her meal.

Willow put the last spoonful of soup in her mouth and forced it down. Her eyes were beginning to droop and she stifled a yawn.

Ames and Tulip exchanged glances.

"You should rest, Willow," Tulip said.

Willow knew that Tulip was only trying to be helpful, but it irritated her nonetheless. "I know that I need to rest. I am a grown woman and can tell when I need to rest."

Tulip's eyebrows rose at her churlish tone.

Ames put a hand on Tulip's arm. "Go home to your family, Tulip. If we need you, I will come get you. All right?"

Tulip fidgeted a little, unsure of whether it would be right to leave them alone. Ames gave her a reassuring smile. At this point, she figured that it didn't matter. "All right. Make sure she rests."

Ames patted her arm. "I promise."

"You listen to him," Tulip told Willow.

Willow scowled at her as she laid down. Tulip took her leave and Ames followed her out. He was relieved to see that everyone else had gone home as well. Picking up the cross-sticks lying close to the tipi flap, he put them out so that they wouldn't be disturbed.

When he went back inside, he took off his boots and shirt, sitting them by his coat. Then he banked the fire for the night and stretched out next to Willow. She snuggled closer to him, laying her head on his chest as he spread the blanket over them and put an arm around her.

"I'm so sorry, Ames," Willow whispered in French. "I would never harm our baby."

He kissed the top of her head. "I know that. There's nothing to feel guilty about."

Willow toyed with his short chest hair. "But if I hadn't been taking that tea—"

"Then you couldn't have helped our tribe, Willow. You wouldn't have fought for them and saved lives," Ames said.

Raising her head, Willow met his gaze. "But I was pregnant while I was fighting. Fierce battle. I took blows, ran, jumped, rode hard. None of that was good for our baby."

"Willow, women work and carry things all the time when they're pregnant. How many times have I been scolded because I wanted to help them? Look at all the times Sky Dancer yelled at me because I tried to help her carry wood or put up a tipi," Ames said. "And that was while she was heavy with her little one. You weren't very far along while you were doing all of that and it was a stressful time. There is no one reason that this happened, Willow. You can't blame yourself. I don't."

Willow blinked back tears. She couldn't keep crying. Ames was right. It just hadn't been the right time for their baby to be born. But that didn't make the loss hurt less. She wouldn't have blamed Ames if he'd held her responsible, but in his typical fashion, he was understanding and supportive.

"What did I do to deserve such a good man?"

Ames chuckled. "It must have been something very good indeed. I am quite wonderful, after all."

Willow laughed and kissed his chest. "Yes, you are."

Exhaustion weighed down her eyelids and she rested her head on him. The steady throb of his heartbeat lulled her down into slumber.

Chapter Ten

"Cricket!"

Growling Wolf's sharp tone snapped Cricket out of his waking vision that he hadn't realized he'd been having. Of course, it wasn't exactly a waking vision. "What? I am sorry."

The rest of the council looked at him, some with amused smiles and others with annoyed expressions. Growling Wolf sported the latter.

"What do you think we should do about Willow?"

Cricket frowned. "Do about her?"

It had been three days since her miscarriage and she was out and about again. She was still somewhat weak after losing so much blood, but well enough to walk around camp and visit.

"Have you not been listening?" the chief asked. "We have been discussing this situation."

Cricket looked back down at the space next to his left side. Bright blue eyes stared back up at him. The spirit child smiled at him and he smiled back.

"Cricket!"

It was tough to concentrate with the little spirit around. "Why do we need to do anything about her?"

Fang said, "It is not just her, there is the question of Ames. They have been deceiving us for who knows how long. This is highly improper and goes against many rules. She has been in combat while pregnant."

The spirit child took Cricket's left hand and he smiled.

"This is not funny!"

His smile quickly disappeared. "No, it is not. I have meditated about this over the past couple of days."

One of their older men, White Oak asked, "And what conclusion have you drawn."

Speaking in front of the council still made Cricket nervous. "I, um, this is hard to explain, but I will do my best. Ames and Willow are meant to be together and their baby must be born."

Lightning Strike, who had recently been appointed to council, shook his head. "What do you mean? She lost the baby."

Cricket looked at the spirit child. "Their baby's physical body might not have survived this time, but it is strong and resilient. It must be born. I do not know why yet, but this child will be important to our tribe. Ames and Willow must be together."

White Oak sat a little straighter. "You have seen this child?"

"Yes. Bison took me to see it."

"Is it a boy or a girl?" Growling Wolf's eyes were full of curiosity.

Cricket arched an eyebrow at the spirit, but it only smiled at him. "I cannot tell. Sometimes I think it is a girl and then other times it seems like a boy."

Fang sighed. "That is all well and good, but what do we do about her fighting from this point forward?"

Lightning Strike said, "We do what we do for any warrior who is hurt; wait for her to get better and resume her duties."

"I do not think that is wise," Fang said. "What happens when she becomes pregnant again? Her and Ames are going to be married. Surely she will conceive at some point."

"We will deal with it at that time," Lightning Strike said.

Fang shook his head. "I think it is dangerous."

"If you take away her duty, it will kill her," Lightning Strike said. "What else will she do? She is not like other women."

Fang brushed his bangs away from his eyes. "I know this, but I am the war leader and I must do what is best for the protection of our people. And if—"

"What is best is to have all our warriors on duty, including Willow," Lightning Strike said. "She has been loyal to our people, even to the point of denying her own happiness! She deserves our loyalty now."

"I am not being disloyal, Lightning Strike. No one knows better than I how many times she has come through for us. But this complicates things."

Growling Wolf cut in. "The problem is that we have forgotten that even though Willow is a warrior, she is still a woman. We overlooked that and somehow never considered that she would find a mate and start a family."

"That is the way she preferred it." Lightning Strike's eyes glittered with anger. "We still need her and she needs to do what she loves to do."

White Oak said, "We will not solve this right now. We must all step back a little and think about it. Let us talk about it again in a couple of days."

The spirit child got up and started dancing around the fire, making Cricket laugh, which drew confused looks from the rest of the council.

"What is wrong with you lately?" Growling Wolf asked.

Cricket shook his head and grinned. "You would not believe me if I told you." He rose and left the lodge. The rest of the council couldn't see it, but the spirit child scampered out after Cricket.

Fang shook his head. "The meeting is not over yet. There are other things to discuss, but he leaves."

Growling Wolf chuckled. "Perhaps he is distracted with thoughts of his betrothed. Do not worry about it. I will talk to him later."

A few mornings later, Ames awoke to discover that Willow was already up and gone. Looking over, he saw that her bow and quiver were gone. Frowning, he rose and dressed. His stubborn woman had snuck away. No matter; he'd find her.

He put on his coat, picked up his own weapons, and left the tipi. As he passed the central fire, he heard a commotion towards the east side of camp and headed for it.

Fang backed away, holding up his hands in surrender. "No, Willow. I will not spar with you."

"Why not?" Willow advanced on him. "I must get back in practice. It is time."

Again, Fang backed up. "It is too soon."

"I will say when it is too soon. I am fine."

She struck out and Fang had no choice but to block the blow. However, he didn't counter attack, which angered Willow. She aimed a kick at his stomach and connected with his lowered arms. Still no counter attack.

"Has someone stolen the stones between your legs?" she taunted. "You are behaving like it."

Fang's jaw tightened, but he didn't take the bait. "Stop this, Willow."

"Fight me, damn you!" she shouted in French. "Why are you being such a coward?"

She went after Fang with a rapid series of punches and kicks. He went down because he wouldn't fight back.

One minute, Willow was standing over Fang, glowering down at him, and the next, she was sent headlong into the snow. Rolling, she gained her feet and turned to face her attacker. She was surprised to see Ames standing there with a grin on his face and she smiled back at him.

"You see, Fang? It is not hard to fight her," Ames said.

Fang rose and glowered at him. "She should not be fighting yet."

"Are you a medicine man?" Ames asked.

"No."

"Oh. Has Tulip said that Willow should not fight?"

Fang walked up to Ames. "No, but I have watched Tulip go through the same thing Willow did. Twice. She should not be doing such strenuous things yet."

Willow joined them. "Then what am I supposed to be doing? Do you want me on sentry?"

"No. Not yet."

Willow's jaw clenched. "When? I cannot just sit around! I am not weak like other women."

Fang met her hot gaze without flinching. "You will return to duty when I say so. Do you understand me?"

Willow let out a loud noise of frustration and whirled away from him. She stomped through the crunchy snow, so angry that she didn't know where she was going. She just needed to keep moving to work off her rage.

"Willow, where are you going?"

She glanced over at Ames. "I do not know. How can he do this to me?"

"Do not be too hard on Fang. He cares about you and is worried about you."

"How long is he going to make me wait? A month? Longer? It is ridiculous! What am I supposed to do with myself? I am bored out of my mind, Ames."

"Come with me, then, and I will keep you occupied. There are traps to be repaired and netting, too." Ames took her hand and led her towards his tipi.

"Why are Firebrand and Panther not helping you?"

He sighed and looked away from her. "They are on sentry duty."

"What?" She ripped her hand from his. "They are on sentry duty, but I am not allowed to be?"

Ames said, "I know you are upset, but there is nothing you can do about it right now. Fang will come around."

Willow ground her teeth together and strode towards his tipi again. She desperately needed to hit something, but she controlled the impulse. Her long legs carried her quickly towards Ames' tipi, but he easily kept up with her.

"Look at it this way; we can spend more time together," he said.

Willow smiled at that. "Yes, that is a good thing."

They reached his tipi and went inside. Several traps lay inside it along with various tools and wood. She'd helped Ames repair traps before, so she was familiar with the process. Sitting down, she picked up a trap and looked it over to see what needed done and how she wanted to go about fixing it.

Ames sat down across the fire from her and tried not to stare at her. It was difficult because she was so beautiful. Ignoring the dart of desire that shot through him, he also started repairing a trap. They hadn't been intimate since the miscarriage and he wasn't sure how to bring the subject up without her feeling pressured. He didn't know when she would be ready physically or emotionally, so he'd decided to wait for a sign from her. That didn't mean he didn't want her, though.

Turning the trap around a few times, Willow couldn't figure out where to start. Her concentration was off and she felt restless. Tulip had warned her that she might feel that way for a few weeks, but that it would fade in time. Not given to crying, Willow became angry when she suddenly felt weepy.

Blinking her tears away, she tried to return her attention to the trap. She needed to remove one of the broken wooden dowels so she could replace it with a new one. It suddenly seemed very complicated even though she'd done it many times. Her shoulders sagged and she put the trap down. Drawing her knees up, she rested her chin on them and just watched Ames.

His brow furrowed as he worked and his large, yet nimble hands skillfully moved over his trap as he shored up the new dowel he'd put in it. His big shoulders rolled under his shirt and she felt the urge to run her hands over them. She wanted to feel his warm skin and taste his mouth.

Heat spread through her as she thought about the way Ames kissed; thoroughly and with the kind of passion that made her tremble with need. The almost reverent way he ran his hands over her conveyed his love for her. She shifted her position a little as her temperature rose.

Ames glanced at her and noticed her perusal. Desire pierced him when he saw the hunger in her eyes. "Are you all right?"

"*Oui*."

The fact that she'd spoken French and was looking at him like he was a delicacy that she wanted to eat made him begin to harden. "Do not look at me that way, *chérie*. You know what it does to me."

A saucy smile curved her lips. "Look at you what way?"

He chuckled. "You know what way."

Willow shrugged. "I like watching you. It is better than crying." She hadn't meant to say that, but it was true.

"Crying?" Ames put down his trap and moved over to her. "Why are you crying?"

"I am not, but I feel like it. Tulip said that my emotions will be erratic, so do not pay me any attention."

Leaning towards her, Ames kissed her cheek. "How can I not pay attention to you when you look at me like that?"

Willow smiled and laid her hand on his leg. "How can I not look at you like that when you are so handsome?"

The way his eyes darkened created a tingle inside. "I can say the same for you." He sobered and took her hand. "You know that I want you, but when is it safe?"

Willow swallowed and looked down. "Not for a while. Tulip said that although having relations is all right, it is better to wait until after my next moon time to try again. I do not know what to do."

"What do you mean?"

"I cannot be a warrior if I am pregnant. If I cannot be a warrior, who am I? I want to make love with you, but even if I take a purging tea, it is obviously not enough to prevent a pregnancy." Tears of misery gathered in her eyes. "I did not want to become pregnant, but now that I lost a baby, I want a baby. I do not know what to do." She shook her head. "I should have stayed away from you from the beginning."

"Why?"

"You deserve a woman who is happy just taking care of the home and rearing children. It is what everyone says women are to be. But I am not and I do not want to stop being who I am," she said, standing up.

Ames also rose. "Willow, I fell in love with you because you are different from other women. I could have taken a wife or several wives long ago, but I only want you."

"Well, you should not," Willow said. "I cannot do this to you or me."

Ames put a hand on her arm. "What do you mean? Willow, I know that this is a terrible time, but it will pass. There is no need to be hasty about anything." He smoothed her hair back from her face. "We will figure this out together, yes?"

Willow wanted to believe that everything would work out, but she didn't see how. "You do not understand. Unless you are a woman, you *cannot* understand. I must choose between two different lives. Either I do not marry the man I love and remain a warrior, or I marry and give up what I love doing, the only thing I truly know how to do. Those are my choices."

The pain in her eyes made Ames' heart hurt. He tried to embrace her, but she pushed against his chest.

"I need to be alone. I need to think," she said and left the tipi.

Ames followed her outside. "Willow, do not shut me out."

"I just need some time," she called back over her shoulder.

Ames rubbed the back of his neck as he watched her break into a jog and disappear around a tipi. He was tempted to go after Willow, but knowing her as well as he did, doing that would be a mistake. Blowing out a breath, he went back inside his tipi.

Lighting Strike ran into Willow as she was on her way to her tipi.

"How are you?" he asked.

"Fine. Bored. Angry. Is there anything else you would like to know?"

He ignored her prickly behavior. "Do you want to go hunting with me?"

"No. I am sure you have more important things to do than to go hunting with a woman," she said.

"Willow, I am not in agreement with Fang, so do not be angry with me."

"It does not matter whether you are or not, you must follow what he says the same as I must." She went into her tipi and gathered her bow, arrows, and hunting knife. Her cousin was still there when she emerged from it. "I am not angry at you, I am just angry."

"Do you want to talk about it? You know that I am a good listener," he said, smiling.

"Talking will not change anything. It comes down to the fact that I have to make an impossible choice about my future and either path I choose will leave me unhappy in one way or another," Willow said.

"Perhaps I can help you see a different solution," Lightning Strike said, walking with her as she headed for the horses. "Fresh eyes, so to speak, cannot hurt."

Willow knew that Lightning Strike was only trying to help, but she was irritated nonetheless. "I either give up being a warrior so that I can marry Ames, or I do not marry him so that I can stay a warrior. I do not know how to be anything else. I do not want to sit in a tipi cooking and making clothing all day. I do not want to organize feasts and do all the things that other women enjoy doing. But it appears I cannot do both things simply because I am a woman. Be glad that you were born a man."

She reached the pasture and whistled for her horse, a big red roan mare, who came trotting through the other horses.

Lightning Strike stopped her from mounting. "Why can you not do both?"

"Because I cannot fight if I am pregnant and if I marry Ames, I will get pregnant. Now do you see?" She shrugged off his hand and mounted her horse. "I need time to figure out what I am going to do."

Lightning Strike stepped back. With a deeply troubled heart, he watched her ride away.

Chapter Eleven

Willow didn't get far before hoof beats sounded behind her. She gritted her teeth and turned to see who was following her. Cricket smiled and waved at her from the back of his pony.

He drew alongside of her. "How are you?"

"Do you want me to lie or do you want the truth?"

Cricket replied, "The truth, of course."

Willow played with her horse's mane a little. "Lousy. I do not want to talk about it, though."

"All right. I will respect your wishes." His smile returned. "I have something to tell you that I hope will cheer you up."

She couldn't help being curious. "What is it?"

"Your baby's spirit is waiting to be born. This child must be born, Willow. Bison has shown me that Sendeh is sending this child to the tribe. I do not know why yet, but it will be important to us," Cricket said.

A shiver ran up Willow's spine. "You have had a vision about this?"

"Yes. Several. Your child's spirit has been following me everywhere. I know how that sounds, but it is true," Cricket replied.

Willow's gaze moved all around Cricket. "Is it here now?"

Cricket grinned. "Yes. I do not know if it is a boy or a girl. It looks a lot like Ames. You must have this child, Willow."

Her forehead creased as conflicting emotions swept through her. She wanted to make another baby with Ames, but she also wanted to remain a warrior. Now Cricket was telling her that she must have the baby in order to help the tribe. Her first responsibility was to her people. Their welfare came before her own personal desires, but it pained her to give up her station.

Cricket was puzzled by her reaction. "What is wrong?"

Willow explained her predicament to him. "I am torn," she concluded.

"Why are you making this more complicated than it has to be?" Cricket asked.

Willow arched an eyebrow. "What do you mean?"

"Marry Ames, do not take the purging tea, and fight whenever you are not pregnant," Cricket said.

Willow rolled her eyes. "I have thought about that, but I do not think that Fang wants me to be a warrior any longer. So, I guess the decision has been made for me."

"Did he say that?"

"He would not spar with me today and he would not put me on sentry duty. I do not think he will change his mind. So, I guess I will marry Ames and try to be happy doing whatever other women do." Her shoulders drooped.

Cricket hated to see Willow this way. He'd never seen her so defeated. "You love Ames, do you not?"

"So very much."

"Then do not be so sad about marrying him," Cricket chided her. "Marry him and be happy. Figure out the rest as you go. I am always here to help you, even if it just to lend an ear."

She gave him a half smile. "Thank you." Then she straightened her spine. "You are right. I must face whatever comes and if I am supposed to have this baby, then so be it." She grinned. "It is no hardship to make love with Ames."

Cricket grew a little embarrassed. "That is a positive thing. When do you want to have the wedding?"

Joy suddenly flowed through Willow. "As soon as possible. Thank you again." She turned her horse around and put her heels to it.

As she cantered away, Cricket smiled, happy to have helped. He, too, set out for camp. The spirit child ran alongside the horse, smiling up at Cricket.

"Soon, little one. Soon you will be born to do whatever Sendeh has planned for you."

The spirit child's smile grew into a happy grin before it disappeared.

Ames looked up in surprise as Willow quickly entered his tipi without scratching. Her beautiful smile mesmerized him, but he wondered what she was so happy about. His eyes widened as she moved the trap he was working on out of the way and sat down on his lap.

Willow slid her hand around the back of his neck and played with his hair. "Cricket says that our baby must be born. He says that it is waiting and that Sendeh has something special planned for it. I want to marry you and make a baby with you. I will figure out everything else later. Make love to me."

Startled at her abrupt change of heart, he gave her a dubious look. "Are you sure? Is this one of those mood swings Tulip warned you about?"

Willow laughed. "I understand why you would think that, but no, it is not. I want to marry you as soon as possible and I want to make love with you...right now. I put out cross sticks."

Raw hunger stole through Ames, but he kept it in check as he lowered his head and pressed his lips to hers. She ran the tip of her tongue over his lower lip and he immediately opened to her, melding his mouth to hers. Molten heat flow through his veins as the kiss deepened.

After a few moments, he reined in his ardor, however. "*Mon amour*, I have missed making love with you and you know how much I always want you, but perhaps it is best to wait until we are married. You said that we should not try again until after you have had your moon time again."

Willow leaned her forehead against his. "Yes. You are right. Will you just hold me for a while?"

Ames kissed her temple and smiled into her eyes. "Of course."

Willow moved Ames' hair back from his face. "I love you."

Ames cupped her cheek. "I love you, too. Our love for each other is the most important thing, yes?"

She nodded her agreement and rested her head on his shoulder. Even more than Lightning Strike, Ames was the man in her life whom she felt that she could count on the most. He was always on her side and only wanted to help her. She thanked Sendeh for bringing the big trapper into her life and vowed to make him happy for the rest of her life. As his strong arms closed around her, Willow felt as though she'd found her true place in the world.

The day of their wedding two weeks later dawned a little warmer than usual. Sky Dancer helped Willow prepare for the special event.

"I cannot believe you kept all of this from me," she said for the fifth time. "Why did you not send for me and tell me about Ames in the first place?"

"I told you; I did not tell anyone about us for fear that it might accidentally get out. And I was also afraid that you would be disappointed in me since we were not married," Willow said. "We had to be careful."

Sky Dancer touched her arm. "I understand being swept away. It was difficult for my first husband and I to wait."

Willow finished with her right braid. "Yes, but you did wait. Neither of us could. It was as though some force that was stronger than us drew us together. We were immediately attracted to each other."

Sky Dancer worked on braiding the other side of Willow's hair, threading a red ribbon through the braid. "If what Cricket says is true, a stronger force did bring you together. I think you are doing the right thing. I know how important being a warrior is to you, but it sounds as though this baby is more important."

Willow's eyes rested on Sky Dancer's middle. "It would be nice if our children would grow up together."

Sky Dancer put a hand on her slightly rounded belly as she finished and smiled. "Yes. I think so, too. Dark Horse is so funny. He tries not to fuss over me, but he cannot help it sometimes. I do not mind. It is nice to know that he is excited about the baby. I am, too. I was afraid to have another child because I did not want to lose a second one, but I realized that I cannot let fear rule me that way. It is also why I kept denying to myself that I loved Dark Horse. I did not want to lose another husband who I loved."

Willow hugged her. "I do not think you have to worry about that. Sendeh has smiled on you and all will be well."

"Thank you. I am sure it will not be long until your little one comes along," Sky Dancer said, drawing away.

Willow played with the fringe on a sleeve. "It is so strange. Before I lost my baby, I did not want one and now...I cannot stop thinking about it."

"I understand," Sky Dancer said, looking up at her. "You look beautiful."

"Thank you." She smoothed down her dress. "Is it time?"

"Are you nervous?"

Willow smiled. "A little. More excited, though."

"All will be well. I will go check to see if they are ready," Sky Dancer said with a smile and left the tipi.

Ames was frustrated with his hair because it was so much shorter now. Normally, it would've been as long as any Indian brave's, but since he'd cut it, he couldn't braid it for the ceremony. He let out a sigh and just neatly combed it.

A chuckle drew his attention from the small mirror he'd been looking in.

"I did not think white men were as finicky about their hair as we are," Dark Horse remarked with a grin.

Ames laughed. "Well, I consider myself half Indian, so it makes sense that I would be. Also, the French are very concerned with their appearances and fashion."

The two men had met several times over the last month and were becoming friends.

Lightning Strike said, "Ames has adopted many of our ways, but you are right. He is rather conceited."

Ames spread his arms wide. "Look at me! I have much to be proud of, yes?"

Dark Horse and Lighting Strike laughed at him. Someone scratched on Ames' tipi flap and he told them to enter.

When he saw Sky Dancer, he swept her into a one-armed embrace while he patted her little belly. "There is the mother-to-be!" He kissed her temple and saw Dark Horse scowl. "I still do not know why you refused my advances. I am much more handsome than him."

Sky Dancer laughed at the dark expression on her husband's face. "It is because you always leave us. Willow is stronger about that than I am."

Ames heaved a dramatic sigh. "So that is why I lost you to the likes of him. Ah, well. So be it. I will just continue to love you from afar."

Sky Dancer playfully swatted him and stepped away. "It is time."

Glad anticipation filled Ames and he couldn't contain a grin. "Finally, I will marry the woman of my heart."

Sky Dancer grew a little misty-eyed. "Make sure you treat Willow right or I will make you regret it."

Ames made a gesture of surrender. "I have no wish to bring your legendary wrath down upon my head. Besides, I want to spoil her as much as she will let me."

"I do not think she will fight you on that," Sky Dancer said.

The men followed her outside and Dark Horse took her hand and kissed it. "It is a husband's right to spoil his wife."

The love the two of them felt for each other showed in the look they exchanged. Ames smiled, glad that his friend had found someone to love again, even if she'd been forced into the marriage. It seemed to have worked out for the best in many ways, he thought as he walked to the central fire area where the wedding would take place.

Cricket grinned at him. "Are you ready to become a married man?"

"More than ready," Ames said.

"Good, because here comes your bride." Cricket gestured to one of the paths leading from the area.

Ames' heart thumped inside his chest at the sight of Willow in her wedding finery. The white calf-skin dress emphasized her slim curves and she wore the gold and turquoise necklace and earrings he'd given her a couple of years ago. She hadn't been able to wear them until now, but she'd told him that she treasured them.

They looked lovely on her and sparkled as they caught the noonday sun. Her black eyes shone just as brightly as her jewelry. The fringes on her dress swayed with her graceful movements and Ames thought that she was more gorgeous than any woman in history.

Willow's full attention was riveted on the man she thought of as a golden god. His intense blue eyes locked on hers and she couldn't look away from him. Unlike many white men, his buckskin ceremonial tunic, breechcloth, and leggings suited him perfectly. He wore a blue-and-red beaded necklace interspersed with wolf teeth. When she joined him and Cricket, Ames held out his hands to her and she gave hers to him.

Cricket had performed a few weddings now, but he was nervous because many of their Lakota family were in attendance, including

Smoking Fire and his future father-in-law, Raging River. He knew that Raging River wasn't happy about his daughter marrying him, which made it even more important that he perform the ceremony well. He needed to make a good impression on him.

He asked Bison to be with him and began the wedding.

"Four winters ago, Sendeh sent us a white fur trader, who we quickly came to love. We did not know what to think of him at first because he acted so strangely," Cricket said, which drew quiet laughter and made Ames grin. "But he fought by our side in times of trouble and has always been generous with us in our business dealings and in teaching us other languages. He is a very good man and we are proud to call Ames Duchamp our friend.

"And now, he will truly become our family by marrying Willow, one of our fiercest warriors and a trusted friend. She has saved many lives and has protected our village from trespassers. She is kind, amusing, and intelligent, and we are glad that her chosen mate is worthy of her." Cricket paused a moment to touch both of their right shoulders with a grouping of three eagle feathers.

"Sendeh has shown me that Ames and Willow were destined to meet and fall in love. It does not matter how or when it happened. The Creator has plans for them and their children that will be important for our tribe. But, just as importantly, it is good to see that they make each other so happy. I pray to Sendeh that it will always be so."

He smudged them both and recited a prayer of thanksgiving over them before leading the gathering in a song of praise to Sendeh. Then he concluded the ceremony with a final prayer.

Ames surprised Willow and everyone else by cupping her face and kissing her firmly right in front of the guests. Chuckles and giggles broke out and then Lightning Strike let out a victory whoop, which was immediately echoed by many others.

Willow and Ames laughed against each other's mouths and broke apart. Caught up in the moment, Willow raised a fist in the air and let out her own victory trill. Ames also raised his voice and then picked up Willow and spun her around in a circle as she laughed.

Soaring Falcon stood by Growling Wolf and leaned closer to him. "Is this a white man's wedding custom?"

Growling Wolf chuckled and lifted a shoulder. "Perhaps, or it might just be something that Ames does. It is hard to tell sometimes."

They laughed together while the celebrants began readying for the feast and dancing. It wasn't long before the food was served and everyone settled down to eat. The women of the Kiowa tribe missed being able to serve the sorts of food they were used to, but since they hadn't been able to bring all the food they'd had stored at their old camp, they were out of certain vegetables.

They also didn't have fresh greens, but the meat and tuber dishes and soups were delicious and enjoyed by all. Compliments were given to the women who had prepared the food. Ames kissed a few of the women in thanks, which only drew smiles and laughter from his people.

The Lakota guests were still amazed that what they viewed as overtly friendly behavior was allowed and even encouraged where Ames was concerned.

However, the trapper never crossed that line with any of the Lakota. He knew that it would offend them and he didn't want to cause trouble. Perhaps one day they wouldn't mind his teasing, but he knew that they had to get used to him first.

While the celebration continued, Cricket went to the medicine lodge to get some salve for a little girl who'd burned her fingers when she's spilled some hot tea on them. As he was getting it, Hummingbird came into the lodge.

"There you are," she said. "I wondered where you went."

He smiled at her. "Keeping a close eye on me, hmm?"

She gave him a coy look. "I have to make sure that no other girl is trying to steal you away from me."

Cricket flashed her a grin and crouched to look through a basket for the right salve. "I do not think you have to worry about that. Even if some girl did try, I would not be swayed by her." Finding it, he stood back up.

"Are you sure?"

Cricket was confused by her question. "Yes, I am sure. What makes you ask? Have I done something to make you doubt me?"

Hummingbird looked down. "It is just that you are growing now and are very handsome. I wondered if any girls had flirted with you."

One of Cricket's eyebrows rose. "I am growing? And handsome?" He looked at himself, but he didn't think he was growing.

Hummingbird giggled and moved closer to him. "Yes. You are a little taller now and not as skinny. You are filling out."

Surprised, Cricket ran his hands over his chest and laughed. "I am! I did not notice it. It is not much, but it is better than nothing."

Looking at Hummingbird, Cricket realized that he had to look down at her a little more than before. He may have grown slightly, but he felt far from handsome. He thought about Dark Horse's younger brother, Spider, and wished that he was handsome like him. Spider was his age, but much taller and muscular, and had an abundance of confidence.

Hummingbird touched his arm. "What is wrong?"

"Hmm? Oh, nothing. I am glad that you find me attractive."

Her smile captivated him. "Of course, I do. Why do you think I steal kisses?"

Heat suffused Cricket's face and he gave a bashful laugh. It was true that she was usually the instigator of the brief kisses they shared. Cricket hated his shyness about it, but he also tried to be respectful of her.

As he met her gaze, Cricket didn't know if it was his happiness over growing or her compliment or both, but he felt a little reckless. He'd once asked Ames for advice about how to kiss a woman and he'd gladly instructed Cricket about the art of kissing. After going over the mechanics of it, Ames had told him that when a man kissed a woman, he should do it like he meant it.

Stepping closer, Cricket cupped Hummingbird's cheek and put his other arm around her waist. He enjoyed the way her eyes widened and he felt powerful somehow. Giving her what he hoped was a charming smile, he asked, "May I kiss you?"

Hummingbird's heart skipped a few beats. He'd never embraced her before and the way he was looking at her was exciting. His palm on her skin was warm and she liked the way he smelled. Mutely, she nodded.

Her eyes drifted closed as his lips touched hers and she put her hands on his shoulders. This kiss wasn't the chaste kind she was used to. No, it was firm and made her feel warm all over, as though it were summer and not the middle of winter.

Cricket had never felt anything so good before. He pulled Hummingbird closer still, enjoying the way her curves fit against him. Trying to recall everything Ames had taught him, he slowly coaxed Hummingbird's lips apart and deepened the kiss.

Apparently, Hummingbird must've had some instruction of her own, because she seemed to know what to do from there. She wound her arms around his neck and kissed him back.

That gave Cricket pause and he broke the kiss. "Have you kissed other boys?"

She met his gaze. "No. My older cousin told me how. Have you kissed other girls?"

He grinned. "No. No other girl has ever wanted to kiss me. Ames told me how."

"I think his advice was very good," Hummingbird said. "Do it again."

Cricket smiled, but shook his head a little. "I would like to kiss you all night, but I do not want anyone to miss us and I have to get this salve to Blossom."

Hummingbird sighed, but moved away from him. "Perhaps before we leave tomorrow you will kiss me again?"

"Why not later when we say goodnight?   I am sure that Three Deer will chaperone you just that long." Cricket winked at her.

Hummingbird giggled as they left the medicine lodge. They went separate ways so as not to raise suspicion. As he walked back to the celebration, Cricket thanked Sendeh again for bringing Hummingbird into his life.

Chapter Twelve

The fire burned lower in Ames and Willow's new tipi later that night as he lay holding her. Their lovemaking had been a slow and tender renewal of their mutual desire. Ames had wanted to make sure that he didn't hurt Willow, but she'd assured him that there had been no discomfort, only pleasure.

Smiling, Willow said in French, "It doesn't feel real that we are married yet."

"I know what you mean." Ames ran a hand over her back. Even when he was sated, he simply enjoyed touching her. "It's been a long time in coming, but perhaps it happened that way for a reason. But you're mine now and I'll never let you go."

She kissed his shoulder. "And I'll never let you go." She sighed.

Ames looked at her. "What's wrong?"

"Once our honeymoon is over, what am I going to do with myself?"

Ames felt badly for Willow. Fang had still not taken her back as a warrior, which made Willow bitter towards the war leader. She avoided him or when she did encounter him, she pointedly ignored any attempts he made to speak with her. Ames had known better than to interfere because Willow could fight her own battles and she wouldn't take kindly to him inserting himself into the situation.

"Well, you can always help me. I'm always grateful when you do."

"I know, but you really don't need me. You have Firebrand and Panther," Willow said.

Ames cleared his throat. "Actually, Panther has been helping a lot with sentry duty and Firebrand wants to go to the Lakota camp for a while to learn some new flint-knapping techniques. So, I really could use your help."

Willow tried to squelch her anger over Panther essentially replacing her as a warrior. She squeezed her eyes shut against the hurt in her heart over it. It wasn't Panther's fault, so she wasn't angry with him. And she was glad that their tribe had another skilled brave to watch over them, but she missed sparring and hunting with the men. She longed to go on scouting runs to make sure that their surrounding area was secure.

She focused on the positive aspect of the situation. Spending each day with Ames would be wonderful, but as much as she would enjoy it, she would still miss her old duties.

"Then I'll be happy to help you. It will be nice to work on your trapping business together," she said.

Ames heard the undertone of disappointment in her voice, but decided not to mention it. Even though he wanted to fix it for her, he knew that this was something that she had to work through on her own. "That makes it *our* business, yes?"

A grin spread over her face. "Yes, it does."

An idea came to him. "You know, Panther could stay here this summer and you could come with me. Would you like to?"

That had never occurred to Willow before. Excitement gripped her. "Yes! I would love to go with you and see how you trade." She hugged him tightly. "We will have so much fun and I'll pull my own weight. You know that."

Ames returned her embrace. "Yes, I do. Otherwise, I wouldn't suggest you going along. It's a demanding trip and not every woman would be able to do it. I hate to say it, but most women would slow us down too much."

She traced his jaw with a finger. "But I'm not just any woman, no?"

The sultry way she spoke in French heated Ames' blood. "No, you aren't just any woman. You are my wife, the woman of my heart." With a grin on his handsome face, he rolled her over. "Just think; we won't have to be apart, *chérie*."

Her heart filled with joy as she wiggled underneath him. "We can make love whenever we want."

Ames groaned and kissed her neck. "I am always so hungry for you. You're going to get tired of my attentions."

He bit her shoulder and Willow shuddered against him. "I'll never get tired of you. My need is just as great." She gasped as he joined them together and lifted her hips. "Love me, Ames."

"Always, *mon amour*. Always."

Sitting out by the dying central fire, Cricket contemplated the heavens in an attempt to calm his raging body. He'd just said goodnight to Hummingbird and he now understood why men and women had such a hard time resisting making love. It was bitter cold, but his robe sat by his side because he was so hot from the heated kisses that he and Hummingbird had exchanged.

He hadn't meant to get so carried away, but it seemed as though his body had taken control and left his mind behind. Hummingbird had finally been the one to come to her senses and halted their passionate embrace. Ashamed of his lack of control, he'd apologized to her, which had made her giggle.

Cricket smiled as he thought about her statement about being as excited as him. She'd jokingly said that they should move the wedding up, which in his desire-fogged brain had sounded like a great idea. He'd been relieved that she hadn't been offended and they'd laughed about the situation.

"Sendeh, please give me the strength to resist that temptation and to do right by Hummingbird. I am grateful that You gave her to me and I do not want to disappoint You by going against Your wishes," he whispered.

He was startled when someone sat down beside him. With wide eyes, he looked at Ten Thunders, their Ojibwa captive. The Kiowa braves had quickly figured out that the Ojibwa had purposely left Ten Thunders behind. He was an odd young man, a few winters older than Cricket. He was muscular and about a head taller than Cricket with slightly sharp features.

Despite being the enemy, he was a friendly, chatty sort who didn't seem to mind that he'd been captured. Ten Thunders had been only too happy to tell them all kinds of information about his own tribe. At first, Fang had been sure that he'd been trying to lead them astray, but when some of their braves had gone to check out Ten Thunders' story, they'd seen that he'd been telling them the truth.

Until recently, Ten Thunders had been kept in shackles to prevent him from escaping, but he'd never complained or asked to be set free. He was always respectful, especially where women were concerned. Even those who had been determined to hate him ended up liking him.

Recently, Growling Wolf had decided to test him by giving Ten Thunders his freedom. So far, he'd shown no inclination to leave or hurt anyone. He helped around camp, but he didn't hunt since he wasn't allowed to leave the camp limits. Therefore, he did other things like gather wood and sharpen and repair weapons.

He was let roam wherever he wanted and he hadn't caused any trouble. Various people allowed him to sleep in their tipi and he seemed content to be a nomad in the camp. Perhaps sensing Cricket's kind heart, he had recently decided that they should be friends. Cricket wasn't yet sure how he felt about that.

"You look sky?" he asked Cricket, pointing upwards. He was learning Kiowa well. "Pray?"

Cricket nodded. "Yes. Trying to."

Ten Thunders didn't seem to catch the sarcasm behind Cricket's statement. He nodded, too. "Good. What pray for?"

Cricket said, "The sick, successful hunts, and our tribe in general. Those sorts of things."

"Good, good. Yes. Pray tribe. Good. You pray me?"

Cricket blinked a couple of times. It was a shock to realize that he'd never prayed for Ten Thunders and he felt ashamed. He might be a captive, but he deserved to be prayed for, too. "How about I pray for you now?"

Ten Thunders' face lit up. "Yes! Yes! Pray me now!"

"All right. Bow your head."

Ten Thunders immediately dropped his chin to his chest.

"Sendeh, I humbly ask that You give Ten Thunders good health in his body, mind, and spirit. Watch over him and keep him from harm. Please reward him for being a good..." Cricket didn't know how he could call Ten Thunders a captive in that context. You couldn't be rewarded for being a good captive. "For being a good man and for being so helpful around camp. We are thankful for him and—" He cut off when Ten Thunders nudged his knee.

"Make my pretty girl like me," Ten Thunders whispered, looking at Cricket with only one eye halfway open.

Cricket almost laughed. He'd never had anyone give him specific prayer requests while he was praying for them. In a slightly thick voice, he went on. "And I would respectfully ask that You perhaps sway the heart of the girl he likes so that she will notice him."

"Thank you, thank you," Ten Thunders whispered.

Cricket barely held his laughter at bay. "We thank You, Sendeh, for all of the blessings in our lives and may we always please You," he finished.

Ten Thunders grinned and clapped Cricket's shoulder. "Good. Thank you."

"You are welcome," Cricket said on a laugh. "Who is the pretty girl?"

Ten Thunders gave him a sly look. "Cannot tell. Prayer not come true."

"That is not fair," Cricket said. "I prayed for you. You owe me. That is my price."

Ten Thunders' crossed his arms over his chest. "I tell, I stay you."

Cricket's curiosity won out and he agreed.

"Love Hummingbird friend, Three Deer. Beautiful."

Cricket was stunned. He'd expected Ten Thunders' love interest to be one of the Kiowa girls, not Three Deer. Over the past few months, Cricket had gotten to know Dark Horse very well and he knew that the war leader wouldn't tolerate an Ojibwa captive sniffing around his little sister.

"Oh, um, Ten Thunders, that is not a good idea."

Ten Thunders smiled and stood up. "Yes. Very good idea. You see. Goodnight."

Cricket scrambled off the ground and grabbed Ten Thunders' arm. "No, it is not a good idea. Her brother will kill you if you try to talk to her." He released Ten Thunders. "I hate to mention this, but you are a captive and a Lakota war leader will not let you court his little sister."

"He will when he finds out that I'm the son of the chief who took your land," Ten Thunder said.

Cricket's eyes grew huge. He didn't understand everything that Ten Thunders had just said because he was pretty sure that the other man had just spoken in fluent English. His chest hurt from how fast his heart was now beating. "You are the son of the Ojibwa chief who killed our people?"

Ten Thunders' expression clouded. "Yes. Son of Ojibwa chief. Gray Cloud."

Cricket tried to stop the trembling in his body and sound authoritative. "Come with me right now."

Ten Thunders obediently fell into step with Cricket. "Where we go?"

"To see Firebrand. He speaks English. You are going to tell us everything."

"All right."

His pleasant tone of voice surprised Cricket and he didn't know what to think as they arrived at Firebrand's tipi. Cricket scratched on the flap and Firebrand said to enter.

Once they were inside, Cricket opened his mouth to speak, but Ten Thunders beat him to the punch.

"Hello, Firebrand. Cricket tells me that you speak English. I think he wants us to talk."

Firebrand looked from Cricket to Ten Thunders. "All right. Please, sit."

Ten Thunders smiled as he sat down and held his hands out to the fire. "I don't know why he sits outside to pray when it's so cold."

Firebrand smiled. "He likes to look at the stars. We should sign so he can follow along."

"Certainly," Ten Thunders said. "He was surprised when I told him that I'm the son of the Ojibwa chief who ordered us to raid your camp."

Firebrand hid his own surprise. "You are?"

"Yes."

"Why didn't you tell anyone?"

Ten Thunders smiled. "No one asked me. They asked me all kinds of other things, but they didn't enquire about my family."

Firebrand couldn't figure out if Ten Thunders was being sarcastic or if he was just simple. "Well, most people want to talk about their families. Didn't you want to talk about yours?"

Ten Thunders made a face and looked down. "I didn't want to be killed and I didn't want to go back. Everyone here has been so nice to me. This is one of the few times in my life when I've felt like I was appreciated for something other than fighting."

Cricket and Firebrand exchanged surprised glances.

"What are you talking about?" Firebrand asked.

"I'm the youngest of my father's seven sons and I've always been looked down on."

Firebrand's cockscomb bounced as he shook his head slightly. "Why?"

"Because, while I'm a very skilled warrior, I don't *like* fighting. I'd rather talk to people to avoid a fight, which angered Gray Cloud,"

Ten Thunders replied. "So my people didn't bother with me a whole lot because I was considered rather worthless.

"Gray Cloud grew tired of it and said that they were going to make a warrior out of me. I was along on the attack against you, but I didn't kill anyone. I could've, but I didn't want to. While I was trying to fight off three of you, my brothers ran off, leaving me to be captured."

Astounded, Cricket and Firebrand simply stared at him.

"That is horrible," Cricket finally said. "How could anyone leave their brother behind that way?"

Ten Thunders patted his shoulder consolingly. "Don't be upset, Cricket. It all worked out for the best. Now you see why Dark Horse will let me court Three Deer."

"No, I do not."

Firebrand's eyebrows shot up. "You want to court Three Deer?"

"Yes. I'm the son of a chief and I know how to do something that none of you do." Ten Thunders' expression turned smug.

"What do you know how to do?" Cricket asked.

"How to make things from iron and gold. I was trained as a blacksmith, but my Ojibwa family didn't know it," Ten Thunders said proudly. "I can help you make better weapons and fix guns, too."

"A blacksmith?" Firebrand felt a shiver go up his spine as he realized just how valuable that could be to them. "We don't have the materials for you to work with."

Ten Thunders said, "I know, but I know where you can get them. However, I don't have any money."

Thanks to Ames, Cricket understood the Europeans' concept of money. The whites would take gold and silver in exchange for goods or services. However, the Indians hadn't understood it when they'd first encountered the Europeans since they didn't have gold or silver. Therefore, they'd only traded goods for other goods or services.

When Ames had shown them gold and told them that they could buy things with it, several people had laughed, not understanding what good a bunch of yellow metal could be except for ornamental uses. It couldn't be eaten, drank, or used for clothing or shelter. Therefore, it wasn't much good to them.

But he'd explained that if they wanted some of the products that the whites made that there was only one thing that Indians had that the whites wanted: pelts and lots of them. However, if they had gold, they could buy more expensive things. Firebrand and Ames had worked hard over the last few years to grow their profits and they'd done very well.

They'd talked about building a small trading post, but they'd known that it wouldn't happen for a few years. However, if Ten Thunders truly possessed metalworking skills and they could get him the equipment he needed, they could set up one between only the area tribes and sell goods locally.

Then the Indians wouldn't have to travel north so much or depend on the English and French for some products. It would also keep whites out of the area—at least for a time.

Before he got too carried away with that line of thinking, Firebrand fixed a steely stare on Ten Thunders. "How do we know that you really know blacksmithing skills?"

Ten Thunders smiled. "I can explain the process, but without the equipment or iron to work with, I have no way to prove it."

Firebrand said, "I'll talk to Ames after his honeymoon. We might be able to acquire some."

"Very good. I'd love to do that sort of work again," Ten Thunders said as he got up. "We'll let you get some sleep. It's good to speak English again. Thank you."

He ducked out of the tipi and Cricket followed him. Ten Thunders started dancing with his arms lifted to the sky in joy. Cricket hadn't seen him dance before and he couldn't help grinning as Ten Thunders stepped and twirled on their way to Cricket's tipi.

Ten Thunders came back to Cricket, put an arm around his shoulders, and patted Cricket's chest. "Thank you prayer. Show what can do. Make you proud. Get Three Deer."

"You are welcome." Cricket was amused by his behavior and confidence about winning Three Deer. "Come, let us go to sleep."

"Yes. Sleep. Dream pretty girls." Ten Thunders winked at him and they grinned as they went inside Green Leaf's tipi.

Green Leaf and Moonbeam were already asleep. Cricket gave Ten Thunders a couple of blankets and they settled down to sleep. Cricket fell asleep with a smile on his face over Ten Thunders' antics and did indeed dream about Hummingbird.

Chapter Thirteen

A week after their wedding, Willow and Ames began settling into their new life. They checked their traps every morning, which usually took until early afternoon. Then they brought their bounty back and skinned the game. Their harvest was highly successful and they were on their way to a great haul to take north for trading in the spring.

Ames and Firebrand had talked things over with Ten Thunders, and if he continued to show good behavior, they would take him along so that he could pick out the blacksmithing equipment he needed. He was looking forward to the trip and to putting his plan to win Three Deer into motion.

Willow sparred with Ames and Lightning Strike to keep her fighting skills sharp. She practiced target shooting every day, too. Just because she wasn't a part of the warrior group at the moment didn't mean that she shouldn't be prepared in case danger arose.

One cold morning, Fang approached her as she came back from hunting.

"Do you want to go back to sentry duty?"

She gave him a cold stare. "No. I am busy helping Ames now. We have a lot of work to do this winter."

Fang's jaw clenched. "I know you think that I have been unfair. I was not trying to offend you. I was worried about you. Despite what you think, I am your friend and I could not stand it if anything happened to you because you had pushed yourself too hard, too fast. As a war leader, it is my responsibility to make sure our soldiers are healthy enough for battle. Do you understand?"

Willow's heart softened a little bit. She knew that Fang wasn't a cruel man, but she'd been deeply hurt by his refusal to let her resume her duties. "Yes, I understand, but you acted as though I did not know my own mind. I needed to keep busy, to not think about losing my baby. I am glad that Ames needed me or I would have gone insane with boredom and grief."

The war leader's expression turned contrite. "I am sorry. I should have listened to you. I should have known that you would be ready soon. Will you forgive me?"

Willow's anger dissipated. "Yes. I forgive you, but I am still helping Ames."

Fang nodded his head solemnly. "Very well. If you change your mind, let me know. I am happy for you and glad that things are going so well."

A grin curved her mouth and her eyes sparkled. "Being married to Ames is wonderful."

"Good. He is a good man."

They chatted for a few more minutes and then Fang left to go back to his duties.

Willow resumed scraping hides. She felt better after talking to Fang. Mending the divide between them was a relief. She appreciated his wanting her back, but surprisingly, she was content working with Ames. Spending each day working by his side towards a common goal gave her a different sort of fulfillment. It added a whole new dimension to their relationship that deepened their bond.

They had fun no matter what they were doing and Willow still mentally berated herself for waiting so long to marry Ames. As she went about her business, she resolved to not let fear rule any aspect of her life. It had already cost her precious time. She wouldn't make that mistake again.

"A tree decorating ceremony?" Soaring Falcon arched an eyebrow at Cricket.

They sat in the chief's tipi drinking tea. Cricket had brought Ten Thunders with him because it would be good for the Lakota tribe to get to know him. He wanted them to know that Ten Thunders could be trusted.

Cricket said, "Ames loves celebrating Christmas, the day that his god, Jesus, was born. Some of the whites celebrate by putting a tree in their houses and decorating it. He did it the first year he came to us and has ever since.

"Everyone makes ornaments and we put them on the tree. We have a feast and dancing, too. It is a fun time and we are inviting you all to attend."

Soaring Falcon smiled. "So you started out humoring Ames, but it grew into an actual celebration?"

Cricket chuckled. "Yes. Ames is very convincing. And he does so much for us that we decided to honor him with the ceremony as much as we honor his Jesus."

Soaring Falcon's wife, Day Star, said, "I think it would be good to participate. We all enjoy a celebration and I am curious to see this one. I will make an ornament for the tree."

"I agree." Soaring Falcon's gaze came to rest on Ten Thunders, who sat silently looking at the tipi floor. He'd barely moved except to drink his tea and he hadn't spoken a word. "Why do they call you Ten Thunders?"

The young man didn't answer.

Cricket said, "Ten Thunders, Soaring Falcon wants to know where your name comes from."

Ten Thunders started a little. He didn't speak Lakota and hadn't realized that he'd been spoken to. He signed, "Hello, great chief. My mother went into labor during a thunder storm. She said that I was born just as she counted ten thunder rolls. So, she named me Ten Thunders."

One corner of Soaring Falcon's mouth lifted in amusement. "It is a good name. I see that you have been behaving yourself."

Ten Thunders smiled. "I am very grateful for my freedom and will not do anything to make my new people distrust me. They have been very kind to me."

Cricket hid a smile at Soaring Falcon's surprised look. "Have you adopted him?"

"Not officially, but I am..." Cricket searched for an appropriate way to explain it to Soaring Falcon. "I am sponsoring him, and if all works out well, I see no reason not to."

Ten Thunders sent him a grateful smile.

"I wish you well with it," Soaring Falcon said and then rose with a frown. "I do not mean to be rude, but I need to speak with Smoking Fire about a few things." A teasing light entered his eyes. "Besides, there is someone else I think you would rather spend time with."

Cricket grinned. "You cannot blame me. She is prettier than you."

Day Star and Soaring Falcon laughed. Cricket and Ten Thunders bid them goodbye and headed for Hummingbird's tipi. As they rounded a tipi, two braves were coming the opposite direction. One of them nudged his companion and, as they went to pass Cricket, his hand shot out, hitting Cricket's shoulder hard enough to spin him around and make him fall to his knees.

As he knelt there catching his breath, Cricket watched with disbelief as Ten Thunders dealt swiftly with the offender. Quick as a cougar, Ten Thunders grabbed the other brave from behind, stole his knife, and held it against the Lakota man's throat.

"He medicine man. Must treat with respect," he said against the other brave's ear. "Tell him I say, Cricket."

Cricket got quickly to his feet, when he saw that a crowd was gathering around them. Their angry faces made him fear for Ten Thunders' life. His Lakota kin wouldn't take kindly to an Ojibwa captive killing one of their braves. It was paramount to diffuse the situation.

Cricked changed to the Lakota tongue. "Please excuse my friend, Ten Thunders' behavior. He mistakenly thought that this man was trying to hurt me. He is very protective." Cricket met Ten Thunders' captive's eyes. "You meant no ill-will towards me, did you? You would not disrespect a medicine man, would you?"

Anger glittered in the brave's eyes, but when Ten Thunders pressed the knife blade against his throat, he said, "No, of course not. It was just meant as a joke. I apologize."

Ten Thunders yelled, "No disrespect Cricket or I make sorry!"

Cricket maintained a straight face. "Ten Thunders, no one means me any disrespect. Please, let him go."

Ten Thunders glanced at Cricket. "You certain?"

"Yes."

"Very well." Ten Thunders shoved the Lakota brave away and then held out the knife to Cricket with a slight bow. "Restitution." He glared at the Lakota brave, daring him to disagree with him.

The brave understood the Kiowa word. "Yes. Please keep the knife as a token of my goodwill towards you, Cricket," he said hastily.

"Oh, it is not—"

Ten Thunders pressed the knife handle into Cricket's palm and smiled. "Very good gift. Fine knife. Now you see Hummingbird. Chief granddaughter waiting for betrothed."

He patted Cricket on the shoulder and motioned to the path. People immediately moved out of the way to let Cricket pass. Deferentially, Ten Thunders followed behind Cricket, turning to give the Lakota brave a fierce glare.

Then he caught up to Cricket and laughed. "We show them. Not be mean no more."

Cricket grinned at him. "I thought you preferred to talk instead of fight?"

"Know his kind. Talking not work. Better this way," Ten Thunders said. "Know how...these things work. Chief son, remember?"

Of course Ten Thunders understood tribal politics. As the son of a chief, he would be expected to. "Yes, I remember. Thank you."

Ten Thunders shook his head. "No. I thank you. Owe you." He clapped Cricket's shoulder as they arrived at Hummingbird's tipi. "You pray me, I keep safe you."

Cricket smiled and shook his head. "Are you suggesting that we make a bargain?"

Ten Thunders' broad smile reminded him of a mischievous child. "Yes. Good deal?"

"No. I have a better one. I will keep praying for you, but you must teach me how to fight. Our warriors have been busy lately so they have not had the time to show me. You will be my teacher now. Do we have a deal?"

Ten Thunders stuck out his arm and Cricket grasped it. Then he scratched on his betrothed's tipi and they entered when given permission.

Willow smiled as she watched Ames work on a little bow that he was making for Quill, one of Tulip's sons. He hummed what she knew was a Christmas carol as he heated and carefully bent the wood into the proper shape. She worked on the set of matching arrows, affixing the dull points to the straight shafts she'd created.

Looking around their tipi amused her further. Neither of them were the neatest people and it showed. All sorts of weapons and trapping paraphernalia lay strewn about. Although they had cooking equipment, it sat off to the side. They were often invited to take their meals elsewhere, so they didn't cook much.

In exchange for the hospitality, they gave their various hosts gifts of pelts or other goods. When they were ready to go to sleep at night, they just pushed things out of the way to make room for their sleeping robes and snuggled up with each other.

Looking at the small arrows, Willow wondered when they would be making weapons for their own children. It amazed her how much she wanted to see Ames hold their baby. She'd known that it was stupid to hope that she would get pregnant right away again, but when she'd had to go to the women's lodge last week, she'd quietly wept in disappointment when she'd been alone in the lodge.

She was distracted from her troubling thoughts when Ames chuckled.

He smiled broadly at her expectant look. "I cannot wait to give you your presents."

Willow had to laugh at that. "You cannot wait to give *anyone* their gifts. You are worse than the children."

"Ah, yes; the children. They are doing well with their practice," Ames said. "What is so funny?"

Willow's eye gleamed with mirth as laughter bubbled from her throat. "I cannot wait to see the Lakotas' faces when they see Kiowa children telling a French Christmas story."

He laughed with her. "I am certain it will be talked about for a long time. I am glad I talked Moonbeam into doing it this one last time even though she is now a woman. She does not seem old enough to be."

"I do not think there is anything she will not do for you. She idolizes you," Willow said.

Ames held the bow over the fire again. "I do not believe in having favorites among children, but I do confess to having a special bond with her and Cricket."

"I know that you love them all," Willow said, laying aside a finished arrow. "But there are times when attachments like yours happen without reason or any intention of playing favorites. I do not think any of the little ones feel slighted."

A frown crossed Ames' face. "I have always felt badly for Cricket."

"Why?"

"You were lucky to have people your own age around while you were growing up," Ames replied. "Cricket was born at an odd time. Most of the young men are—or were—either older than him, or several years younger than he. And his lack of inclination towards fighting and his small stature made it hard for him to make friends."

Willow hated to admit it, but Ames was right. "Yes. He has seemed lonely sometimes, but he never seemed to hold it against any of the boys that they were not interested in becoming friends with him."

Ames chuckled. "I think he has one now."

Carefully, so as not to split the wooden shaft, Willow affixed an arrowhead onto the end of it. "Yes. It makes sense that he and Ten Thunders would become friendly. Our warriors are not ready to befriend him yet, but Cricket has a kind heart."

"Cricket is wise to befriend Ten Thunders. If he truly does know metal working, he will be influential around here one day. A friendship with him will be advantageous to Cricket," Ames said.

Willow nodded. "And Ten Thunders knows that being friends with a medicine man also benefits him. However, he does seem to genuinely like Cricket."

"I agree."

They were startled when a furry head poked through the tipi flap.

Willow smiled and patted her leg. "Come, Jacqui."

A very pregnant tan and black dog waddled her way into the tipi and carefully picked her way over to Willow. She laid down with a grunt and leaned against Willow. Her breathing was labored and she whined and licked her lips.

"Willow, what have I told you about letting the dogs stay in here?" Ames gave her a disapproving frown. "It will make them soft if you do."

"It is just one night," Willow said.

Ames sighed. "One night turns into another and on and on."

Jacqui got up, turned around, and lay back down. She whined and rose again, pawing at the hides covering the floor.

"Jacqui, stop that," Ames scolded her.

Jacqui paid him no mind, instead turning to snap at her rounded flank.

"Ames, do not be harsh," Willow said. "She is having her puppies."

"What?" Ames gave her a startled look. "No, she is not. She has never once wanted to have her puppies inside. In fact, we never knew when she had them until Gray came to tell us where she was."

"That may be, but I am telling you that she is in labor." Willow stroked the furry canine as she laid down beside her again.

Ames scratched his jaw, looking agitated. "If that is the case, then something is wrong. She is telling us so."

Jacqui groaned and crouched. She pushed for several moments, but nothing happened. Exhausted, she lay down again. Her panting had grown even heavier.

"That is not a good sign," Ames said. "I think she has been in labor for some time. I did not see her at all today, but we were so busy that I did not think much of it."

He moved over to Jacqui, but she snarled at him.

"Shh shh. It's all right, Jacqui," he said softly. "I just need to look at—"

Jacqui snapped at him and he jerked his hand back.

"Come, now," he said. "I only want to help you."

Willow leaned over and tried to lift Jacqui's tail, but she growled. "How can we help you if you will not let us?"

"Hold her head while I look," Ames said.

He didn't make it far before Jacqui struck, sinking her fangs into his left hand. Although he cried out, Ames didn't pull away. If he did, Jacqui's teeth would rip right through his flesh, doing further damage.

"All right, all right," he said as quietly as he could.

Jacqui slowly released him and then whined as she wagged her tail a little in apology.

Ames swore vehemently and sat back on his haunches. His hand throbbed and burned. Willow grabbed a soft cloth and wet it. She wiped away the blood from his hand, but more came out of the two puncture marks.

Turning his hand over, she saw two more wounds. "I think you should go see Cricket. I do not have any yarrow to stop the bleeding."

She gave him an apologetic glance. "I am not a very good wife. I should have these things on hand."

Ames smiled through his pain. "You are a wonderful wife. Having such things here is easily remedied. I will go see Cricket." His eyes clouded with concern as he looked at Jacqui, who lay on her side panting. "Perhaps Green Leaf will know how to help Jacqui. I will ask her and return just as soon as Cricket is finished with me."

"I will stay with her."

Ames kissed Willow's cheek before leaving. She sighed and sat down as she looked at Jacqui. After losing her own baby, she felt a kinship with the dog and didn't want anything to happen to any of the puppies. Willow gathered dried sage and a few cedar chips and added them to the fire.

Once their aroma filled the tipi, she bathed in the smoke and proceeded to pray for the mother dog and her unborn pups. It might be silly to some people, but all animals were sacred and Willow wanted a successful delivery for Jacqui. She closed her eyes and lifted her voice in a song of entreaty to Sendeh.

"I can help with Jacqui."

Ames gave Ten Thunders a dubious look. "I tried to help her, but this is what happened when I did."

In English, Ten Thunders said, "There was a small white settlement near our people. They're the ones who taught me English and how to work with metal. Their leader raised Pembroke Welsh Corgis and taught me about their care, including whelping and how to deal with difficulties when they arose."

Surprised again by how fluently Ten Thunders spoke English, Ames could only conclude that he'd spent a great deal of time with them. "You know white man's ways extensively. Why?"

Ten Thunders' expression grew wary. "I'd rather not talk about it right now. I assure you that I can help Jacqui."

Ames looked at his bandaged hand. Cricket had applied a salve of agrimony and calendula after thoroughly washing the wounds with witch hazel tea. "All right. You can try, but I doubt that she'll let you any closer to her than she did me."

A smile returned to Ten Thunders' face. "Let's go then."

As they walked through the cold, windy night to his tipi, Ames tried to figure out the puzzle of Ten Thunders. He spoke English fluently, was extremely familiar with white man's ways, and knew metal working; something that Indians did not. He didn't have time to ponder it further because they arrived at his tipi.

Cricket and Ten Thunders followed him inside.

"Ten Thunders says that he can help Jacqui," Ames said in response to Willows questioning gaze.

Ten Thunders surprised them by dropping to all fours and then onto his belly. Jacqui's ears pricked forward when he began whining. Ames' was taken aback by how accurately Ten Thunders mimicked a dog's whine.

The younger man wiggled forward, inching his way over to Jacqui, who watched him with great interest. Ames realized that Ten Thunders was approaching her the way a submissive dog would a dominant one. As Ten Thunders drew closer, Jacqui snarled at him.

Undaunted, Ten Thunders whined and rolled over. Jacqui quieted and wagged her tail. Only then did Ten Thunders reach out a hand to her. She sniffed it and licked it a little. The others were surprised when she let Ten Thunders scratch behind her ears and stroke her side.

Ten Thunders hummed while he repeatedly ran his hand over her swollen belly. "She'll have at least eight puppies. It's possible that the first one in the canal might be breech."

Ames signed so that the others understood. "Eight? That many? How can you tell?"

"Call it an educated guess. I can't really explain it to you."

Ten Thunders went back to humming and moved his hand farther down Jacqui's body to her hind quarters. Then he sat up and scooted down until he could lift Jacqui's tail. She growled once, but Ten Thunders cut her off with a whine.

Willow cringed as he began examining Jacqui, but other than whining a little, she didn't object.

Cautiously feeling around, Ten Thunders quickly discovered the problem. "The first puppy's head is very large. Must be a male. I have to get it out so that the rest can follow." He smiled. "He's alive. I can feel him moving."

"What are you going to do?" Ames asked. His face was taught with anxiety.

"Pull it out. Have Willow move over and put Jacqui's head in your lap. Whine at her. It tells her that you mean her no harm," Ten Thunders said. It was easier speaking English so that Ames could translate.

Willow did as he asked. Jacqui made no objection this time and rested her head on Willow's leg.

Satisfied, Ten Thunders went to work. As gently as possible, he maneuvered his fingers until he could get them around the puppy's head. Jacqui whined and cried out sharply at one point, but she didn't become aggressive. Bit by bit, Ten Thunders worked the puppy out of the birth canal until he could slide it free.

It let out a loud squeal as Ten Thunders gave the wet pup to its mother. Jacqui immediately began washing the male puppy.

"You did it!" Willow exclaimed quietly. "Please stay in case she has more trouble."

Ten Thunders smiled. "Yes. I stay. Want see...more dogs."

As it turned out, the rest of Jacqui's labor went smoothly and by morning, she'd delivered eight more.

Ames yawned as he watched Jacqui with her litter. "What am I going to do with them? We cannot put her in a den since she is already here. But they cannot stay here, either."

Ten Thunders said, "I take. Give me tipi. Stay with me."

Cricket asked, "You would keep them with you?"

"Yes. Make...place for them." He turned to Ames, but also signed. "I'd make a whelping box for them so that the puppies would be contained in one place and not wander off. They would be warm and safe and I could watch over them."

Willow surprised Cricket by saying, "You can have my old tipi. You could keep them there."

He'd never seen her vulnerable side so much as he had the past couple of months. The canine family's welfare was obviously very important to her and he surmised that it must be because of her miscarriage.

"I will help you set them up," he said to Ten Thunders. "Just tell me what to do."

Ten Thunders beamed as he jumped to his feet. "Come. I show you."

The two young men left and Willow chuckled at Ames' puzzled expression. "I think you have lost your dogs, at least for a while."

Ames smiled. "I guess so. I have the feeling that this will be very amusing for our people."

"What do you mean?"

He gave her a mysterious grin. "You will see."

Chapter Fourteen

"Your people are very strange."

Growling Wolf hid a smile by taking a sip of coffee as the other chief and Day Star sat in his and Sleek Doe's tipi on the night of the festivities. "What do you mean?"

Soaring Falcon took a bite of fry bread and chewed thoughtfully for a moment. "You are having something called a Tree Decorating Ceremony and a Christmas Play. Now you have an Ojibwa captive raising puppies as a white man would. Is Ames trying to assimilate you into his culture?"

"Soaring Falcon! Do not be impolite," Day Star admonished him. "I am certain that that is not the case."

He frowned at her. "I am just saying that it seems odd that he would keep introducing all these things from his own culture to all of you. Even odder is that you allow it."

Anger flashed in Sleek Doe's eyes. "Forgive me, but you know nothing about our history with Ames and what he means to us. I do not think it is your place to question my husband or our council about our choices regarding him."

Shocked by her rebuke, Soaring Falcon looked at Growling Wolf who said, "I gave up trying to hold my wife's tongue many winters ago. She is right. If you are going to constantly question our friendship with him, this is going to strain our alliance."

Soaring Falcon chuckled. "There is no need for unpleasantness. It is just very strange to me."

Growling Wolf grinned. "That is part of Ames' charm, as you can see. We are always wondering what he will do next."

Sleek Doe said, "At the heart of it, these ceremonies are no different than ours. They tell the stories of his traditions, the same way our stories do ours. They are very interesting, too." She smiled.

"And the children have come to love being in the Christmas Play. It is so sweet to watch."

Soaring Falcon was very curious to see this celebration. Perhaps he was being too suspicious. For the time being, he decided to put aside his misgivings and just enjoy the evening. "I am looking forward to it."

When someone scratched on the tipi flap, Sleek Doe bid them to enter.

Moonbeam came inside and smiled at them before averting her eyes. "Chirping Cricket says that it is almost time to start."

Sleek Doe was amused by her excited expression. "Then we should not keep everyone waiting. We will be right there."

Moonbeam ducked back out and they chuckled.

"She will never get used to Cricket's new name," Sleek Doe said.

Growling Wolf nodded and rose stiffly to his feet. Although not as creaky these days, his arthritic knees still plagued him. "He has stopped correcting her about it."

As they left the tipi, drums started up, letting everyone know that it was time to gather. They made their way to the central fire, where a huge tree had been erected. It was a splendid specimen that had been chosen with great care by Ames. He'd trimmed the branches himself the previous day, going over it until he'd deemed it perfect.

Soaring Falcon had never seen a trimmed tree before and its symmetry was beautiful. It had never occurred to him that such a thing should be done to a tree, but he had to admit that it was pleasing to the eye.

A mixed throng of Kiowa and Lakota milled around the tree, with the Kiowa proudly explaining to their new kin what was about to take place. Soaring Falcon and Day Star noticed that the Kiowa all wore expressions of happy anticipation. As they drew nearer to the tree, they saw Ames off to the side, surrounded by the children.

He appeared to be giving them instructions about something. Then he finished and they dispersed. Ames strode in front of the tree and held up his hands until the crowd had quieted.

"Greetings, relatives! My heart is gladdened that our Lakota kin could join our Christmas celebration this year. We hope you enjoy yourselves. This is a season of joy and light in my other culture. The time when we honor the birth of Jesus Christ, the Son of God and come together in unity.

"Now, in France we do not often celebrate with a Christmas tree. However, my mother is Swedish, and in her country, they do. Papa loved her dearly, so he indulged her in teaching me the Swedish tradition of putting up a Christmas tree. It is decorated with ornaments and treats and is a symbol of hope for the coming new year.

"I appreciate you all indulging me in bringing a little of my other culture to you, just as my father did with my mother. I hope you enjoy our Christmas Play, as well. The children and others have worked diligently to entertain you and to also tell you the story of Jesus' birth. This is a time of gaiety and thanksgiving, so please have fun. My Kiowa kin will show our Lakota family how this is done. Now, we will have a song before we begin decorating the tree."

The Kiowa raised happy whoops and trills by way of applause and the Lakotas joined in showing that they were good sports about the strange festivities. Ames ran over to the side of the clearing, took something from Willow, and returned to his previous position. Lightning Strike saw what he was up to and let out a happy yelp. Ames raised his fiddle in the air and his family set up a ruckus for a few moments before settling down.

The children gathered around him as he began playing a very old French Christmas Carol, *Entre le Bœuf et L'âne Gris* (Between the Ox and the Gray Ass). Moonbeam and one of the younger boys who'd caught on well to various languages had been chosen to sing the song in Lakota so that everyone could understand it.

Ames played the first verse through before the youngsters lifted their voice in song:

Between   the   ox   and   the   gray   ass,
Sleeps,   sleeps,   sleeps   the   little   son,
A   thousand   divine   angels,   a   thousand   seraphs
Fly around this great God of love.

Between   the   nice   shepherds,
Sleeps,   sleeps,   sleeps   the   little   son,
A   thousand   divine   angels,   a   thousand   seraphs
Fly   around   this   great   God   of   love.

Between   roses   and   lilies,
Sleeps,   sleeps,   sleeps   the   little   son,
A   thousand   divine   angels,   a   thousand   seraphs
Fly   around   this   great   God   of   love.

Between   the   two   arms   of   Mary
Sleeps,   sleeps,   sleeps   the   little   son,
A thousand divine angels, a thousand seraphs

Ames' rich baritone voice mixed with those of the children, who smiled at their audience, not a bit bashful about performing. Their pride shone in their dark eyes and they sang with gusto, pronouncing the French words as accurately as possible.

By the time the last verse was sung, some of the Kiowa adults had joined in, unable to refrain from adding their voices. Cricket watched with a huge smile on his face. But it wasn't only because of the joy hearing the young ones sing that made him happy.

The spirit child stood unseen with the other children, singing along. It shimmered and glowed and its sweet, pure voice gave Cricket goosebumps. Shock shot up his spine when he saw a little boy next to the spirit child smile at it and take its hand. They grinned at each other and went back to singing, their hands still joined.

Cricket intently watched the other youths to see if they also saw the spirit child, but none gave it any notice. He shivered as he felt Bison's hot breath on his neck.

"Do you see?" Bison asked.

Cricket nodded. "Yes, I see."

"But do you understand?"

It was always an awe-inspiring experience when Bison let him into His consciousness. Another power joined that of Bison and Cricket felt faint from its intensity.

"Who is that?"

Bison chuckled. "The One whom you have been sensing lately. Do not worry. There is nothing to fear, Good Cricket."

Both presences faded away. Cricket blinked a couple of times and took a deep breath to clear his mind. The children finished their song and the spirit child darted off into the night. The little boy it had been standing with looked after it with a sad expression.

I need to talk to him tomorrow, Cricket thought. Then his attention was diverted when Hummingbird touched his hand.

"Are you all right?"

He smiled. "Yes. Fine."

Her eyes held his. "Did something just happen? You seemed so far away. I said something to you, but you did not respond."

"I am sorry," he said, contritely. "Yes, something did happen, but I cannot talk to you about it just yet. I hope you understand."

Although curious, Hummingbird nodded. "I understand. It is the same with Smoking Fire. I will respect your wishes."

"Thank you," he said. "Now, come with me. It is time to decorate the tree!"

They moved forward with the rest, surrounding the tree. Laughter and lively conversation flowed around the area as spots were chosen for the various decorations and their significance was explained. Several of the men lifted children up so they could stand on their shoulders to reach the uppermost branches of the tree.

It didn't take long for the tree to be covered. Once it was finished, Ames, Lightning Strike, and Fang went around placing small lit candles on some of the branches. Once they were done, they stepped back with the rest and gazed at their handiwork.

A hush fell over the crowd gathered. Many of the ornaments were made with glass beads, copper, and gold. The beautiful decorations reflected the candlelight. It flickered over the shiny surfaces, making the tree appear as though it was moving. A light breeze started up and some of the ornaments brushed against the others, creating faint, musical chimes.

The Lakota had never witnessed anything like the beauty that stood before them. Even though the Kiowa had, it still transfixed them. Soaring Falcon gazed upon the tree and understood why the Kiowa enjoyed Ames' holiday celebration. It had certainly brought both tribes together in a positive way and it had been fun, too.

He looked at Growling Wolf and caught the knowing twinkle in his eyes.

"There is no need to be smug," he said.

Sleek Doe snorted, drawing a frown from him, but she was unfazed and just smiled back.

Ames stood with his arm around Willow's shoulders as they looked at the tree.

"I think that is the most beautiful tree yet," she remarked.

He gave her an affectionate squeeze. "I agree. The Lakota made some very fine ornaments."

"Yes, they did."

Ames chuckled. "Do not sound so disappointed."

She smiled. "I am trying to get along with them. I am much better about it than I was at first."

He cocked an eyebrow at her. "Could that be because you are seeing that there are good people among them?"

She turned her attention back to the tree. "Yes, there are good people among them. It is easy to like those people. But there are some of them who I will never like. You must accept that."

He said, "Of course there will be those you do not get along with it. No one likes everyone."

"You do."

Laughter rumbled in his chest. "Is that what you think? No, no. There are many people I have met that I do not like, but for the sake of my business, I had to be diplomatic."

"I hate being diplomatic."

"I know, but I have to say that you are improving."

Glancing over at where the two chiefs and their wives stood, Willow grunted. "There will never be any improvement when it comes to some people."

Ames didn't respond because the finest tenor voice he'd ever heard started singing *O Come, O Come Emmanuel* in English. His eyes went wide and his heart beat faster as he watched Ten Thunders walk towards the tree with his hands held up to it. The young man didn't just mumble the words; he sang with confidence and power.

Laughter rippled through the onlookers, but Ten Thunders kept singing. Ames took up his fiddle again and started playing along when Ten Thunders began the second verse. Slowly, he walked out to Ten Thunders and gave him an encouraging smile.

On the third verse, he joined his baritone with Ten Thunders' tenor:

O	*come,*	*Thou*	*Dayspring,*	*from*	*on*	*high,*
And	*cheer*	*us*	*by*	*Thy*	*drawing*	*nigh;*
Disperse	*the*	*gloomy*	*clouds*	*of*	*night,*
And	*death's*	*dark*	*shadows*	*put*	*to*	*flight.*
Rejoice!		*Rejoice!*		*Emmanuel*
Shall come to thee, O Israel.

Ames played two more verses before drawing the song to a close. He tucked his fiddle under his arm and clapped while grinning at Ten Thunders.

"You have a splendid voice, friend," he said. "Well done, indeed."

Following Ames' lead, his family started clapping as well. The Lakota hesitantly followed suit.

Ten Thunders looked bashfully around. "I couldn't help it. It's been so long since I heard that song, but I'd know it anywhere. It brings back very good memories for me, as does the tree. I couldn't resist singing. I miss that, too."

"How long were you with your white family?" Ames had concluded that the only way Ten Thunders could've known so much about white man's ways was if he'd been assimilated at some point.

"Seven years. It is a long story."

The pain in his eyes touched Ames' heart. "Perhaps you will tell me one day."

"Perhaps."

Ten Thunders gave him a tight smile and moved off through the crowd. People gave him curious looks as he did, which made him feel uncomfortable. He didn't want to be the subject of their scrutiny, so he found a spot off alone from which to watch the play.

Chapter Fifteen

The "stage" was set up quickly and the play started. Ames had talked Firebrand into narrating the story of Christ's birth. He started reciting it, beginning with the Angel of the Lord's visitation upon Mary. Moonbeam played a very believable Mary while, Jumper, a boy a year younger than her filled the role of Joseph.

Using one of Ames' smaller mules, they portrayed Mary and Joseph searching for a place to stay for the night. The youngsters had practiced hard and it showed. There were only a couple of times when Ames had to prompt them.

Willow was filled with pride over their performance, but also for the skillful way Ames directed them. His love for the children was evident and he was thoroughly enjoying himself. It made her wonder if he ever missed living among his own people.

As she watched Moonbeam hold a pretend baby Jesus, a pang of longing shot through her. It reminded her of her baby and she furiously blinked away tears, hiding her pain behind a smile as the performance ended. She clapped and whooped with everyone, but on the inside she cried for the lost little life.

She needed to get out of there before she broke down and embarrassed herself. Quickly, she made her way through the crush of people who were pressing forward to talk with the performers. Her chest hurt from holding in her grief and her breath hitched as she finally reached clear space.

Desperately seeking a distraction, she headed for Ten Thunders' tipi. She loved visiting Jacqui and the puppies. Their eyes and ears had opened a couple of days ago and they were becoming more active now.

She scratched on the tipi flap and he told her to come in.

"You left the celebration early," she said.

"Yes. Too...crowded. Needed space."

Being back in her old tipi was both comforting and upsetting. It was where she'd lost her baby, but also where she'd spent so much of her time when not seeing to her duties. She smiled understandingly as she sat down by the wooden whelping box that Ten Thunders and Cricket had built.

Jacqui thumped her tail as she lay on her side nursing her pups. Five of them looked like her with her black and tan markings, but three of them resembled Gray with their silver fur. The other one, the runt, had shorter gray hair that was peppered with black. His white underbelly and four white paws made him stand out from the others.

Willow petted the feeding canine babies, enjoying the softness of their fur and the sounds of their suckling. Occasionally, one would whine because one of its siblings had stolen its place.

"You get away, too?"

Ten Thunders' question drew her attention away from the dogs. "Yes. Bad memories. I needed space, too."

He smiled and chin-nodded at the whelping box. "Puppies make me feel better."

Seeing that the runt was done feeding, Willow picked him up and held him in her arms. He whimpered and sniffed around a little, but the warmth of her buffalo robe comforted him and he soon fell asleep.

"How do you know how to take care of dogs this way?"

Ten Thunders put a little more wood on the fire. He let out a resigned sigh. "When I was five winters old, our tribe was attacked by white men. They captured some of us to use as slaves," he signed. "They took us back to their village and sold us off. I was lucky that the spiritual leader there took pity on me. He refused to buy me. Instead, he adopted me."

Willow's eyes rounded in surprise. "A white man adopted you?"

"Yes, he named me Luke and he was very kind to me. He gave me a good home and taught me how to read and write. I made a few friends there, but most people only tolerated me."

"How did you come to be with the Ojibwa?"

Ten Thunders propped his forearms on his drawn-up knees and rested his chin on them. The firelight illuminated the tears that shimmered in his eyes. "They attack town. Take me since Indian. I was fourteen winters old. Now nineteen winters old."

The crackling of the fire and the quiet grunts of the puppies were the only sounds in the tipi for a few moments.

Willow couldn't imagine being taken captive three times in her life. "And then we took you captive from them."

"Yes." He shrugged in confusion and started signing. "I do not remember what my first tribe was. I do not know if I was Lakota, Kiowa, Hidatsa...I have no idea. I am not white, but I miss my white father. He was so good to me and he loved me, not like my Ojibwa father. I was a disappointment to him from the beginning. I am glad to be away from him. But I do not know who I am. I do not remember my first family very much. What culture am I? I am caught between so many."

His sorrow made a lump form in Willow's throat. "I am very sorry for what you have endured, but I think you have found your home. I would never leave you behind the way the men who called you a brother did."

Brushing away a tear, Ten Thunders said, "Thank you. I hope I have finally found where I am supposed to be."

"I wondered how you knew that song that you and Ames sang. It was very beautiful."

Her compliment made him self-conscious, but he knew that she meant it. Willow didn't say things that she didn't mean. "I am glad you enjoyed it. I went with my father every week to the worship ceremony and I enjoyed their songs very much. As soon as he heard me sing, he began training me and the other members liked to hear me sing. I missed singing like that."

Ten Thunders wondered why he felt comfortable telling Willow all of this when he hadn't wanted to discuss it with Ames.

"I am sure you have." Her mouth curved in a smile. "Feel free to sing anytime."

He smiled as he watched her pet the puppy. "I think he is yours. He has your smell now and he is comfortable with you."

"He has my smell? He is so little."

He started speaking out loud again.. "It not matter. Puppies can smell soon as born. He knows you now. Time new moon, Jacqui wean puppies. You take home then."

Although Willow had always played with the camp dogs, she'd never had one of her own before. The idea of raising her own dog warmed her heart. She picked up the puppy and looked into its little dark eyes. Gently, she blew into his face so that he inhaled her breath.

"You are mine now."

A wide smile curved Ten Thunders' mouth. "What are you going to name him?"

"I do not know yet." She kissed her puppy and put it back in the box with the rest of his family. "I should go find my husband before he comes looking for me. Goodnight, Ten Thunders."

"Goodnight."

She stepped outside the tipi and stopped short when Soaring Falcon blocked her way. "What do you want?"

One of his eyebrows rose at her sharp tone. "I came to see this puppy box."

Just the sight of the Lakota chief set her blood boiling. "Fine, but the little one with the white paws is mine. You cannot have it."

"Willow, no one will take your puppy," Day Star said kindly.

Without warning, tears burned Willow's eyes. "You might not, but he would."

"Willow!"

Growling Wolf's displeased voice came from behind Day Star, which explained why Willow hadn't seen him.

"Apologize, right now!"

"No." She gave Soaring Falcon a hard, direct glare and stomped off.

Soaring Falcon shook his head. "I know that our tribes have bad history between us, but I do not understand why she directs her hatred at me. She likes the women and most of the braves. Except Slither. They came to blows once. But her and Dark Horse and Rushing Bull are friends. I cannot figure it out."

Growling Wolf said, "I do not know, but she is going to stop this. I know she has not been feeling well lately, but I will not tolerate her insolence. She has never disobeyed a direct order before."

Soaring Falcon made a dismissive motion. "Do not worry about it. It is of no real consequence. Let us go see these puppies."

Growling Wolf followed his friends into Ten Thunders' tipi, but he fully intended to get to the bottom of Willow's hatred of Soaring Falcon.

Ames leaned against a wicker backrest, his long legs stretched out before him as he ate a bowl of stew and wondered where his wife was. He'd look around for her after the festivities, but then he'd gotten distracted by people who wanted to talk to him.

He'd just swallowed a bite when Willow came into their home. Her wild-eyed gaze made the hair on the nape of his neck stand up. "What happened?"

"He is going to kill me. Or have me killed." Willow crossed over to her things and picked up her large, buckskin bag. "We have to leave."

Ames sat forward and set his bowl on the floor. "Who are you talking about? Where have you been?"

"I went to see the puppies. I saw my puppy. I am keeping one. And then he was there and he wants my puppy. I just know he does," Willow said, stuffing a rolled-up pair of leggings into her bag.

"Willow, stop packing. You are not making sense. Who is going to kill you?"

Willow dropped her bag and sniffled. "Growling Wolf. I disobeyed him. Now I will be punished. Good warriors do not disobey their chief."

Ames stood up and stretched. He jumped a little when she whirled around and pointed a finger at him. "He wanted me to apologize, but I will never tell that man I am sorry about anything."

There was only one person other than an enemy tribe who brought out Willow's wrath that way. "What did Soaring Falcon do?"

Her chin rose. "He was going to steal my puppy."

Ames' forehead creased and he rubbed his jaw. "Why would Soaring Falcon steal your puppy? They have dogs in his camp."

"Exactly. I told him that he could not have it. I gave him my breath and I breathed in his."

"Why were you giving Soaring Falcon your breath?"

"No! The puppy! I gave the puppy my breath." She threw up her hands. "You are just like all men. You do not listen."

Ever since he'd met Willow, she'd been virtually unflappable. Yes, she could be testy, but she'd never acted so irrationally before. "Are you feeling well?"

"I feel fine. Why do men think that women must be sick just because they do not pay attention when women speak?"

Ames took a deep breath. "Let's start at the beginning, *mon amour*," he said. "I promise to pay very close attention."

His confusion deepened when tears gathered in her eyes. "Ames, I think I am going crazy. I know that I am not making any sense. Maybe something *is* wrong with me. Oh. You spoke in French, so I should respond that way."

Placing a hand on her shoulder, Ames said, "Do not worry about that. Take a deep breath and then start at the beginning."

"Now you are speaking Kiowa. Which language are we speaking?"

He sat down and patted the place next to him. "Kiowa. Now, tell me what happened."

Willow huffed out a breath and lowered herself down by his side. "I was feeling sad—stew! I am so hungry." She picked up Ames' bowl and ate a spoonful. "Mmm. Very good. Thank you for bringing it for me."

Ames opened his mouth to object, but decided against it. "Why were you sad?"

"Because the birth of Jesus reminded me of our baby," she said between bites. "I did not want to cry in public, so I went to see the puppies. I picked the little one with the white paws."

"I am following so far. Go on."

"We had a nice talk. Ten Thunders and me, not me and the puppy, although I talked to all the dogs, too."

Ames frowned. "Focus, Willow. Then what happened?"

"I left to come find you, but Soaring Falcon was there. It startled me and I hate him. I told him that he could not have my puppy. I was very rude. Growling Wolf reprimanded me and told me to apologize, but I refused and walked away."

Ames watched her polish off the stew with gusto. "I do not think Growling Wolf will have you killed for that."

She sat the bowl down and chuckled. "I know. Why am I acting like a crazy woman? I feel better now, though."

"I am glad you feel better. Willow, getting over the loss of a baby is not easy. I still grieve, too. But, even though we will always miss that little one, we will have other babies." He embraced her and kissed her forehead. "Neither of us are patient people, but be patient we must. It has not been very long."

"I know. I am getting fat, Ames."

"What?" While it was true that her normally slim waist had thickened somewhat, Ames didn't think she was fat in the least. "You are not. You are just not doing the same things as before. Your body will adjust."

"I still hike miles every day and spar, although I have not feel like it the past few days," she said.

"You are allowed to be a little tired now and again. I am," Ames said.

Willow covered her mouth as she belched. "Sorry." She put a hand to her stomach as a weak wave of nausea flowed through her. "I do not think that stew agreed with me. I must have eaten too fast. I was so hungry."

"Do you want me to make tea?"

The nausea subsided. "No. It is going away." Willow looked around the tipi. "We are very messy."

Ames laughed. "I know. I try not to be, but I think it is hopeless."

The dancing flames of the fire had a slightly hypnotic quality to them and Willow suddenly felt very tired. She yawned until it felt as though her jaw would crack. "I guess it is time for bed. It was a long day."

"I agree."

They spread out their sleeping robes and Ames took off his tunic. Willow crawled onto their sleeping pallet and stretched out fully clothed. She didn't have the energy to undress. Instead, she pulled the blanket over her as Ames banked the fire.

As she watched the play of his muscles while he worked, a brief glimmer of desire flared but quickly died. It simply wasn't in her that night to make love with Ames. She tried to keep her eyes open, but the effort was too much and she slipped into slumber.

Ames finished with the fire and lay down so that he was spooning her. As he put his arm around her, Willow let out a soft snore. She'd recently started falling to sleep quickly, but not that fast. Her odd behavior of late was worrisome.

He kissed her cheek and rolled over on his back. As he lay there listening to his wife's even breathing, he decided that she should talk to Cricket the next morning. Hopefully, he'd be able to figure out the trouble.

Chapter Sixteen

Cricket groaned in protest when someone shook his shoulder. "Moonbeam, leave me alone. I just got to sleep."

When he heard a young child giggle, Cricket opened his eyes a little. The spirit child sat near him with a mischievous smile on its face.

"Why are you waking me?" he asked.

"We have to go."

Cricket lifted his head from the grass on which he lay. There was a decided nip in the air and leaves floated on the cool breeze. "Where are we going?"

The child smiled and cocked its head to the side. "Not you. Us. We wanted to say goodbye, but we will see you again soon."

Cricket gazed intently into its blue eyes as its face kept changing. He now understood why it sometimes looked like a girl and sometimes like a boy. It wasn't just one child: there were two separate entities.

They must have realized that he'd figured it out because they laughed and suddenly broke apart.

Cricket shook his head. "I do not understand."

The spirit girl said, "It is time. We are stronger now and she is ready."

"Our mother is now ready to bear us," the boy said. "You must tell her."

Standing up, Cricket asked, "Willow has become pregnant again?"

The girl smiled at him. "We have never left her."

"We will see you soon." The boy smiled at Cricket and took his sister's hand.

They ran off together, fading from sight as their laughter carried back to him. Cricket felt an acute sense of loss. He was going to miss having them around. But even as he felt sadness, he was happy for Willow and Ames and that Sendeh's will would be carried out.

"Thank you, Sendeh, for honoring me with the task of watching over them until now. I will do my best to help them grow strong and guide them," he said before the familiar white light engulfed him.

The next morning, Cricket listened to Willow as she explained her symptoms to him. She'd found him in the medicine lodge and he'd gladly agreed to give her his advice. He was amused over her rambling because it was so different than her usual focused, articulate way of speaking. However, trepidation gnawed at him over how she was going to take what he was about to tell her.

She rubbed at her tired eyes. Even though she'd slept like a rock, she was exhausted. "What is wrong with me?"

Cricket squared his shoulders. "Willow, you must trust me even though what I am about to say will shock you. You must believe me, because I would never lie to you."

His statement made her feel queasy. "Am I dying?"

He smiled kindly. "No. Far from it. You are going to live, especially because you carry life within you."

An annoyed sigh escaped her. "I am too tired for riddles, Cricket. Please just tell me."

Cricket took her hand. "Look into my eyes."

She did so with an expectant expression.

"Willow, you are pregnant. That is why you are so tired and your moods are so erratic."

His declaration stunned her, rendering her speechless for long moments. Eventually, she whispered, "So soon after losing our baby?"

"Willow, you only lost one baby. You are still pregnant," he said, smiling.

Anger filled her eyes and she squeezed his hand hard. "What kind of sick game are you playing? I lost my baby. I am not pregnant!"

Her painful grip made him grimace. "Willow, I would never lie to you, especially over something so important. I know how terrible losing your baby has been for you and Ames. Do you remember when I told you that your baby's spirit visited me a lot?"

"Yes."

"At that time, I did not understand that it was not the spirit of the baby you lost. I thought that it was waiting for the next time you conceived. I did not realize that it was the spirit of the baby you still carried. Willow, please let me go."

Willow released his hand, but still regarded him suspiciously. "I cannot be pregnant. I had my moon time last month."

"You also had your moon time during your whole pregnancy. Like their mother, your babies are tenacious. They have been fighting for their lives even though you took a purging tea."

Her eyebrows drew together in a ferocious frown as she fought back hope and confusion. "Why do you say 'babies'?"

"It is rare, but you conceived three babies," Cricket replied. "You only lost one. It must have been too weak to resist the purging tea, but the other two have hung on. They have been gaining strength since you stopped taking the purge. With you now wearing winter clothing, I cannot tell whether you are gaining weight, but your face looks a little fuller."

Putting a hand to her cheek, Willow tried to see if he was right, but she couldn't tell. However, there was no doubt that her waist was thicker. "I have not felt any movement. I would have felt movement before now."

"Not necessarily. If the babies were stunted a little, you would not have felt them move yet. Movement can also be mistaken for other things, such as gas or nausea," Cricket said.

Pressing her hand to her abdomen, Willow's gaze locked on his. "I have been nauseous, but I thought perhaps I had a stomach ailment. And then there are times when I am so hungry and..." Her eyes misted over as hope and guilt warred within her. "Cricket, what if I am still pregnant? I have been sparring and hiking and lifting heavier things than most women do when they are pregnant. What if I have hurt them?"

Cricket sat straighter and his face settled into somber lines. "Willow, I tell you without a shadow of a doubt that you are still pregnant. They came to me and told me so. They said that they have never left you. Your babies are so strong, Willow. Just like you and Ames."

Tears rolled down her cheeks. "You have seen them?"

A smile lit his face. "Yes, and they are beautiful. Your babies love you, Willow."

The conviction in his voice finally convinced her. A sob hitched in her throat as she grabbed him in an impulsive embrace. "Thank you, Cricket. May Sendeh bless you with everything you ever want or need. I will take care of my babies and they will be born. Nothing will stop me from making that happen."

Cricket returned her embrace and he had to blink back tears. "There is no need to thank me. I am only doing my duty. I am so happy for you and Ames."

Willow released him, but held onto his arms. "No, Cricket. You do not just do your duty. You may have power and knowledge, but what sets you apart from other medicine men is your generous heart. You have truly given yourself to your calling and you always put your whole being into it. Besides that, you are a good friend and I am honored to call you such." She clapped his shoulder and stood up. "I cannot wait to tell Ames. I will never be able to repay you. Thank you again."

He responded to her broad smile with one of his own as she left. It remained on his face for some time as a warm glow filled his heart. After years of feeling like an outcast, first because of his lowborn status and then his slight build, it was a wonderful feeling to be held in such high regard.

It wasn't pride that made him so happy, it was finally feeling accepted for who he was inside that gave him so much joy. He went about his work, making Willow a tincture that would strengthen her blood and help with her fatigue. As he did, he hummed a song of thanksgiving for all the positive changes in his life.

Waiting for Ames to return home that day made Willow irritable, so she went to visit the puppies. Ames had left early to check traps with Firebrand since he'd come back from the Lakota camp. Since it was taking them so long, she assumed that they were having great success.

Once her mood had improved, she went for a walk and was drawn to her other baby's grave, which she had done a couple of times since the miscarriage. She sat down by it and put a hand on her stomach.

"I am so sorry. If I had known that I was pregnant, I would not have taken the tea. I would never do anything to hurt you," she said.

She heard someone coming up behind her and turned to see Tulip approaching her. "I did not mean to eavesdrop, but I heard what you said." She sat down by Willow. "There was no way for you to know since your moon time never stopped. You never had morning sickness or any other signs of pregnancy."

"I still feel responsible," Willow said. "We have not talked about it, but I know that you must have been disappointed in me because I was intimate with Ames before we were married."

Tulip took her hand. "Willow, from the time we were children, you have always done as you wished. You have obeyed most tribal customs and rules, but you have pushed against those lines sometimes. I was shocked, at first, but I was so worried about you. And angry with Ames."

"Yes. He and Lightning Strike argued a couple of times." Willow patted Tulip's hand. "But what everyone needs to understand is that women are capable of deciding when they are ready to make love to a man. People seem to think that we need to be protected, but we do not. If I had not wanted Ames so much, we would not have become lovers. Other men have made passes at me, but I had no interest in them. I punished those who were too forward." She smiled. "Do you remember the first time you kissed Fang?"

Tulip laughed. "Of course. We had been flirting quite a bit the spring before we married. One evening, when I was coming back from gathering firewood, he caught me alone on the path. He made it seem like it was by chance, but I knew better. And he knew that I knew."

Willow laughed with her. "What happened then?"

A faraway light come into Tulip's eyes. "Magic. I thought that my heart was going to gallop right out of my chest when he kissed me. He gave me every chance to say no and rebuff him, but I wanted him to kiss me. It was the most wonderful thing I had experienced until then. He started courting me that very night."

"See? You knew what you wanted," Willow said. "I was twenty winters old, more than old enough to know my own mind."

Tulip gave her a smile filled with curiosity. "When did you fall in love with him?"

"The first moment that we met," Willow replied. "We grasped arms and looked into each other's eyes and I knew right then that I wanted him to be mine." She looked away shyly and then back at Tulip. "He had been here for a couple of weeks when he asked if he could kiss me. He did not just take it for granted that I wanted him to. Not like some men had. He was so patient and gentle and not just about kissing me. I will never regret giving myself to him. The only thing I regret is not marrying him the first time he asked me to."

Tulip gasped quietly. "Why did you refuse?"

Willow told her cousin her reasoning. "I was stupid to have turned him down for so long. Maybe I would not have lost our baby."

"There is no way to know that. Many women lose their first baby. And other women who have taken purging teas have had the same sort of thing happen. You cannot continue to blame yourself. Why did Ames not go to Lightning Strike and ask to marry you?"

Willow smiled. "He wanted to. We argued about it often, but he wanted me to be ready to marry him in my own time. He would not force me into it by going behind my back to Lightning Strike. He is so considerate and accepting of me. I doubt any other man would put up with me."

"His love for you is easy to see," Tulip said. "When you were sick, we could not keep him from you."

Willow grinned. "I know. That will always be the case."

Tulip rose and put a hand on Willow's shoulder. "I must go make the evening meal. Will you eat with us tonight?"

"No, thank you. I have something to discuss with Ames."

Tulip nodded. "Do not sit here too long. It is getting colder."

"All right." Willow's eyes returned to the little grave when Tulip had gone. "I promise to take good care of your brother and sister. We will meet one day when I come to you in the next life. I love you so much and I will never forget you."

As Ames looked around his tipi, he thought at first that he'd accidentally entered the wrong home. All their possessions were neatly arranged and something that smelled heavenly was cooking in a pot that hung over the fire. Apparently, Willow had found her domestic side that day.

"*Há:cho*, husband."

He'd been so focused on the cleanly state of the home, that he'd somehow failed to notice Willow sitting off to one side. A spear of desire ran through him as he looked at her. She wore a pretty, dark doeskin dress with white quill work and red beading. From her ears dangled a pair of gold earrings that he'd given her the previous year. The golden feathers caught the firelight as she moved.

She'd trimmed her bangs and the right side of her hair, but the rest of the long, sooty tresses, she'd braided with red thongs. Although she always looked gorgeous, Willow practically glowed and Ames was mesmerized by her beauty.

"Are you hungry?" She took the lid off the pot and stirred the savory-scented contents inside.

Ames snapped out of his fog. "Yes."

He looked around for a good spot and sat his pack there. He took off his coat and put it with his pack. Willow had gone to a lot of trouble to clean their tipi and he didn't want to mess it up again. Everything looked so nice and smelled fresh, too.

"Come, sit."

He sent her a charming smile. "I do not feel presentable enough to sit by such a beautiful woman. I have been out in the woods hauling traps and skinning dead animals all day." He held up a finger. "I will return shortly."

Once outside, he ran to Firebrands tipi and hurriedly scratched to enter. Barely had Firebrand given permission than he went inside.

"I need to borrow one of your clean linen shirts and wash up," he said. "My wife has something unexpected planned for tonight and I reek of dead beaver."

Firebrand laughed, but refrained from making jokes. "You are lucky that I just put water on to heat. There are some cloths and the soap I bought in Grand Forks are over in that basket."

Ames whipped off his shirt and retrieved the toiletries. He took a little extra time and washed his hair, too. It would dry while he and Willow ate. Then he donned the clean, white shirt that Firebrand gave him and combed his hair.

"I am afraid that is the best I can do on such short notice," he said. "How do I look?"

Firebrand grinned as Ames turned around once. "Very handsome. She will not be able to resist you, not that she has ever been able to, as you keep telling me."

"So I do. But only because I cannot resist her, either. Thank you, brother."

He took his dirty shirt and hurried back to his home. Dropping the soiled shirt near the tipi entrance, he straightened his shirt and ran his fingers through his hair a little. Then he rolled his eyes at his vanity and joined his waiting wife.

The appreciation in her midnight eyes made him very glad that he'd spruced up. His father had told him that the secret to a happy marriage was for a man to constantly woo his wife. Acquiring her was only half the reward; keeping her was the challenge. Ames fully intended to keep his wife forever.

As he sat beside her, he kissed her cheek and spoke in French. "You're ravishing. What are we celebrating?"

"Our love." Willow dipped out a bowl of pheasant stew and handed it to him. "And the many blessings bestowed upon us."

"I won't argue with any of that." Ames took the bowl and inhaled the aroma rising from it. "We're very blessed indeed and you are my greatest treasure."

Willow blushed over his compliment. She knew that no matter how many winters they were together that he would always affect her so. "And you're mine. Did you have a profitable day?"

"Yes. The amount of plentiful game here is amazing. We must do our utmost to make sure our location is kept secret when we go to *Les Grandes Fourches* in the spring. The trek there is shorter than the one to our old trading post. We'll leave as soon as the weather breaks and we'll be able to return sooner. We won't have to be away from home as long.

"At this rate, we'll soon have as many pelts as we can carry without attracting attention." Ames paused to take a bit of stew. "Mmm. Even more delicious than it smells, Willow."

Willow didn't comment on the trip north because she didn't want to spoil his enthusiasm. She loved listening to him talk about his trade. Although she was disappointed that she wouldn't be going with him and Firebrand, the reason why more than made up for it.

"I'm glad you like it. Will you go to the trading post separately?" She also began to eat.

"I think it would be wise," he said. "I don't want them to know that we travel together. If we split our goods, it won't tip anyone off how well we did. And since Ten Thunders is going with us, we'll be able to further divide up our haul.

"He'll be able to negotiate well, too. You and I will go in together, though. Trappers' wives don't normally go to the posts there, but there are exceptions. No one will make much of you being with me. We'll meet up with the other two when we're ready to leave. We'll depart before first light."

"That sounds like a good plan." She sat her bowl off to the side and took the stew off the fire so that she could make some fry bread.

Ames watched her, thinking what a well-rounded woman his woman was. She could fight with the most fearsome warriors and fix weapons, yet she also knew how to take care of a home. And she looked like an angel no matter what she was doing. Sometimes it was a fierce, avenging angel, and other times she was a womanly, caring angel. Ames loved all her sides equally.

When the bread was ready, she put some on small plates to cool and then drizzled some maple syrup over it.

"You spoil me, *mon amour*."

"No more than you spoil me."

When they finished their stew, Ames picked up a piece of fry bread and held it out to her. "I want to feed my queen."

Willow giggled and took the bite he offered her.

As she chewed, he leaned closer and kissed her earlobe. "I have some ideas about what we could do with this delicious syrup."

His suggestive remark and his warm breath against her ear made Willow shudder. "I'm sure you do."

Ames went to lick his fingers, but she took his hand and brought it to her mouth. His pupils dilated as she sucked syrup from one of his fingertips. Watching his sky-blue eyes darken with desire gave her a feeling of power.

"If you keep doing things like that, I'm going to have you for dessert."

She smiled and kissed him lightly. "You can do that as soon as I tell you something very important."

He groaned. "Please hurry. You know that I'm not a patient man."

Trailing her fingers down his arm, she said, "That's not true. You were very patient the first time we made love."

Heat surged directly to his loins and he suppressed another groan. "Wicked, wicked woman to remind me of that after denying me."

Willow laughed and hugged him. "You'll be glad that I denied you."

"Hmm. I doubt that, but go ahead."

Putting a little space between them, Willow began telling him about her visit with Cricket that morning. A myriad of emotions played over his face as she spoke. By the time she finished, he'd gone from wary, to relieved, to incredulous, and then completely blank.

Willow fell silent and waited from him to speak.

Coherent thought escaped Ames at the moment. "I..." He cleared his throat. "Cricket is certain?"

"Yes."

"I see."

His quiet reaction was beginning to scare her. She was startled when he rose quickly and left the tipi.

Ames paced outside, unmindful of the bitter wind that blew. He thrust his fingers into his still-damp hair as he tried to wrap his mind around her news. *Willow is pregnant. Has been pregnant all this time. With twins. How is this possible?*

He stopped pacing and stuck his head back inside. "Cricket is absolutely positive about this?"

Willow nodded and he withdrew again.

"She only lost one baby. How could there be three? Is my essence that strong? Or—what does it matter?" he asked himself before popping his head inside again. "Two babies? Twins?"

"Yes. Twins."

He calmly nodded and resumed pacing outside. "Two. We made three, only lost one. Still going to be a father. To two babies." As it became more real to him, joy made his heart pound and he let out a shout of laughter.

Bursting back inside, he was stopped short at the sight of Willow sitting completely nude by the fire.

She put her hands against her softly rounded stomach. "Ames, see what our love made?"

Love, joy, awe, and desire coalesced inside his heart, making him slightly dizzy. He fell on his knees before her and put his hand over hers where they rested on her belly.

"You said that we were celebrating our love and we certainly are." Tears gathered in his eyes, blurring his vision, and he blinked them away. "Do you know how much I love you?" He took her face in his hands. "Do you? So much, my Willow." He kissed her forehead, her eyes, the tip of her nose, and then finally, her lips. "You were already the most wonderful blessing in my life, but now, I am triply blessed by the two little lives growing inside of you. My three treasures."

Willow held onto him as he embraced her, his words easing her fear that he would be unhappy with her announcement. "I'm just as blessed, Ames. So very much to have found such a wonderful man. A man I'm proud to call my husband and the father of my children."

"I'm going to be a father," he said softly as tears slid down his face. "I can't believe it."

Willow sniffled against his shoulder. "Me, either, but I'm so happy."

"As am I. As am I." He drew back and met her gaze. "Are you feeling well? Are you tired? Do you need to lie down? Are you still hungry?"

Her lips twitched at his rapid questioning. "I am fine. I am full and feel well. Wonderful, in fact." She moved her hands to the buttons of his breeches. "The only way I'll lie down is if you make love with me."

His brows puckered with uncertainty. "Is it all right to make love? Will it hurt the babies?"

Willow lifted his shirt and kissed his chest. "It is fine."

She bit him and he growled. "Are you sure?"

"Take off your shirt and make love to me, damn it," Willow said.

Ames grinned at her swearing. "I shouldn't, but I enjoy hearing you curse."

"It's your fault for teaching me to."

He smiled and tossed his shirt aside before taking Willow in his arms. As the fire burned lower, the flames of their passion rose higher when they kissed. Ames skimmed his hands over Willow's silky skin, admiring every curve and relishing the way she felt against his own naked flesh. Her lips tasted of maple syrup and he wanted to devour her.

Willow leaned back and pulled Ames down to their sleeping robes with her. "You are the most virile, gorgeous man I have ever met." She ran her hands over his shoulders as he lay half on top of her. "I want to show you how much I love you."

Her soft lips on his flooded Ames with need for his wife, but he forced himself to take things slowly. Although his body wanted to quickly consummate their mutual longing, his heart demanded that he thoroughly love his woman. He took his time kissing and caressing her, telling her how much he loved and desired her.

Willow was of like mind and didn't mind the leisurely pace of their lovemaking that night. There was no need to rush, no reason to not fully enjoy one another. Her questing hands traveled down his muscular back when he finally covered her body with his. And still, they didn't rush, moving in a lazy rhythm that created exquisite sensations.

Worried that his heavy weight would harm the babies, Ames rolled over, putting Willow on top. She smiled down at him and began moving, resuming their easy pace. When the steadily building tension reached the peak, ecstasy washed through them in long, undulating waves that carried them into a sea of bliss.

Easing further down on top of Ames, Willow kissed him thoroughly as he ran his hands over her shapely thighs. One of the things she loved most about Ames was that he still made love to her after they were satisfied.   He continued to touch and kiss her, conveying his deep feelings for her.

Sometimes it rekindled their desire and sometimes they just talked while being so close. That night, it wasn't until the fire had burned down to embers that they were completely sated and fell into a pleasantly exhausted slumber.

Chapter Seventeen

Christmas would take place in two days in the Kiowa village. Although Dark Horse had brought Sky Dancer and her mother, She Sings, to celebrate, the only other members of the Lakota tribe who would attend were Rushing Bull, Dark Horse's younger siblings, Spider and Three Deer, and Hummingbird.

Hummingbird's parents hadn't wanted her to go to the strange event, but she'd persisted. Although she was a dutiful daughter, she was also stubborn and felt that she should go out of respect for her future husband. She was also intensely curious about what Cricket had told her was a "holiday".

Sky Dancer and She Sings had interceded on the young woman's behalf. She Sings had employed her considerable skills of diplomacy and convinced them that the young woman would be safe and well looked after. It had annoyed her that they were resistant even though they'd been to the Kiowa village several times and had no reason not to trust her people. However, she kept those thoughts to herself.

Hummingbird's parents had finally relented, but her father had informed She Sings that if anything happened to his daughter that he'd hold her personally responsible. Hummingbird had been furious about her father's attitude, but had held her tongue lest he change his mind.

Spider had been relegated to the role of chaperone for the younger people, which annoyed him. He'd have much rather gambled with the Kiowa braves than watch over Three Deer and Hummingbird. However, he did as Dark Horse told him and stayed close as they entered the Kiowa village the day before Christmas.

He called out greetings to people he'd come to know, but when Cricket approached, his demeanor changed. Outside of saying a polite hello to the medicine man, he remained aloof.

A frown briefly darkened Cricket's expression before Sky Dancer embraced him, distracting him.

"You are growing, Cricket," she said, her eyes shining with fondness. "You are as tall as me now."

Although he was a little embarrassed, he laughed. "You are growing, too." He gestured towards her thickening midsection. "How are you feeling?"

"I feel wonderful, which I repeatedly tell my husband. He keeps trying to interfere in my work."

Dark Horse shrugged. "You would think she would be happy to have a doting husband."

"I do not need a doting husband where my duties are concerned."

She Sings intervened. "Stop it. I have never seen two people who profess to love each other argue as much as you do."

Others soon surrounded them, happily welcoming their family. Anxious to see Willow, Sky Dancer broke away from the group and went to her friend's tipi. Standing outside, she imitated a yellow warbler and waited.

In just a moment, Willow pulled the flap back and emerged with a big smile on her face. "Sky Dancer! I wondered when you would arrive."

They embraced and Sky Dancer noticed that there was a little more of her friend to hug.

"I have the most wonderful news to tell you," Willow said. "Come inside. I will make us some tea and tell you all about it."

Sky Dancer followed her into the tipi and was surprised at how orderly the home was. The last time she'd visited, they'd had to shove traps and other equipment out of the way to make sitting space. Now, the tipi was largely devoid of such things and new cushions surrounded the fire pit. She saw that there were also two large sleeping pallets made up.

Willow noticed her perusal and laughed. "Surprised you, did I?"

Sky Dancer chuckled as she sat down. "Yes. Do not be offended, but you have never been interested in domestic pursuits. You and

Three Deer are cut from the same cloth, although she has shown more interest as of late. There is a young man she has her eye on."

Willow put a pot of water over the fire and sat back. "Sometimes it just takes the right motivation to make a woman interested in such things."

Sky Dancer nodded. "There is something different about you."

Willow beamed. "You have no idea how different. What I am about to tell you sounds impossible, but it is the truth."

Sky Dancer listened intently as Willow told her story, trying to absorb the fact that Willow had conceived three children, but had lost only one. She'd never heard of such a thing, but she didn't doubt Cricket's vision. She'd witnessed his abilities and believed in him.

Sky Dancer was filled with happiness for her friends and hugged Willow. "You have to take care of yourself now. No fighting or hunting."

Willow frowned at her. "I know that I cannot fight right now, but I can still hunt small game. I know my limitations and I cannot just sit around all the time any more than you can."

Sky Dancer laughed. "You will never change. Stubborn as ever."

"I can say the same about you," Willow shot back. "Besides, after losing one baby, I will not take any chances of losing these two."

"It is hard to believe. You will have your babies before I have mine." Sky Dancer's eyes filled up. "Our children will grow up together."

Willow also grew misty-eyed. "I know. Now stop crying. I hate crying. I rarely ever cry, but since becoming pregnant, I blubber over the silliest things."

Sky Dancer grinned. "Poor Ames. I can only imagine your mood swings."

"For a while, I thought I was losing my mind." Willow poured their tea. "I think Ames thought I was, too, but he was too kind to say so."

"Other than seducing you, he is a very good man." Sky Dancer regretted her words as soon as she saw Willow's frown. "I am only joking, Willow."

"Why do people insist on thinking that women are not smart enough to know when they want to have sex with a man? Why does everyone think that if a woman gives herself to a man before marriage that he tricked her into it somehow?" She folded her arms. "I knew exactly what I wanted and I wanted Ames to make love with me. He did not trick me into anything. Did Dark Horse trick you into making love with him the first time?"

The glint in Willow's eyes told Sky Dancer to tread lightly. "No, Willow, he did not. I was not trying to offend you. I truly meant it in jest."

Willow lowered her arms and smiled sheepishly. "I am sorry that I am so touchy. I just cannot stand the idea of anyone thinking badly of Ames about it." She made a dismissive gesture. "That is all in the past. Just ignore me. So, tell me what is happening in the enemy camp? Anything that our warriors need to know about?"

Sky Dancer laughed at her term for the Lakota tribe. "Not that I know of, but I am sure that you would be notified if there were."

"I keep worrying that the Ojibwa will come after us," Willow said. "Fang sends out scouts every week to make sure that we are not caught with our guard down."

They fell to talking about tribal matters and exchanged gossip for a while. Then Sky Dancer said that she wanted to go see her grandparents. Willow felt tired and declined to go with her, telling her that she would make a nice meal for them that evening and that she and Dark Horse would be staying with her and Ames.

When Sky Dancer left, Willow tidied up a little and laid down. She hated being so tired after doing so little, but she couldn't help it. She smiled as she closed her eyes. After the past couple of nights in Ames' arms, what woman wouldn't be tired? Her smile remained in place as she drifted off.

Cricket considered himself to be an even-tempered, patient person, but Spider was greatly annoying him with his condescending behavior. As they'd gone about their visiting that day, Spider had barely spoken to him, only giving perfunctory responses when he'd spoken to the brave. They'd eaten the evening meal at his home. While everyone else had conversed, Spider had kept largely quiet. Cricket had finally quit trying to engage him in conversation, focusing on the others present.

When the meal was over, Spider thanked Green Leaf for her hospitality and left the tipi. Fed up, Cricket followed him.

"Spider, wait. I would like to speak with you."

Spider turned back to him with a wary look. "Yes?"

"Do you have something against me?"

One of Spider's eyebrows rose. "No. Why?"

"You act like you do. If not, why do you barely talk to me? Have I offended you in some way?"

Spider crossed his arms and lowered his gaze. "I like you, Cricket, but you, um, make me uneasy."

That wasn't the answer Cricket had expected. "I make you uneasy? How so?"

"Medicine men in general make me uneasy. The spirit world scares me and you communicate with the spirit world all the time. People say that you are very powerful and have visited the spirit world many times," Spider said.

He's afraid of me? He's much bigger than me and better looking and yet he's scared of me. That made Cricket feel powerful yet badly. He didn't want Spider to be afraid of him. How could they become friends if Spider wasn't comfortable around him?

"Spider, I do not know how powerful I am, but yes, I do go to the spirit world quite a bit. But you have nothing to fear from me. I am just a young man, the same age as you are. I am interested in many of the same things you are," Cricket said.

"No, you are not. You are much more mature than I am. I mean, you have important duties to perform for your tribe and you already have enough coup to be eligible for marriage. You helped forge an alliance between our tribes, Cricket. No, we may be the same age in winters, but you are older than me in many ways," Spider said.

Cricket thought about that for a moment and saw himself through Spider's eyes. "Spider, all of that might be true, but does that mean that we cannot be friends? Even though I am a medicine man, it does not mean that I do not like having fun or sparring. Well, I am learning about sparring. People have been teaching me lately. In case you have not noticed, I am not exactly built to be a warrior."

Spider responded to Cricket's self-deprecating smile. "I might have noticed."

"I am sure you have. I cannot believe that someone like you would be afraid of a skinny medicine man," Cricket teased him.

"The spirit world has always scared me and Smoking Fire terrifies me," Spider admitted.

Cricket grunted. "I am no Smoking Fire. I am just Cricket. There is nothing to fear. I promise not to curse you. All right?"

He held out his arm to Spider, who grasped it after hesitating for a few moments. "All right."

"Good. Now, I will get the girls and Ten Thunders. I am sure that Lightning Strike and some of the others are playing games in the council lodge." Cricket smiled and went back into his tipi.

Spider felt a little better about being around Cricket and he started looking forward to creating a friendship with him.

Christmas brought a heavy snow with it, but that didn't dampen the spirits of the Kiowa one bit. Everyone went around to each other's tipi, exchanging gifts and eating the various dishes that had been prepared. A few of their people had traveled to the Hidatsa village, which was several days away, to trade for vegetables and dried fruits. Therefore, they were able to make mashed sweet potatoes and add carrots and other tubers to their meat dishes and soups.

The Lakota guests enjoyed themselves immensely, participating in the gift exchanges and they'd even brought some food supplies with them so that the women could make some food to contribute.

The village rang with laughter and lively chatter all that day. Snowball fights struck up all over the place and even the women participated. The camp dogs joined in the melee, their yips and barks adding to the festive atmosphere.

Hummingbird loved the whole experience and she was amazed at the number of presents bestowed upon her. And just when she thought that she'd opened the last one, Cricket gave her several packages when they'd returned to his tipi. He'd also wanted to give them to her in private and had asked Ten Thunders to stand right outside the tipi flap. That way they'd still be chaperoned, but it would give them a little time alone together.

"What are these?"

He gave her a lopsided smile. "Presents, silly. Open them." He'd purposely waited to give her his presents last.

Hummingbird opened the first one and gasped when she saw the beautiful beaded bag inside it. "Oh, Cricket! It is lovely. Thank you."

"I am glad you like it. Open the others."

She giggled at his impatience and unwrapped the next one, which contained a journal and two pencils.

"I want to teach you how to read and write. Ames has been teaching us and I have a feeling that it will come in handy one day. You should know how, too," he said.

Hummingbird was deeply touched. First, because he was concerned for her welfare and secondly, because he deemed her intelligent enough to learn something so important. She held the journal against her chest. "I cannot tell you how much this means to me. I will do my best to learn well."

"I have no doubt about that."

She carefully wrapped up the journal and pencils and went on to the next package. It was small yet heavy. Cricket's excited smile made her very curious about what it contained. What she uncovered stunned her.

She lifted out a gold necklace with a rose-shaped pendant on it and matching earrings. There was also a bracelet and a fine leather headband adorned with small gold flowers. Hummingbird gaped at the exquisite jewelry.

"Cricket, you said that gold is very expensive. How could you afford these?"

"I traded with Ames for them. Do not worry about it."

"But they must have cost you a fortune," she said. "They are too much."

He put a hand on her shoulder. "Nothing will ever be too good for you." Moving closer, he gazed into her eyes. "You are everything a man could want and so much more. I am very fortunate to be betrothed to such a fine woman. I thank Sendeh for you every day. What I am trying to say is that I have fallen in love with you."

Hummingbird's heart flooded with light and joy. Tears rose in her eyes. "I love you, too, Cricket."

His eyes widened in surprise. "You do?"

"Yes. How could I not? You are so good to me. Kind and considerate and you make me laugh. You are handsome and intelligent and you make my heart race when you kiss me," she responded. "What women could resist falling in love with a man like you?"

It amazed Cricket that she found him handsome and thought so highly of him. "I am so happy when I am with you and when I am not, I am always thinking about you. Both because I just enjoy being near you and talking with you, but, yes, kissing you is amazing. I have trouble restraining myself." He laughed. "Now I know how difficult it is to keep things appropriate between two people who desire each other."

They traded bashful smiles and Cricket couldn't resist embracing her. "I love you, Hummingbird, and I am so glad that we are promised to each other."

"So am I." She boldly pressed a brief kiss to his lips, mindful that Ten Thunders was just outside the tipi. "I love you, too."

Awareness flowed between them, but they reluctantly parted, trying to behave properly.

"We should let Ten Thunders come in out of the snow," Cricket said.

"Yes."

Cricket called out to him and the Ojibwa man entered the tipi, brushing snow from his hair.

"You have nice time?" His eyes gleamed as he gave them a mischievous smile.

Hummingbird ducked her head a little, but replied, "Yes. Thank you for allowing us a little time alone."

"Happy to help."

Their conversation turned to other things, but Cricket and Hummingbird exchanged meaningful glances that conveyed their mutual feelings for one another. Neither of them would ever forget the magical Christmas when their relationship had deepened, bringing them unexpected happiness.

Chapter Eighteen

Several days later, Willow had trouble waking up. Although she'd gone to sleep early the previous night, she was still exhausted. Dragging herself from the sleeping pallet, she put on some coffee and stretched.

Putting a hand on her stomach, she was amazed at the way she'd started to show seemingly overnight. She guessed that the twins were trying to catch up now that they were growing well.

She heard Ames moving around behind her as he too rose. Then he sat behind her, stretched out his long legs on either side of her, and pulled her back against him.

She smiled as he kissed her cheek. "Good morning."

"Good morning," he responded. "Did you sleep well?"

"Yes, but I do not feel as though I did."

"You are growing two babies. No wonder you are so tired," Ames said.

"I know. I am glad—"

A fluttering sensation in her abdomen surprised her into silence. Could it be? Placing her hands on her stomach she waited. Faintly, she felt movement under her palm.

"Ames!" She took his hand and guided it to where she'd felt the movements. "They are starting to move."

He rubbed his hand over her belly. "Right here?" Immediately, he felt a bump against his palm. "My God! They are!"

The movement became stronger and Willow laughed with joy. "Ames, it is your voice. They hear you!"

He laughed as he caressed her stomach. "Hello, little ones. I am your papa and I love you."

The whole time he spoke, the babies shifted around, which made them laugh.

Ames hugged Willow close. "I love you, *chérie*, and I love our babies. I can't wait until they're born."

"I feel the same way," she said.

The babies settled down and Willow broke away from Ames because she had to visit the trenches. She bundled up and left the tipi. On the way back, pain shot up her back, stealing her breath and forcing her to stop. Sleek Doe had also been at the trenches and had caught up to Willow.

"Are you all right?" she asked, noting Willow's pained expression.

The pain eased, but Willow was scared. "I-I do not know. I have been so tired and I just had a bad back spasm."

Sleek Doe took her arm. "Let me help you. You should lie down."

Willow was comforted by the older woman's presence. She hated being afraid. It went against her warrior nature to show fear, but at that moment, she was glad that Sleek Doe had come along.

Another spasm gripped her a short distance from her tipi and she had to stop again. She clung tightly to Sleek Doe's hand as she gasped for breath. "Something is wrong."

Sleek Doe didn't want to alarm Willow, but she wondered if the back pain indicated labor. She hoped not. "Can you walk?"

"Yes."

They reached the tipi and Sleek Doe helped Willow inside. Ames sat at the fire, cooking something in a pan. He looked up and his expression immediately registered concern.

He rose quickly. "What happened?"

Willow let him help her to their sleeping pallet. "I had some back pain. I feel better now."

Ames assisted her in laying down. "Rest while I make breakfast."

Sleek Doe said, "I should take a look at you, Willow."

The elderly woman was a skilled midwife and Willow trusted her judgment. "All right."

Sleek Doe had Ames step outside and began her examination. When she was finished, she sighed. "You are bleeding a little. You need to stay lying down as much as possible."

Willow covered her face with her hands. "This cannot be happening! Am I going to lose our babies?"

Sleek Doe put a blanket over Willow. "Not if you do as I say. You must rest and eat well. Try not to worry or get upset. It is not good for the babies."

"But I have things to do," Willow said.

Sleek Doe took her hand and patted it. "What you must do now is follow my advice. If you want your babies, you must fight for them, and the best way to do that is to rest and take care of yourself. Do you understand?"

Determination took hold of Willow and she nodded curtly. "I understand and I will do as you say."

"Good. You will have plenty of help," Sleek Doe assured her. "I will be back later to check on you." She gave Willow a smile. "Let your handsome husband pamper you."

Willow chuckled. "He certainly does that."

Ames met Sleek Doe as she stepped outside, questions filling his eyes. She gave him her assessment and told him that she would return to see Willow later.

"Thank you for your help, Sleek Doe." Worry shone in his eyes. "I will make sure she behaves."

Sleek Doe smiled and shuffled off and Ames went inside. Willow smiled at him.

He knelt by her. "You must not be stubborn about this. Please, Willow?"

She reached for his hand and kissed it. "I promise not to do anything that will put our little ones in jeopardy."

He was reassured by the honesty in her gaze. "Good. Now, we will have some breakfast and then you can rest. I was not planning on going to check traps today. Instead, I was going to fish since the streams are not frozen over yet. The fish will make a good change for the dogs and us."

"Ames, please do whatever you need to do. Sleek Doe will be back and I am sure that she is spreading the word. I will have more help than I need. Do not worry," Willow said.

Easier said than done. "I cannot help it. If I know that you are safe, I will not worry."

"I will be safe." Although she was trying to alleviate his anxiety, Willow had her own misgivings. However, she would fight tooth-and-nail for her babies.

Ames nodded and went back to making breakfast, wondering how he was going to go about his business when he wanted to be with Willow to protect and help her. When the warmed up roasted venison and tubers were ready, he gave Willow her plate and made one for himself.

Willow was ravenous and quickly downed the meal, washing it down with the chokecherry tea Ames had made.

"Now, lie down until Sleek Doe comes back. Promise me that you will behave? It is the only way I will leave you," he said.

Exhaustion tugged at Willow and she smiled sleepily. "I promise."

Ames watched her eyes drift shut as he gathered his fishing supplies. He was just about to head out when Moonbeam arrived.

"Sleek Doe said that Willow needs help. I am not busy, so I came to sit with her."

Ames hugged her and kissed the top of her head. "My little Moonbeam has come to my rescue. It makes me feel better that she will have such capable help."

Moonbeam's eyes were filled with pride as she grinned at him. "I will take good care of her."

"I know. I will be back before dark," he said.

"All right."

With a last long look at Willow, Ames nodded and left.

"Come, Willow, you must eat."

Willow looked at Ames from where she lay and forced a smile to her lips. He'd had to shake her twice to wake her. In the past two weeks, her health had rapidly declined. Complications had started plaguing her. She was spotting and had abdominal twinges. The twins were sapping her strength, but she never complained. Her love for them overrode any discomfort, her desire to successfully bear them mattering more to her than her own welfare.

She struggled into a sitting position and sighed. He would've helped her, but she was adamant about doing as much as possible for herself.

"Are you hungry?" he asked hopefully.

There were times when she wolfed down food and others when it took her an hour to choke down a meal. Tonight, she could've eaten all the roasted bison herself.

"Famished." She accepted the plate he handed her. "How was your day?"

Ames hated lying to his wife, but he wasn't going to worry her. He wasn't getting much work done because he couldn't sleep at night. Instead, he laid awake into the wee hours of the morning, terrified to drift off for fear that something terrible would happen. During the day, he was tired and sometimes grabbed a nap in Firebrand's tipi.

"It was fine. The traps yielded a good harvest. I repaired some netting for fishing and I am thinking about building a boat," he said.

"A boat? What for?"

Ames gave her a plate of the food that Moonbeam had made. "Fishing and to take small trips up to the Hidatsa for trading. It will be more convenient and faster, especially coming home."

Willow swallowed a bite of meat. "That is a great idea. I am lucky I married such a smart man."

His mouth curved upwards. "And I am lucky to have married the woman of my dreams."

A trifle embarrassed, Willow snorted. "I am hardly dream-worthy right now. I know that I look horrible."

Ames couldn't deny that her fatigue showed in the dark smudges under her eyes. While the babies were growing at an alarming rate, Willow was growing thinner throughout the rest of her body. Her dresses hung slightly loose around her shoulders. Her hair wasn't quite as shiny and her eyes were a little dull. Even so, she was still lovely.

"Willow, you will always be beautiful to me." He gave her a second helping of food. "And you are especially beautiful to me right now because of the life you carry within you."

Willow rubbed her swollen midsection. "Thank you. You are very kind."

"No, just truthful."

She smiled and worked on her meal. By the time she was finished, she was exhausted again, but at least she'd fed the twins. Looking at the dishes, she wanted to go wash them, but she didn't have the strength. Apprehension about the future filled her.

With her whole being, she wanted to bear these babies and watch them grow. She'd never seriously thought about becoming a mother, but now she fiercely desired children. Her warrior's heart recognized that the fight ahead of her to deliver her children was going to be arduous. But she resolved to rise to the challenge and come out the victor.

On a day at the tail end of the month that Ames called January, Willow sat sipping on some broth that Tulip had brought her. She wasn't at all hungry, but she drank as much of it as she could.

She was bored and cranky. Being cooped up inside all the time was starting to wear on her. When she slept, she often dreamed about hunting, the thrill of bringing down a bison flowing through her. But when she woke in her tipi, reality would descend on her and she felt stifled again. The good news was that she'd stopped spotting: one little battle won.

As she swallowed another sip of broth, Ten Thunders showed up. With a broad smile, he pulled out a squirming ball of fur from under his robe.

"This little one told me that he wanted to come see you."

Willow grinned and put aside her broth. Ten Thunders sat the puppy in her lap. She petted the young canine, who enthusiastically tried to climb up her so he could lick her face.

"He has gotten so big!" Willow laughed as she stroked his fluffy fur.

"He is not as big as his siblings, but he bullies them," Ten Thunders said. "He is getting pretty good at doing his business outside. I have been working with all of the puppies, teaching them their manners."

"Their manners?" Willow asked.

He sat down. "Yes. My white father taught me that there are several things that every dog should know how to do. Sit, lie down, stay, and to not make a mess in the tipi. You need to name him so you can keep training him."

Willow looked into the puppy's dark eyes. "What is your name?"

He yipped a little and jumped up at her playfully. He lost his balance and collapsed back down in her lap, making her laugh.

"He is also the funniest out of the litter," Ten Thunders said. "He does such odd things sometimes."

"I will think about a name," Willow said. "Oh! I know. What do you think of 'Trapper'?"

Tulip and Ten Thunders laughed.

"I think that is very appropriate," Tulip said.

Ten Thunders nodded. "It is a good name."

Smoothing a hand over the puppy's back, Willow said, "You are now Trapper, fierce dog of the warrior, Willow, and the strong fur trader, Ames. Do you like your name?"

Trapper cocked his head to the side and then let out a puppy bark.

Willow smiled. "I will take it that you do."

Tulip said, "You should rest now, Willow."

Ten Thunders said, "I will bring Trapper to see you tomorrow, Willow."

However, when he reached for Trapper, the pup backed away and leaned against Willow's leg.

Willow chuckled. "Leave him with me. He has to get used to being here."

Tulip said, "You do not need a puppy wearing you out, Willow."

Lying down, Willow said, "He will be a good boy."

As if to agree, Trapper curled up against her large belly.

Willow petted him and smiled. "See? It will be fine."

"All right, but if he gets to be too much, just have someone bring him to me," Ten Thunders said.

Willow agreed and Ten Thunders went on his way.

Chapter Nineteen

Ames laughed until tears stood out in his eyes as Trapper "killed" a small beaver pelt he'd been given to play with. The three-month-old puppy had been with him and Willow for a week now and was settling in well. Trapper proved to be highly intelligent and caught on to things quickly for a dog so young.

He shook the pelt, growling fiercely. Then he released it, backed up and pounced on it again. This time he shook it so vigorously that he knocked himself off balance and fell over. Willow laughed from where she lay, enjoying Trapper's performance.

Watching Willow's eyes shine did Ames' heart good and he was grateful to Ten Thunders for bringing Trapper to her. The puppy seemed to sense that Willow was not well and was careful around her. He liked to sleep against her stomach and when the babies were active, he licked her belly. No doubt his keen canine hearing could detect them moving about.

He'd only messed in the tipi once, which they found impressive, and he was quickly learning that he wasn't supposed to get into food baskets or chew on arrows. When she was awake and bored, Willow worked on teaching him to fetch and he was starting to pick it up.

Trapper brought the pelt over to Ames and pressed it into his hand. Ames grasped it and they had a game of tug-of-war.

"One day, he will help you with the trap lines," Willow said.

Ames nodded. "I had a dog once who did that, but it takes a special dog to learn what to do and not run off game. Perhaps he will learn."

Willow was about to respond, but let out a gasp when hot pain shot through her abdomen. It didn't last long, but it was powerful enough to make her slightly short of breath.

Ames was by her side in an instant. "What is it?"

"Just a bad cramp," she said, rubbing her stomach. "Please help me sit up. I am not comfortable."

Carefully, Ames assisted her and had her lean against him. "Is that better?"

"Yes. Thank you."

Trapper approached her, but he wouldn't completely close the distance between them. Instead, he sat down and whined.

"Trapper, it is all right. Come," Willow said.

The puppy let out a half-growl and batted the air with a front paw, but he wouldn't come closer.

The pain came again and Willow inhaled sharply. She felt immense pressure in her back at the same time. Ames supported her until the pain relented.

Their gazes met. "It is too early, but I think I am in labor."

Ames heart lurched into faster rhythm, but he kept a hold on his emotions. "I will go get Tulip and Green Leaf." Slowly, he lowered her down to the cushioned sleeping pallet. "I will be right back."

She nodded. "All right."

As soon as he was outside, Ames took off running, fighting back panic as he sprinted to Tulip's tipi. He scratched furiously on the flap and Fang granted him entrance.

He looked around, but Fang and his son, Spotted Pony, where the only ones in the tipi. "Where is your wife? Willow is in labor."

Fang rose. "She went to see Sleek Doe. I will go there and send her to you."

Ames said, "I will go get Green Leaf then."

Spotted Pony spoke up. "I will get her for you. You go back home to Willow." The young boy thought very highly of Willow and he wanted to help her.

Ames ruffled his hair. "You are a good boy. Thank you."

He left then, rushing back home. Entering the tipi, he saw Willow's face creased in pain and knelt by her, holding her hand until it eased.

"They will both be here, my love." He kissed her hand and let it go. "I am going to put water on to boil."

Willow saved her breath and just nodded.

Ames had just hung a large pot over the fire when Tulip arrived with Green Leaf right behind her.

Tulip smiled. "We will take good care of Willow and your babies, Ames. Fang and some of the other men will help you pass the time until they are born."

Ames knew that Indian men didn't attend the birth of their children, but he didn't give one fig about custom right at that moment. Although he'd never witnessed a birth, he also knew that Indian women rarely laid down to deliver their children.

He leveled a defiant stare at both women. "I am not leaving. I will help bring our children into the world. Willow is not strong enough to deliver in the usual way without assistance and neither of you are strong enough to hold her yourselves while the other catches the babies. I will help support her."

Willow let out a low groan. "Do not bother arguing with him," she said through clenched teeth. "It is no use. Besides, he is right. I am almost as heavy as a man." She groaned again.

Ames lifted an eyebrow in challenge.

Tulip sighed. "I do not like it, but I suppose it is best. You should take the dog to Ten Thunders so he does not get in the way."

Ames looked at Trapper, who sat halfway behind one of the privacy panels, looking on with interest. "He is fine. He should be here. He knew that Willow was in labor."

Green Leaf shook her head. "Men and dogs attending births. It makes sense since nothing about you and Willow is normal."

Willow laughed as Ames scowled at Green Leaf. However, her mirth turned into another groan and Ames gave her his hand. Long moments passed before Willow relaxed again.

Ames bent down and kissed her forehead. "I am going to help you each step of the way. You are so incredibly strong, but do not hesitate to use my strength, too. We will do this together, yes?"

Willow smiled briefly. "Yes."

Green Leaf said, "Ames, you must do as we say."

"I will," he promised. "Just tell me what to do."

Willow sweated profusely as she gritted her teeth and pushed. Ames helped support her as she crouched and she was thankful for his strength and encouragement. After almost eight hours of grueling contractions that had made her feel as though a huge serpent had been squeezing her, the time had finally come to push.

As was befitting for Indian women, she rarely made a noise louder than a moan. She took joy in knowing that all the pain would be worth the reward. With every contraction, she thanked Sendeh for the opportunity to bear these children, to have the honor of raising them. The loss of one baby made her acutely aware of how precious these two were and she wouldn't complain about the agony she was being put through in order to bring them into the world.

She grasped Ames' powerful arms tightly, using him as leverage as she bore down harder. He held her steady and counter-pulled to assist her even more. Her energy was flagging, but grim determination propelled her onward.

"I see the head, Willow," Tulip said. "Keep pushing."

Willow took a deep breath and pushed with all her strength, letting out her first scream. All of them recognized that this wasn't a sound of pain, it was a war cry. Agony worse than anything she'd endured thus far slashed at Willow, and she almost stopped pushing.

No! I cannot give in! Sendeh, please give me the strength to do this. I need Your help. Please help me! Drawing on her inner reserves, Willow took another quick breath and kept going. Something gave way and she grew dizzy.

"You have a daughter, cousin," Tulip announced as she tied off and cut the umbilical cord and handed the baby to Green Leaf.

Ames slowly lowered Willow onto the temporary pallet that had been spread out to allow her to rest a little in between babies.

Willow raised her head, tears of fear standing out in her eyes. "Is she all right. Please, tell me she is healthy, Tulip."

The baby let out a thin cry at first, but as Green Leaf cleaned her, the infant objected more loudly. "She is just fine," Green Leaf said.

As she collapsed back in relief, Ames caught her and they clung together as joy surged through them.

"Ah, my love, you did so well. My brave warrior." Ames rocked his wife a little as he held her. "I have never seen anything so beautiful."

Raising her up a little, they watched Green Leaf work with the baby while Tulip tended to Willow. When Green Leaf was done, she gave the little girl to Willow, who cradled her lovingly.

Willow couldn't tell the exact color of the baby's hair since it was still damp, but it looked much lighter than hers. She was small, but appeared to be healthy. Willow lightly stroked her cheek with her forefinger, awestruck at the precious little life she held. "*Há:cho*, my daughter. It is wonderful to meet you. It has been a hard path, but now that you are here, all will be well. I love you so much."

A tear fell on the baby's forehead and Willow looked at Ames. Tears rolled down his face and one had dripped off his cheek.

"She looks like you." Willow smiled as tender love for both her daughter and husband washed over her. "Perhaps we will have our blue-eyed Indians."

Ames laughed a little and kissed her temple. "Perhaps we will. She is so beautiful. So tiny!"

Willow lifted the baby towards Ames. "Here, Papa. Hold your daughter."

With infinite care, Ames took the baby, settling her in the crook of one arm. He stared at her in wonder, amazed that he and Willow had created such a perfect little person. "*Bonjour, ma belle petite fille. Votre Père vous aime beaucoup.*"

Watching Ames tell the baby he loved her brought more tears to Willow's eyes. A contraction took her by surprise, making her grunt.

"It is time for our son to be born," she said, gathering her strength again.

Green Leaf took the baby from Ames and he helped Willow back into position. Exhaustion weighed on her as her abdomen was squeezed by fiery pain again. For the first time, doubt that she could get through this crept into her brain. She raised her eyes to Ames'.

He stared back. "I am here, Willow. You are the woman who has fought many battles to protect your people. To keep the people you love alive. You will also win this battle. You have helped our daughter win hers, now help our son win his. They have fought to stay alive, and now you must finish the battle. You are not alone. I am fighting alongside you."

Bolstered by his encouragement, Willow nodded and bore down when the next contraction started. Willow grunted, groaned, and swore softly, but she didn't scream until the very end when she let out another war yell.

A very odd thing happened just then. A bunch of trills answered her from outside. Buoyed by the support of her fellow warriors, Willow used the very last of her strength to bring forth her son. As she felt him leave her body, dizziness engulfed her and she collapsed in Ames' arms.

Carefully, he laid her down, brushing her sweat soaked hair back from her face. "Rest now, Willow. Rest."

He watched his son wave his tiny arms as Green Leaf washed him, but the baby still hadn't made a sound. "Is he all right?"

Green Leaf smiled. "Yes. I do not think he realizes that he has been born yet. His color is good and he is breathing well."

Ames sagged in relief. "Do you hear that, Willow? Our son is just fine."

She didn't respond and Ames grew alarmed. Gently, he shook her shoulder. "Willow?"

Willow tried to rouse, but only succeeded in briefly opening her eyes.

Tulip said, "She has lost a lot of blood."

"Is she going to be all right?"

Green Leaf said, "We will do everything we can for her. She is strong and stubborn, Ames. Two things that will help her right now. We will take good care of her. Would you like to hold your son?"

Ames was deeply concerned about Willow, but there was no denying that he wanted to meet his son. Taking the baby from Green Leaf, he smiled when he saw that his hair was also lighter.

"*Bienvenue dans le monde, mon fils. Votre papa vous aime, aussi,*" he said.

Tulip asked, "What does that mean?" She hadn't mastered very much French.

"I welcomed him to the world and told him that I love him," Ames replied.

Green Leaf smiled kindly at him. "Ames, you have been wonderful. I have never seen a man attend a birth, but I think somehow that you were meant to be here for the birth of your children. Go out and let everyone know that they are well and please send someone for Sleek Doe and Lilac."

"Do you need Cricket?" Ames asked anxiously.

Green Leaf smiled again. "This is for the women to do now. Please do as I ask. We will let you know when you can come back in."

Reluctantly, Ames gave his son back to Green Leaf and kissed Willow's cheek. Standing up, he looked down at her and for the first time, he thought she looked truly fragile.

"Ames, go," Tulip said firmly.

He gave her a curt nod and exited the tipi. The cold air struck him hard after being in the cloying heat of the tipi for so long. The breeze felt good to him, though. Quite a few people sat at a fire that had been built near their tipi and they looked expectantly at him.

Walking over to them, he sat down at an empty spot. "We have a healthy son and daughter."

A round of cheers and congratulations rose and he accepted them with a broad smile.

Lightning Strike noticed that it didn't reach his eyes. "What troubles you?"

"Green Leaf asked that someone be sent for Sleek Doe and Lilac," Ames replied.

Fang instructed Spotted Pony to fetch them.

Ames rubbed his forehead. "Willow is very weak. She was weak to begin with, but now..." Everything suddenly crashed down on him. He groaned and dropped his head into his hands. His shoulders shook from the quiet sobs he couldn't stifle. The almost constant worry and stress of the last couple of months caught up with him and he couldn't contain it. He cried with joy over the birth of his children, but it was mixed with the fear of losing Willow.

Someone sat down next to him, settling a comforting arm around his shoulders. "Take heart. I have known Willow since she was born," Growling Wolf said. "She is the most stubborn person I have ever met and she never backs down from a fight. She may be wounded right now, Ames, but she will not quit fighting. Willow will come through this and you will spend many happy winters together."

Ames brought his emotions under control and lifted his head again. "Yes, you are right. I just cannot stand to see her like this." He wiped his tears away with his shirtsleeve and inhaled a shaky breath. "Just the thought of losing her..."

Lightning Strike said, "You will not. Nothing stops Willow from doing what she wants and what she wants most in this world is to be with you and your children."

Ames smiled. "Aside from Willow being in so much pain, helping bring them into the world was the most beautiful thing I have ever experienced. I will do it again, too."

Some of the men sent him curious looks, but it was Cricket who asked, "What was it like?"

Ames rubbed his chin and laughed a little. "I cannot really describe it. Incredible, scary, magical. That does not do it justice at all, but I am not sure how else to put it."

Growling Wolf chuckled. "You are a brave man, Ames. There are very few of our men who have been present during the birth of our children."

"I could not leave her. I needed to help her," Ames said. "I should go purify myself."

Cricket said, "Come to the medicine lodge and I will do a cleansing for you."

"Thank you." Ames started following Cricket, but then turned back to the group gathered. "Please send for me if...if I am needed."

They all understood exactly what he meant. Lightning Strike promised to come get him if need be and Ames went with Cricket.

Chapter Twenty

An infant's cry cut through the fog in Willow's mind as she regained consciousness. She battled to open her eyes and finally won. Her vision cleared and she saw Tulip sitting near her left-hand side, holding a baby. *My baby.*

Everything came flooding back to her and she wondered how long she'd been unconscious. She struggled to raise herself up, but couldn't quite manage it.

"Easy, Willow."

Turning her head to the right, she looked into Ames' eyes. "I need to feed them."

He smiled and took her hand. "I know, but let me help you."

"I can do it," she insisted and tried again. Pain clawed at her and she flopped back again.

Ames cleared his throat. "You were saying?"

She gave him the scariest scowl she could muster, but he just chuckled. "Fine! Help me. Please."

Ames grasped her under the arms and slowly pulled her into a sitting position against a wicker backrest. "There, my love. Are you comfortable?"

Willow nodded. Suddenly, she was nervous. She'd never paid much attention to how women breastfed their babies. "What do I do?"

Tulip gave Ames a pointed look. "Would you please step out?"

"Why?"

"Because Willow is a new mother and needs some instruction. It is a private time for a woman at first," Tulip said.

Ames opened his mouth to object, but Willow put a hand on his arm. "Please, Ames. Do as Tulip says."

The uncertainty in her eyes convinced him that leaving would be the best thing for her right now.

"I will not be far away," he said and kissed her forehead.

Willow watched him leave and smiled at Tulip, however, when she saw Tulip's serious expression, her smile evaporated. "What is wrong?"

Tulip said, "I have just been so worried about you. We all have."

"How long was I unconscious?"

"Several hours. I am glad you woke up. The babies need to eat."

Willow's smile returned. "I know. Tell me what to do."

She listened carefully to Tulip and it wasn't long until her daughter suckled at her breast. Willow was relieved that she'd taken to the breast so quickly. She remembered that there were times when Sky Dancer had had trouble getting Minnow to eat. Hopefully that wouldn't happen with the twins.

She played with her daughter's hand as she nursed, marveling at how much she looked like Ames despite her much darker complexion. She had wispy, light brown curls and Willow wondered if they would darken or turn lighter.

Looking over at Tulip, who held the other baby, Willow wondered the same about him. Would they both have Ames' blue eyes or would they be dark like hers? Or would one have brown eyes and the other, blue?

Her daughter finished and Tulip traded her babies. The little boy was very eager and started eating right away.

Willow grinned down at him. "You eat like your father."

Tulip chuckled. "Yes, he has a good appetite."

"I must find names for them."

"You will," Tulip said.

"I was in so much pain that I did not hear anything except for you and Ames. And all I saw was him because he was helping me so much," she said.

"Do not fret. Names will come to you."

Tulip finished burping Willow's daughter and laid her down on the sleeping pallet beside Willow. A whine drew Willow's attention. Trapper peeked out from behind one of the privacy panels.

"Trapper, come meet your new family members," Willow said softly. "Come."

Trapper crept forward slowly, unsure of the situation.

"He has been here the whole time," Tulip said.

Willow watched Trapper approach. "He has been watching over us. It is all right, Trapper."

The puppy drew close enough to sniff the baby girl's hair. After a few moments, he backed up and sat down. Cocking his head, he put a paw up in the air and whined.

"Come, Trapper," Willow coaxed.

Trapper cautiously walked to her side and she let him sniff her son.

Willow pet him with her free hand. "They are your family now, too. You must watch over them."

Trapper yawned in response and lay down, leaning against one of Willow's legs.

Once the baby had eaten his fill, Willow burped him and Tulip changed both babies. Willow appreciated her help and knew that it was necessary. However, she became determined to regain her strength as soon as possible so that she could care for her children.

She smiled as she looked at each baby in turn and thanked Sendeh for the two healthy, beautiful children. It had been a grueling battle, but she'd come out the victor with two precious little lives as the rewards. In the end, it was all worth it and she would strive to give her children the best of herself every day and love them with her whole heart.

Over the next couple of months, the twins grew rapidly and Willow's health improved. She felt stronger every day and took care to eat properly and became active again. The babies were the center of her and Ames' world and they were completely in love with them.

Willow had wanted the babies' names to honor both of Ames' parents' heritages. Therefore, they'd named their son, Lucien, which meant "light" in French, and their daughter, Mia, Swedish for "beloved".

Ames tended to his business during the day, but hurried home to his family every night. Sometimes Willow and the babies weren't home and he had to track them down. He was a great source of amusement because of his eagerness to see them and how reluctant he was to share them.

He sang and talked to the twins, sometimes using them as comic avoidance tools so he could tease someone without directly speaking to them. No matter how hard he worked, he always helped Willow at night when the babies needed to be fed. Often in the evenings when they were home, he and Willow lay together against a backrest, holding the twins and talking.

Although some days were challenging for Willow, she relished her role as mother, even when she was tired. She had plenty of assistance, but she liked to be as self-sufficient with the twins as possible. Moonbeam was a great help to her, sometimes cooking the evening meal so that Willow could feed the twins and do some cleaning. Moonbeam loved the twins and she happily watched them while Willow napped or took a short walk.

Around the beginning of April, Ames started planning for the trip to Grand Forks. He always hated being parted from Willow, but it was a hundredfold worse now that he had children.

"They are going to grow so much while we are gone," he said to Willow one evening. "I will miss so many things."

Willow nodded as her heart constricted. She didn't want him to leave, but there was no way around it. "I know, but I will tell you everything when you come home and you will have fall and winter with them."

He put an arm around her. "And you. Do not forget how much I love you."

She looked up at him coyly. "I have already forgotten. It has been so long since you loved me."

Heat spread through his body. "Are you saying that it is time I remind you?"

Her sultry smile set his blood on fire. "You are such a smart man. As soon as the twins are asleep."

Ames grinned. "I plan on reminding you for a long time."

"I will hold you to that," she responded.

Once the babies were fed and deep in slumber, Ames took Willow in his arms, kissing her tenderly.

"I have missed you so much," he said.

Willow caressed his jaw. "I have missed you, too."

Ames kissed her palm. "You are so beautiful."

Her gaze lowered. "I do not feel beautiful."

"Willow, let me show you how beautiful you are to me," Ames responded.

Returning her gaze to his, Willow saw the familiar desire in his cobalt eyes and was reassured. She let him lead her over to their bed and undress her. Slowly, and tenderly, the passionate side of their relationship was rekindled and by the time the flames of desire burned down to embers, there was no doubt left in Willow's mind that Ames' attraction to her was as strong as ever.

As April ended, Willow was devastated to find that her milk was drying up. Thankfully, they'd been able to save one of their cows and supplemented the babies' diets with its milk, but it wasn't going to be enough to sustain them.

"Why is this happening to me?" she lamented to Green Leaf when she'd stopped by to see the twins one day. "I do not understand. Is it not enough that I had such a difficult time giving birth to them? What am I going to do? My babies are going to starve!"

Green Leaf put a consoling hand on her shoulder. "We must find a woman with milk to nurse them. Unfortunately, we do not have any women in our tribe right now who are breast feeding." She sighed, hating to broach the subject. "We must ask the Lakota if they have anyone who is willing to feed Lucien and Mia."

Anger and distaste mingled in Willow's expression. "I will not go to live there. I could not stand being surrounded by Lakota all the time. I do not know how Sky Dancer and She Sings do it."

Green Leaf patiently said, "Because it was necessary and they are happy there now. You must put your children's welfare ahead of your needs. It would not be for forever, Willow. Just until they do not need to breast feed any longer."

Looking at Lucien, who rested in Green Leaf's arms, Willow's heart filled with worry and sorrow. She enjoyed the closeness she felt when she fed the twins. It made her feel defective as a woman that she wasn't going to be able to continue providing them with sustenance herself.

"I will discuss it with Ames and see what he says," she said.

Green Leaf's heart went out to Willow. She knew that it was a terrible blow on top of all the difficulty she'd gone through to have the babies. "I think that is wise."

She stayed for a few more minutes and then left to go start the evening meal. Willow took the twins inside. She fed them what little she had and laid them on the thick buffalo robe to take a nap. They gurgled, kicking their little legs around and waving their arms.

Willow kept her tears at bay by playing with them until they tired and went to sleep. Ames arrived home soon after.

"Hello, my beauty," he said with one of his charming smiles.

She responded with a wan smile. "How did you do today?"

He sat his pack off to the side and sat down by her. "Fine, fine. We pulled all the traps now, though. We have plenty of hides, so we decided that we are truly done for the season."

She couldn't look at him. "You will be leaving soon."

"Yes. How are the little ones?"

There was no avoiding the subject. "Hungry. We need to find a woman with enough milk to feed them. None of our women are breast feeding. I must ask the Lakota if there are any women who would be willing to nurse them." The thought of some other woman feeding her children twisted her insides. "We may have to move there so that she can feed them."

Ames absorbed this information, shocked that Willow would even consider such a thing given her hatred of the Lakota, especially Soaring Falcon. His worried gaze rested on his children. He knew that the situation was growing desperate if Willow was willing to live with the Lakota. Although he didn't want to move, they might have to until the twins were past breast feeding age. But could they find a woman who was willing to feed children of mixed blood who weren't a part of their tribe?

"You should find another wife," Willow said, her expression stony.

His eyebrows shot up. "Why would I do that? I do not want another wife. I love only you."

Willow shook her head. "What kind of wife and mother am I if I cannot feed our children?"

He put an arm around her, but she pulled away from him. "Willow, sometimes these things happen. It is not your fault. You are a wonderful wife and mother. I love being married to you."

Clenching her fists in her lap, Willow said, "There is something I need to tell you. Something that may make you change your mind about that."

"I will never change my mind. Nothing you say could make me love you less."

Willow tried to believe that, but fear crowded her mind and heart. She swallowed hard. "I can no longer bear children. There was too much damage done when I had the twins. I will not conceive again. You need to find a wife who can give you more children. You deserve that."

Anger and hurt built inside her until she felt that she would explode. Averting her eyes from Ames, she rushed out of the tipi and took off running. It didn't matter where she went, she just needed to get away.

Her long legs carried her swiftly over the ground even though she was somewhat out of shape. Her muscles remembered the motions and adrenaline flooded her body as she ran through the dark. The urge to escape overrode her usual caution and she didn't pay attention to her surroundings as she neared the edge of camp.

Willow collided with someone in the dark and they both almost went down. Managing to keep her feet, she stumbled onward until someone grabbed her shoulder, bringing her to a stop and spinning her around.

"Willow, what is wrong? Why are you running?"

She tore out her nemesis' grasp. "Why are you always here? Go back to your own tribe! You have done enough damage to us!"

Soaring Falcon alarm turned to anger. "Why do you hate me? Just because I am Lakota? Because our tribes have fought in the past?"

"Yes! And because your blood runs through my veins!" she yelled. "I hate you because of what you did to my grandmother and because I have Lakota heritage! You have taken everything from us! We just wanted to be left alone, but you just could not do that, could you?" Her breathing had grown labored and a painful stitch started in her side.

The chief stepped back as if she'd struck him. "What are you talking about? You are no relation of mine. Have you gone insane?"

"Does the name Blue Feather mean anything to you?"

Soaring Falcon completely stilled and his face went slack as he stared at Willow.

A cruel smile twisted her lips. "I see that it does. You are the man who raped my grandmother. She had a daughter, my mother! On her deathbed, my grandmother told my mother who her real father was. You! The minute I laid eyes on you, I knew it was you. Do you want to know how?" Willow's fists balled at her side. "Because Mother looked just like you! She was your spitting image and I am hers! That is why I hate you. Because you are a despicable animal and we had to leave our homeland!"

Recovering himself, Soaring Falcon approached her. "I have never raped anyone, Willow. Yes, it is true that I knew Blue Feather, but I never raped her."

A crowd had gathered, but Willow didn't notice. "You are a liar! A filthy, lying Lakota!"

Soaring Falcon managed to keep his anger under wraps. He hid it under a blank expression. "When you are ready and you can be reasonable, we will discuss this, and I will tell you the truth about what happened with Blue Feather."

He turned to leave, but she followed him. "Are you saying that Grandmother was a liar? How like a Lakota man to try to cover up his cowardly misdeeds!" she hurled at his back.

Slowly, Soaring Falcon stopped and faced her again. His eyes glittered with an intense light. "Little girl, if I were you, I would shut my mouth before you say something that you regret. I have been lenient with you ever since we met, but I will only take so much."

Willow marched up to him, her eyes drilling into his. "I am no little girl. I am a warrior. You need to remember that."

Soaring Falcon cocked an eyebrow and then looked around dramatically. "Warrior? I see no warrior here. Just a woman who cannot control herself and does not know when to keep her mouth shut. A woman who has forgotten her manners and disrespects her elders. That is what I see."

He blocked the fist she threw at him, spinning her around and wrapping an arm around her neck while forcing her arm up behind her back. "Stop it! I have fought far more battles than you and against braves twice as deadly. I have no wish to hurt you, Willow, but I will not let you attack me without fighting back."

"Excuse me, but that is my wife you are manhandling. I would prefer that you let her go so that I do not have to blow your brains out."

Fury burned even hotter inside Willow when she heard Ames' voice. She didn't want him to save her. She didn't want *anyone* to save her. She wanted to give Soaring Falcon what he deserved, to mete out the punishment she'd been dreaming about since the moment she'd met him.

"Leave it be, Ames," she ground out between clenched teeth. "I can take care of myself. I have gotten out of much tighter circumstances."

"I cannot do that, my love. I will not stand for any man putting his hands on you. You will just have to accept that," Ames said. He cocked his pistol and aimed it at Soaring Falcon's head. "Unhand her."

Soaring Falcon's chuckle as he let her go enraged her even more, but before she could hit him, Ames stepped between them, taking the blow to his midsection instead of the object of her fury. He grunted and bent forward from the force of the hit.

"Willow, stop."

Soaring Falcon said, "As I said, when you can rationally discuss this, we will talk, but not before then. Ames, you are a good man. Husbands should always protect their wives, even if it is just from themselves, like now. I harbor no ill-will towards you."

Willow tried to go after him as he walked away, but Ames stopped her.

"No, Willow. Enough damage has been done. We are going home."

Drawing herself up, Willow gave him a cold smile. "No, *we* are not. *I* am going home. You can sleep somewhere else tonight."

He started to smile until he saw that she was deadly serious. "Willow, please do not be like this. I know you are angry—"

"Angry? No, Ames. I am not angry. There is no word for how furious I am right now. So, unless you want to find yourself a divorced man, I suggest you do not return home until tomorrow morning," she said and walked away.

All that night, Willow sat awake thinking about the horrible situation. Her children were going to starve if she didn't find a solution. The cow's milk wasn't going to sustain them much longer. She would've preferred to go live with their Hidatsa kin for a while, but they were too far away. The twins couldn't wait a few days. They needed to eat now.

Therefore, the Lakota tribe was her only option. But after the terrible scene between her and Soaring Falcon, she was certain that he wouldn't allow her to come live there. Her stomach churned just thinking about it, but the only course of action she had left was to apologize to him and throw herself on his mercy.

Only her powerful love for her children made her even consider swallowing her pride. By morning, she'd made up her mind.

Ames arrived just as dawn broke. "You said not to return until morning. It is morning." His determined expression told her that he wasn't going to let her kick him out again.

Willow stood up. "So it is. I am going to apologize to Soaring Falcon and to ask if he will allow me to move to his village so I can find a woman, or perhaps several, who are willing to feed Lucien and Mia."

Ames gave her a dubious look. "You are? Why would you do that?"

She met his gaze. "Because a mother's first concern is for her children and I love my babies enough to put my pride aside so that they might live. I hate him, but I will do what I must for their welfare."

Running a hand through his hair, Ames let out a sigh. He looked as tired as Willow felt. Stepping around her, he went to the twins, kneeling by them. They looked adorable as they lay next to each other. Like Willow, he would do anything for their babies. "You are right. We must put them first. We will get through it together."

Willow's chest hurt as she watched him with Lucien and Mia. "I must go before he leaves."

Ames stood up. "I will go with you."

"No. This is something I must do on my own. I do not need you or any man to save me all the time."

"Willow, you know that I was right to stop you last night." He came over to her. "You were out of control. You embarrassed our chief as well as Soaring Falcon."

She couldn't stop her upper lip from curling. "I would like to do much more than embarrass him. Because of you, I was also embarrassed. You should have let me fight."

Ames shook his head. "Willow, there are two reasons why I interfered. You are not in top fighting shape. Much as you hate it, you are still recovering, both physically and mentally. I also know that you have no use for politics, but the fact is that our alliance needs to remain strong and beating up their chief would have created an irreparable rift between our tribes."

"Mark my words, Ames: one day I will put a knife through his heart," she said. "He will pay for his crimes. But for now, I will use him the way he is using us, the way he is using you. Now, I must go."

"Willow, you cannot allow hate and anger to fester like this. Besides, he said that there is more to the story," Ames replied.

"You believe him over me?"

"I did not say that. I am asking you to be rational. Our children's lives depend on it."

"I am aware of that," she said. "I will listen to him, but I will not believe a word he says about the subject. I will be polite, but nothing more."

Ames supposed that was as much as he could ask of her. "All right. When you come back, we will discuss the other issue you told me about last night before you ran out of here."

Willow shrugged. "There is nothing to discuss. I am barren. I cannot change it so there is no sense in crying about it anymore. Crying will not change anything. I have cried far too much the past several months. My eyes will shed no more tears. I will be back as soon as I can."

Sorrow took hold of Ames as she left. She was erecting walls around her heart and shutting him out. He knew that it was a defense against all her pain, but it hurt to see her like this. He'd always been the one she'd let in completely, but he sensed that she was fast locking up her feelings for him and he had no idea what to do about it.

Mia began fussing and he picked her up, smiling at her despite his low spirits. Holding her made him feel better, but his heart was filled with worry that he was going to lose his wife.

Chapter Twenty-One

Growling Wolf reluctantly admitted Willow into his tipi, furious with her for creating such a scene last night and offending their guests.

Keeping her eyes downcast, Willow said, "I have come to apologize for my actions last evening."

Growling Wolf lifted an eyebrow in surprise. "You have?"

"Yes."

"Very well, but you had better be on your best behavior. I am almost out of patience with you."

Willow nodded. "I know."

Growling Wolf stepped aside and let her come further into the tipi.

Anger rose in Willow's breast as she approached Soaring Falcon. Thinking of her children's welfare was the only thing that kept her from attacking him. "May I sit?"

Soaring Falcon regarded her suspiciously, but her neutral expression gave nothing away. "Yes."

Willow lowered herself to the floor and gathered her courage. She forced herself to say the words that galled her. "I am sorry for attacking you last night. It was wrong. I am sorry I embarrassed you."

Soaring Falcon took a sip of tea. "I do not believe you. You accused me of being a liar, yet here you sit before me telling me that you are sorry when you are not. At least I now understand why you hate me so much. It is because of the lies you were told."

Willow burned with hot rage, but she held her tongue.

"I have no doubt that if Ames had not gotten involved that you would have kept fighting. And you would have lost. Not because I am stronger or faster, but because you were fighting without focus. You fought in blind anger, which makes you weaker. But you do not need me to tell you that."

Picturing her hungry children, Willow held her silence, but she didn't disagree with him, either.

Soaring Falcon finished his tea and sat the cup down. "Tell me why you are really here. What is it that you want?"

"I need your help."

His short laugh held only sarcasm. "You want the man you hate to extend help to you? Why would I do that when you have made it perfectly clear just how much you want to hurt me?"

Sitting erect, Willow met his eyes defiantly and pushed through her humiliation. "Because your great-grandchildren are starving. I have very little milk for them and we have no woman in our tribe who is breast feeding."

Shock stabbed Soaring Falcon. He understood that only something so dire would make Willow come to him like this. "I am sorry to hear this, but what do you want me to do about it?"

Willow bit the inside of her cheek as she fought back tears. She would not show weakness in front of him. "Would you allow me to move to your village so that I can find someone who will feed the twins until they are old enough to be weaned?"

Soaring Falcon inhaled sharply and he was once again reminded that only a parent's love could make someone do something so drastic. He knew how much this was costing Willow to ask for such a favor.

"What does Ames say about this? Why is he not here?"

"Because this was something I needed to do. This is between you and me. Not him. I do not need him to speak for me," Willow said. "You were right. I hate you and I always will."

Growling Wolf groaned. "Willow—"

Soaring Falcon held up a hand. "No, let her speak honestly. I would rather that than have her lie to me. Go on."

"I hate you, but I love my children more than I hate you. It is for their sakes that I ask this, not mine."

"I figured as much," Soaring Falcon said. "I did not rape Blue Feather, Willow. She came to my sleeping robes willingly. She was an Iroquois captive whom I fell in love with. I thought that she loved me, as well, but she did not. She made me think she did so that I would marry her, which I did. However, not long after we married, she ran away.

"She was very crafty. No one could find her trail. I looked for a long time before I gave up. I even hoped that she would return. I would have forgiven her and taken her back. But after a few months, I knew that she was not coming back. I had no idea that she had conceived, nor did I know where she had gone."

Willow shook her head. "No. Grandmother was Kiowa."

Sleek Doe said, "He tells the truth, Willow. Your grandmother came to us much the same way Ames did. She was scared, tired, and hungry, but otherwise healthy." She chuckled. "She was also brave and beautiful. Much like yourself. The man you regard as your grandfather, Black Elk, had lost his first wife and was eager to marry again. He married your grandmother and they grew to love each other very much.

"The timing of your mother's birth was such that we knew that Black Elk was not her father, but he did not care. He raised her as his own and loved her with all his heart. We had no idea who your mother's real father was. I did not know until last night when you essentially told the whole camp."

The censure in Sleek Doe's voice made Willow feel a twinge of guilt. She was also very confused. "Why would she tell Mother that you had raped her if you had not?"

Soaring Falcon's face settled into sad lines as he shrugged. "I cannot tell you what I do not know. I was raised to hold women in high regard the same as any other man, Willow. I would never force a woman to sleep with me. I truly did love Blue Feather and I am sorry that I did not know your mother." He sighed. "I wish you had just talked to me about this, but I understand why you did not. I would have felt the same way. You may come live with us. I am sure that there are women who can help feed your babies."

Willow's shoulders sagged with relief and defeat. Nothing about her life made sense anymore. She'd had one tragedy after another visited upon her and she'd been so angry and sad over the unfairness of it all. But at least she'd had somewhere she could direct some of that anger. However, even that had been taken from her. Suddenly, she was very tired and she just wanted to sleep and hope that it was all just a nightmare.

"Thank you. I will go today and stay with Sky Dancer. I know she will help, but she cannot feed her baby and mine, too," Willow said quietly.

Day Star said, "I know some women who can help, Willow."

Willow nodded woodenly and rose. "Thank you. I must go pack so we can leave as soon as possible."

Her dejected manner as she left deeply saddened the two couples.

Tears slid down Sleek Doe's wrinkled face. "She has endured too much sadness in such a short time. A lesser woman would have gone insane from it all the tragedy she has suffered."

Soaring Falcon's brow furrowed. "What are you talking about?"

Sleek Doe exchanged a look with Growling Wolf. "They should know."

Growling Wolf nodded his assent and she began telling Soaring Falcon and Day Star Willow's tale of woe.

Ames listened to Willow as she told him Soaring Falcon's story with cool detachment. Her lack of emotion worried him. There was no anger in her dull gaze or in her voice as she started packing.

"At least you know the truth and you do not need to hate him anymore," Ames said. "You have the opportunity to get to know your grandfather."

Calmly, Willow said, "I will always hate him and hate the fact that I have Lakota blood. It seems that I have a lot of enemy blood running through me. Iroquois and Lakota. I am barely Kiowa." She shook her head. "I have no idea who I am anymore. I'm a woman who cannot bear or breast feed children. I am no longer a warrior and I am a poor excuse for a wife."

Ames put a stilling hand on her shoulder. "Willow, women sometimes lose their milk, but that does not make them less of a mother. As for bearing more children, you do not know for certain that you cannot have more, but even if you cannot, it does not matter to me. We have two beautiful babies and I am grateful to you for fighting so hard to have them. I am perfectly content with them."

She nodded and tried to move away from him, but Ames grabbed her arms and turned her to face him.

"Listen to me, damn it!" His eyes blazed blue fire. "You're my wife and I love you whether you want me to or not. I know that you still want me to take another wife, but I will never do that. Ever. You are the only woman I will ever want and I will touch no other. So, give up this ridiculous idea of me doing so. It will not happen."

"Very well. If that is your decision, so be it," she said. "I must finish packing and get the twins ready."

Ames searched her face, but her expression was devoid of emotion. He cupped her cheek. "Do not shut me out, Willow. You know that I am always on your side and that I love you. Let me help you through this."

She smiled sadly. "You cannot. No one can. No one understands. Besides, I do not want to dwell on it and neither should you. You must finish preparing for your trip."

Ames' jaw clenched. "I am not going. Not with you like this. I cannot go when you are in so much pain."

"I will be fine. You must go. It is your duty to our tribe and you will not shirk your duty to stay and hold my hand." Willow hardened her heart at the hurt and anger in his eyes.

His hand dropped and he backed away from her. "Fine. I will go get the horses so we can pack them and leave soon."

"There is no reason for you to go with us. You will only need to come back here to get everything for the trip to the trading post. It does not make sense for you to do that."

His expression tightened. "I will not allow you to cut me out of your life or your heart, Willow. And I will not let you cut me out of our babies' lives, either. I will go with you and help you settle in, and that is final!"

He stomped out of the tipi and Willow went back to packing, refusing to acknowledge her aching heart.

Sky Dancer watched Willow with Lucien and Mia, thinking what a wonderful mother she was. However, she was concerned about the obvious disconnect between Willow and Ames. He tried to engage her in conversation, but her responses were perfunctory and her tight smiles never reached her eyes.

Glancing at Dark Horse, she saw that he'd also noticed. Sky Dancer knew that Willow was upset about many things, but she'd never thought that Willow would be indifferent to Ames. They'd always been so close and loving. It was painful to see the rift between them.

"We will set up a tipi for you tomorrow, Willow," Dark Horse said as he held his son, Little Bow.

"Thank you," Willow replied.

Sky Dancer said, "There is room for one near ours."

"That will be nice." She kissed Mia's forehead and smiled at her babbling. "We will be close to your aunt and uncle, little one. And your cousin." She looked at Ames. "You have enough time to get home before dark if you leave soon."

A muscle in his jaw jumped as Ames ground his teeth together. "I think I know when to leave. I do not need you tell me as though I am a child. I have been traveling since before you became a woman. Do not condescend to me."

His harsh words created an awkward silence in the tipi, but Willow seemed not to notice as she put Mia down and picked up Lucien. Dark Horse and Sky Dancer exchanged uncertain glances.

When Willow didn't respond, Ames let out a disgusted noise and rose. "You want me to leave? Fine!" He picked up Lucien, kissed his cheek, and held him close. "I'm going to miss you so much. Don't forget your papa, eh? I'll come home just as soon as I can and I'll bring you something nice. Don't grow too much." Carefully, he laid Lucien back on the blanket and took Mia from Willow. He repeated the farewell with his daughter before laying her next to her brother and turning his attention to Sky Dancer and Dark Horse. "Thank you for all of your help. I am very grateful to you. It puts my mind at ease that Willow and the children will be with family."

Sky Dancer rose and embraced him. "Please have a safe journey and do not get yourself in trouble."

Ames grinned even though he didn't feel like it. "Me? Get in trouble? I think you have me confused with someone else."

Sky Dancer chuckled and stepped back so Dark Horse could grasp arms with Ames.

"I think my wife is wise to remind you to behave."

Ames shrugged a little. "Perhaps."

Dark Horse smiled. "Safe travels, my friend."

"Thank you."

Ames said goodbye to Little Bow and then turned to find Willow on her feet with a resigned expression on her face. She went outside and he followed her over to his horse.

"I know you will be, but please be careful."

He changed to French. "I don't believe you give a shit what happens to me right now. You just want me gone so that you don't have to talk about anything. Go ahead and lock your feelings up. I'll give you a couple of months to sulk, but when I come home, I won't be put off. Even if I must tie you up and force you, you're going to listen to me. But right now, anything I say would fall on deaf ears. I'd be wasting my breath."

Cupping the back of her neck, he yanked her to him, covering her mouth with his in a demanding kiss. She couldn't quite resist his advance and kissed him back for a few moments before breaking the embrace.

"You can try to cut me out of your heart, Willow, but you never will because you know that no one could ever love you as much or as well as me." His voice was raw with emotion and his blue eyes had grown stormy. "Have a good summer, *mon amour*."

He mounted, whirled his horse around, and put his heels to its flanks. Willow watched him ride away for a few moments, but only felt a little guilty for sending him away. She had nothing more to say about recent events and didn't have it within herself to care about much outside of her children.

Feeling a little relieved, Willow went back inside Sky Dancer's tipi and tended to Lucien and Mia.

Willow walked along the stream near the Lakota camp a week later. She'd started taking the twins to whomever was going to feed them and then going off for an hour by herself. Watching another woman feeding her babies was too painful. It made her feel even more defective and damaged.

She looked up as a flock of crows flew overhead, their noisy caws reaching her ears. Finding a good spot where she had a good view of the stream, she sat down, enjoying the warm, early spring sun on her shoulders and back.

Faint movement from behind her made her turn around. Much to her annoyance, Slither walked towards her. She turned back to the water.

"I see that you have finally learned where your rightful place is instead of playing at being a brave."

Willow ignored him, instead watching the rippling water as it moved around a couple of large rocks that jutted up out of the surface.

"I hear that our chief taught you a lesson. I am glad he finally got fed up with your insolent behavior and gave you what you deserve." Slither chuckled. "I guess you are not so tough after all."

Willow kept her voice mild. "I pity your wives. Not only are you ugly, you have a nasty streak."

"You are wrong. I love my wives very much and treat them accordingly. They will tell you that," he said. "They are good women."

"Yes, they are, despite being married to you. I give them credit for the tolerant way they put up with you. I only hope your children do not follow in your footsteps. As far as your chief goes, it is surprising that your nose is not permanently brown from how far your nose is up his conceited backside," Willow shot back.

"*I* am hard to put up with? Tell me, who is in charge in your marriage? You or Ames? How does he like being married to a man? Or maybe you are just fighting against your *winkte* nature. It is never good to try to be something you are not," Slither taunted.

His barbed comments hit their mark, but instead of making her angry, they brought tears to her eyes. She wasn't *winkte*, but she didn't feel very much like a woman right then. "Just go away, Slither. Leave me alone."

Slither had been expecting one of her sharp retorts. He was confused by her odd behavior. Coming around to face her, he was surprised to see tear tracks on her face. "Why are you crying?"

"None of your business."

He crouched close by. "I never thought I would see you cry."

She stared at the stream. "Well, now you have. Happy?"

"You would think I would be, but I am...disturbed by it."

"Disturbed. You do not know what disturbed is, Slither. You have no idea."

"Try me. I am a good listener. You cannot live with two wives and not be. They give you no choice."

Her lips twitched at his funny remark. "I think not. I have to go back to Lucien and Mia."

"Willow—"

"What do you want from me?" she yelled. "Do you enjoy kicking dogs when they are down? Do you? Can you not see..." She growled and then said, "Screw you!" in French as she got up.

"Wait." Slither put a hand on her arm.

It was the last straw for Willow. Spinning around, she swung, channeling all her anger and frustration behind her fist. She hit Slither squarely on the jaw and he dropped to his knees.

"I tried to tell you to leave me alone. Maybe you will listen from now on."

She stalked away, her long strides taking her quickly back to the village. It had felt good to hit someone, to vent some anger, and she wanted to do it again. She wanted to pound and pound until she had no more anger left and she'd annihilated her opponent. However, she couldn't do that right now.

Arriving at the tipi of the woman who'd fed Lucien and Mia, Willow scratched on the flap. Rippling Grass told her to enter. The sight that greeted her made her heart stop. Rippling Grass held Lucien, who smiled up at her.

"*Han*, Willow." Rippling Grass smiled at her. "He is such a happy baby. They both are. And I think their eyes will stay blue, too."

Lucien looked so happy to be with this woman who wasn't his mother. A woman who could feed him and give him everything he needed. Unlike her, who couldn't feed him in the middle of the night when he was hungry. She had to bandy him and Mia around, disturbing people from their slumber. Jealousy turned her stomach sour, but she forced herself to smile.

"Yes. They look much like their father," she said.

Rippling Grass smiled. "He is very handsome...for a white man," she teased.

"I will take them if they are finished," Willow said, brusquely.

"Yes. Of course."

Mia was already in her cradleboard. Willow picked her up and kissed her hello. Mia smiled and blew bubbles at her, making her laugh. She ducked through the doorway, with Rippling Grass following her.

Willow took Lucien from her and thanked her for her help. Taking her leave, she took her children home to the new tipi that had been set up for her. The things that she'd brought with her had been organized nicely around the tipi. She started a fire and changed the twins.

Someone scratched on the flap.

"Come." Willow groaned when Soaring Falcon entered. "First Slither, now you."

Soaring Falcon restrained a smile. "Yes. He has a nasty bruise on his jaw."

"Good. He has a nasty mouth."

The chief laughed. "Sometimes, yes. But then again, so do you."

She flicked a brief annoyed glance at him. "Would you like some tea?"

He put hand on his chest. "Who? Me? Are you actually inviting me to sit down?"

"I assumed you would whether I did or not."

Spying the twins, Soaring Falcon asked, "May I?"

Willow's first instinct was to refuse, but remembering that he was helping her, she nodded.

With a big smile, he sat down near them and took Mia from her cradleboard. Holding her in his large hands, he examined her thoroughly. "It looks like her eyes will stay blue like Ames'. And her hair is light like his."

The easy way he handled Mia convinced Willow that he was used to holding babies. "I am glad that they have his eyes because they are such a beautiful shade of blue. The same with their hair. I do not think Lucien's is going to be as light as hers. Perhaps the same lighter brown as Cricket's."

"Were his eyes what attracted you to Ames?"

Willow frowned, surprised by his question. "Why do you want to know?"

His lips thinned as he settled Mia comfortably in his arms. "I know that you hate me, but I do not hate you. You are my granddaughter and I do not hate any of my children or grandchildren. I may get put-out with them, but I do not hate them. And you owe me. The price of you staying here is to let me get to know you and my great-grandchildren."

"Fine! Everything about Ames attracted me. His eyes, his golden hair, his handsomeness, but even more than that, his laugh and kindness were his most attractive qualities to me. He was so charming and different than any other man I had ever met. Open with his feelings and thoughts. He is also easy to talk to." She dipped out a cup of tea and sat it near him.

Soaring Falcon took a sip of his drink. "He is also a very intelligent man and a skilled trader."

"Yes, he is. And I doubt that there is a better lover anywhere."

It gave her great satisfaction when Soaring Falcon choked on his next sip of tea.

She shrugged when he turned a wide-eyed stare on her. "You said that you wanted to get to know me."

"There are some details that I could do without."

"What details *would* you like to know? How I plan to kill you? Or how I regret not doing it when I first met you?"

His expression darkened. "I am trying to be civil. Why can you not do the same?"

"Very well. How was your day?"

"What are you doing?"

She raised an eyebrow. "Being civil."

He frowned and rubbed his forehead. "I think I preferred it when you were mean to me."

"With a knife through your heart."

"What?"

"That is how I plan to kill you."

"Are you always this fickle?" he asked.

"Me? You are the one telling me to be civil one moment and then wanting me to be mean the next."

"Mia, do not grow up to have your mother's personality. I pray that you are genial and charming like your father."

"Ames thinks that I am very genial and charming, especially—"

"Stop being crude and tell me how you came to be a warrior."

Willow sighed. "It is not much of a story. I am no different than Three Deer. I never liked doing the things that girls were supposed to do. Scraping hides, making clothing, keeping a home. Boring. Racing ponies, hunting, fighting; those were the things I enjoyed the most. I went on my first raid when I was fourteen and I stole two ponies from a Cheyenne camp. Lightning Strike was so angry because he had only gotten one." She smiled at the memory. "My father was furious that I had gone on a raid and I was made to stay close to home for a while. I grew tired of it, though, and started sneaking off."

Soaring Falcon grunted as he put Mia back in her cradleboard. "I am not surprised. It seems as though you have never behaved as you should."

Willow watched him as he picked up Lucien. "I went on three more raids that year, each time bringing back three ponies. I counted sixteen winters old when I earned my first coup in battle."

Soaring Falcon was impressed. "Not bad for a girl."

"By a couple of years later, I had counted enough coup to be eligible for marriage, had I been a man. Ask Growling Wolf if you do not believe me. He is the one who awarded it to me and allowed me to be a warrior. Father was furious, but he soon came to see that it was what I was born to do." Willow sobered. "Or I was. Now, I am not anything, really. I have no function."

"Why? You will go back to being a warrior when the time is right," Soaring Falcon said.

"I doubt it. Fang does not truly believe that I am able to perform those duties any longer. He stripped me of my status a while back."

"Why would he do that when you are so skilled?"

"Because I miscarried one of my babies and he did not think I was ready to return to duty. I felt fine after a couple of weeks, but he would not listen to me. And no one has been listening to me ever since," she said.

The chief said, "I guess Fang was right to not allow you back since you were still pregnant."

"Perhaps, but he did not know that at the time. No one did. Not even me. It does not matter now. That life is behind me."

The wistfulness in her voice spoke volumes. "You miss it."

"Yes. For a while, I worked the trap lines with Ames and I was happy. Then we discovered that I was pregnant, so I stopped. And then all of the difficulty began with my pregnancy." She touched Mia's cheek. "I fought so hard to keep her and Lucien. I love them so much."

"I can see that. You are a good mother, Willow."

She smiled a little, but remained silent on the subject.

Sensing that she was done talking, Soaring Falcon gave Lucien to her and rose. "When you are done being sad and pitying yourself, come see me."

Fire leapt into her eyes. "Do not think you understand what I am going through."

"Everyone suffers loss in one way or another, Willow. Loss of loved ones, loss of health, loss of faith. Loss is a fact of life. How you react to that loss is what shows a person's true character. If you are the warrior you say you are, you will fight your way out of this...depression you are allowing yourself to be stuck in. I have a job for you, but only when you are ready."

"How can I take up any duty? I have children to raise," she said angrily.

"Figure it out. You will earn your keep while you are here," he said coldly and left.

Willow battled to keep her composure. She needed to move, needed to work out her frustrations, but she couldn't leave the twins. But she could just run around her and Sky Dancer's tipi. She would be close enough to hear them cry.

Settling them down for a nap, she exited the tipi and stretched, limbering up her muscles a little before setting out. It wasn't a very big area to run in, but it was better than nothing. On her tenth lap, Sky Dancer came out of her own tipi holding Little Bow.

"Why are you running in circles?" she asked.

Willow stopped. "I was angry so I needed to run, to move."

"Why do you not go to the foot races then? I will watch the twins," Sky Dancer said.

"I cannot ask you to do that," Willow said. "They are my babies."

Sky Dancer cocked her head and gave her a wry smile. "I think that you have forgotten that it is every woman's responsibility to help rear the all of children in a tribe. Little Bow just ate, so if Mia and Lucien need fed after a while, I will have plenty of milk."

Sky Dancer's innocent statement sliced through Willow's heart, but she forced a smile. "All right. I will not stay long." She took off running before tears gathered in her eyes.

Chapter Twenty-Two

Two nights later, Willow returned to the racing area, intending to just be a spectator. However, Slither had other ideas.

"Well, if it is not the cry baby herself," he said when he saw her.

"And there is the man with a glass jaw," she shot back.

"Are you here to race?"

"No. Just to watch."

He smirked at her. "Not feeling up to racing, hmm? Too out of shape. Having babies will do that to a woman."

She shoved him. "Do not talk about me like that or I will give you a bruise on the other side of your face."

"Lucky shot."

"No luck needed. Just skill and fast reflexes."

Slither grinned. "Like the skill you showed with Soaring Falcon that night?"

"He would be dead now if Ames had not interfered."

"I highly doubt that. You had some fun playing brave, but you really should go back to your children where you belong." Slither's mocking gaze moved over her. "Yes. Definitely out of shape."

Rushing Bull had been watching their tense exchange. "Are you two racing? I thought I heard you say something about it."

"Are we racing, Willow, or are you too tired?" Slither asked.

"I am never too tired to beat you at anything."

Rushing Bull grinned. "What are you betting?"

Willow's face fell. "I do not have anything valuable to bet. All of my expensive things are at home."

"Then we will just race for honor," Slither said, shrugging. "That will suffice, especially when I put you in your place."

Rushing Bull raised an eyebrow over his remark and waited for Willow's response.

She gave a curt nod. "For honor then."

Slither laughed. "This will be fun."

Rushing Bull announced the race and raised his hands in the air. Willow ignored Slither as she waited for the big brave's arms to start downward. The moment they did, she took off, leaving Slither behind. He soon caught up, smiling over at her. Willow focused on the track ahead of her, listening to the blood pounding in her ears.

She settled into a steady pace, conserving her energy for the homestretch because, based on the easy way Slither ran beside her, she was going to need it. Slyly, she made it look as though she was floundering and Slither slowed his pace with a patronizing smile. She shot him a scowl but smiled inwardly.

As they rounded the far turn and the finish came into her sight, Willow forged ahead, putting daylight between her and Slither. The crowd had quieted over what they had viewed as a boring race, but as Willow streaked over the ground towards the finish line, a roar went up.

When Slither caught her this time, he wasn't running as easily as before, but he still looked strong. Willow dug deeper, and, even though her thighs burned and her lungs felt like they were on fire, she pressed on. She ran flat out, but Slither moved ahead, winning by several strides.

Willow's heart sank as she slowed down and came to a stop. Her defeat drove home the fact that she was woefully out of shape. Ignoring the jeers of the crowd, Willow made her way from the racing area and sat down on a fallen log to catch her breath. To her great dismay, Slither had followed her.

She glared at him. "What do you want now? Is it not enough that you won? Did you come to gloat?"

He sat down next to her. "No. You did not give me a chance to congratulate you."

"Congratulate me? I lost."

"Is that the first time you have raced since you gave birth?"

Willow nodded as she worked to bring her breathing under control.

Slither laughed. "I thought so. If you can run like that without being in condition, I can just imagine how fast you are when you are in good shape. From what I can see, it would not take much for you to get back into condition. If you have the guts, that is. Thank you for a good race." He thumped her shoulder and jogged off.

Watching Ten Thunders get plastered for the first time was immensely entertaining to Ames and Firebrand. They sat in the nicer of the two ale houses in Grand Forks, playing the part of three men who'd happened to meet there and taken a liking to one another. Their trading was going well, but they were far from finished.

Ten Thunders had let it slip that he'd never been drunk before and his companions had immediately set about rectifying that. After two pints, Ten Thunders was on his way to becoming good and soused. The strong ale hit him hard because he wasn't used to alcohol.

No sooner was he done with the second pint than Firebrand bought him another one.

"Drink up, Ten Thunders," he said.

Ten Thunders gamely downed a couple of swigs and let out a loud belch. "How's that?"

"You're doing well, lad," Ames said. "You're going to feel great in the morning."

They spoke English since they were all fluent in that language.

"You're a damn liar," Ten Thunders said. "I'm going to feel as though someone is hammering on my head. I've heard tales of that. But for right now, I feel great. That tavern maid keeps looking at me. I think she fancies me."

Ames said, "I hate to dampen your spirits, but she's actually looking at Firebrand. I think she likes his hair."

Firebrand turned around and winked at the pretty redhead, who colored and smiled.

"I'll be damned," Ten Thunders said. "Maybe I should wear my hair like that."

He petted himself and Ames burst into laughter. Taking hold of Ten Thunder's wrist, he stopped him. "Don't do that. You'll make the other bar wench rethink her obvious plans for you."

"Huh? What other bar wench?" Ten Thunders asked loudly.

"Quiet down. I don't think they heard you across the street."

Ten Thunders missed Ames' sarcasm in his drunken state. "What bar wench?" he asked in a stage whisper.

Firebrand grinned and shook his head. "You don't know anything about the fairer sex, do you?"

Ten Thunders sent him a lopsided smile. "I know penty...prentny." He laughed at his muff-up. "Plenty. I know plenty and I can say it, too."

"Oh, so you're experienced with women then?" Ames asked.

"That's right." Ten Thunders nodded emphatically. "They smell good, well, most of the time. And they're soft and warm. And comfortable."

Firebrand let out a hoot of laughter. "Comfortable? I don't think I've ever heard anyone describe a woman that way before. I guess you could say that, though."

Ten Thunders gave a sigh. "I miss women, but I'm saving myself."

Ames arched an eyebrow. "Saving yourself? What for?"

"Not for what, for whom," Ten Thunders responded and raised a hand. "Don't aks...ask because I'm not telling you. Cricket's been praying for me and if I tell you it won't come true. Of course, things sort of changed there, so I don't know exactly who I'm having him pray for."

Ames chuckled. "I think you're confusing prayers with wishes."

"No, I'm not. My white father taught me that prayers are private and we're not to go around telling everyone what we pray for and draw attention to our woes and troubles. It's conceited and fake. It's in the Bible somewhere, but I don't remember the place right now," Ten Thunders said.

Ames' gave him a confused look. "You're half-white?"

"No. My adoptive father was white. He was a minister, a very kindly man and I greatly miss him." Ten Thunders' slightly glazed eyes shimmered with sudden tears. "He loved me despite me being an Indian. I don't know who my first people were, so he's the only one I remember loving me."

Feeling sentimental himself, Ames grew a little misty-eyed. "I'm sorry for your loss, Ten Thunders. Perhaps you could find him."

Ten Thunders shook his head and cleared his throat. "No. The only way there is through Ojibwa territory and I won't risk being captured again. Three times in a lifetime is enough. I'm accepted now and I'm happy."

Firebrand nudged his foot under the table. "I think you're about to get even happier. Here comes the other tavern girl."

A young woman of indeterminate heritage approached their table with a flirtatious smile on her pretty face. She executed a little curtsey. "Do you gentleman need anything else? Perhaps more ale to slake your thirst?"

Her dark eyes sparkled as her gaze settled on Ten Thunders. Ames and Firebrand grinned at each other over the shy way Ten Thunders smiled back.

"I'll take another ale and perhaps some bread and cheese if it's not too much trouble," he said.

"Not at all, love." She looked at Ames and Firebrand. "And for you gents?"

Ames said, "Just more ale."

"The same for me," Firebrand said.

She smiled at them and went to fetch their order.

Firebrand clapped Ten Thunders on the shoulder. "Are you telling me that you're going to turn her down? She's beautiful and most certainly inviting you."

Ten Thunders shrugged. "I'll see how I feel about it in a little while."

Firebrand laughed. "Well, I plan on spending the night with that comely ginger lass over there." He looked over at her and winked. She giggled and blushed. Firebrand rose. "I'll see you both in the morning. I'll meet you here for breakfast."

Ames raised his mug in acknowledgment and drained it just as the other serving girl returned. She put their food and drink on the table and shocked Ten Thunders by sitting in his lap. Picking up the bread, she tore off a small piece and held it out to him.

"Hungry?" she asked.

Her shapely bottom resting on his lap warmed Ten Thunders' blood. "Starving."

Ames didn't need to see anymore to know that he'd be spending the rest of the evening alone. With a sigh, he got up. He'd rather get drunk in private. He leaned down so he could speak into Ten Thunders' ear. "Have a good time, my friend. See you in the morning."

Ten Thunders' absently responded, his attention mostly focused on the serving girl who was now stroking his shoulder while she fed him. Ames chuckled and strolled over to the bar.

The barkeep smiled. "What can I get you?"

"A bottle of good whiskey."

The barkeep pulled one out from under the bar and Ames paid the man. He made his way across the street to the stable where he'd rented a stall for his dogs, who guarded his wares. As he greeted his beloved canines, he thought of his wife and children and felt a pang of longing for them. How stupid he'd been to leave with angry words between him and Willow.

As he took off his shirt and hung it on a nail, he cursed his volatile temper. He should've stayed and made her talk to him, but his pride had gotten in the way. The dogs milled around him as he settled down in the clean straw, sitting up against the stone wall at the back of the stall.

He took a parfleche of wasna out of his pack and gave some to the dogs. Petting them made him wonder how Trapper was getting along at the Lakota camp. Gray put a big paw on Ames' knee, distracting him from his musings.

"You're a glutton, do you know that?"

Gray looked at the piece of wasna in Ames' hand and licked his chops. Ames divided up the rest of the snack between the dogs and took a long pull from his whiskey bottle. He calculated that they should be able to leave in two weeks. They were making good progress with their trading and, so far, no one suspected where they'd gotten their hides or that Firebrand and Ten Thunders knew him.

As far as Ames knew, various Indian tribes came to Grand Forks to trade their pelts, but no French tappers went as far south as he did. It was entirely possible that a few might, but he'd never met any. He'd heard of Francis and Louis-Joseph Verendrye, who'd traveled among the Mandan, Sioux, and Fox Indians approximately eight years before in 1743, but there hadn't been any other tales of French explorers undertaking such an excursion.

Ames didn't want to lead white people into his kin's area, not only because the land south held such a preponderance of game, but mainly because he was very protective of them. He knew that all the land-hungry Europeans would love to get their greedy hands on such fertile territory. After his first winter with them, Ames had vowed to keep his family's lands as secret as possible, even from his own countrymen.

They would destroy the Indian settlements with disease and alcohol and undermine their way of life, just as they had in the French and British Colonies. He'd seen it often enough during his travels with his father and the thought of that happening to the Kiowa tribe sickened him. However, he knew in his soul that it was only a matter of time before their land was encroached upon since whites of all nationalities were flooding into the continent.

Like his father, Ames loved being a fur trader because of all the different people he encountered and the chance to see various lands.

He didn't desire great riches or fame. Making his yearly trek suited him just fine and he intended to stick to his way of life, the same as he wanted the Kiowa and other Indians to continue theirs.

He and Firebrand had gleaned valuable information last year in *La Baie Verte* or The Green Bay. Tensions were mounting even higher between the French, English, and some Indian tribes, and there were rumblings of more wars. Ames had no wish to get involved in any conflicts, preferring to live his quiet life as a fur trader.

It was yet another reason that he didn't live near any of the larger trading posts. He couldn't stand watching the Indians basically give away their valuable pelts because the French and English at the posts swindled them. Often, they plied the Indians with alcohol and traded when the Indians were too drunk to make wise deals.

Some of his countrymen would've called him a traitor, and he supposed that he was since he'd largely defected from France. His allegiance was now to the Kiowa, especially his wife and children. The Kiowa enjoyed many of the products he procured for them, but he knew that they largely wanted to stick to their old way of life. They might appreciate the knives, hatchets, cloth, needles, and ornamental materials he bought for them because they made their lives a little easier, but they still wanted to live on their own terms.

Although he enjoyed celebrating Christmas with them, he would never give them a Bible or try to force Catholicism on them. That was usually the first step toward colonizing the Indians and Ames wouldn't take any part in such devious actions.

He felt badly that they hadn't been able to secure all the materials needed to set up a small blacksmithing operation. Getting an anvil, hammers, and pliers hadn't been a problem, and charcoal could be made from burning pine and other kinds of wood, but without iron, the equipment did them no good. Ames knew that he could've gotten it in The Green Bay, but Grand Forks had been closer.

He knew that they'd be making the longer trek to *La Baie Verte* next year to secure the metal they needed. In the meantime, the tools would come in handy for copper working and various other endeavors.

Ames figured that if they left Grand Forks in two weeks, they could make it home by the first or second week in August.

He ran a hand through his hair as impatience set in. After a few more swigs of whiskey, he corked the bottle and put it aside. Laying down, he smiled as he thought about Ten Thunders' surprised expression when that tavern girl had brazenly sat down on his lap. No doubt the boy was right now enjoying how "comfortable" she was.

Willow was comfortable to lay on as they recovered from lovemaking. Yearning for his wife, Ames shifted in the straw a little. He'd meant what he'd said to her about discussing the whole situation through when he returned. *No more will you put me off, my little bird. We'll get to the heart of the matter and, by God, you* will *talk to me.*

Ames lay awake for a long time that night, composing what he would say to his wife when he arrived back in the hills that their Lakota kin called Paha Sapa.

Rushing Bull spat grass from his mouth as he picked himself up off the ground and looked at Willow.

"Stop that!" she ordered loudly.

"Stop what?"

She threw her hands in the air. "Letting me win!" Pointing at him, she said, "Do not deny it. You are taking it easy on me."

Rushing Bull looked chagrined. "It is not that I am taking it easy on you, it is just that..."

Willow waited, but he looked at the ground in silence. "It is just what?" she prompted.

"You are a woman."

"Not right now I am not. I am a warrior and we are sparring."

Rushing Bull said, "You are always a woman, whether we are sparring or not."

Willow and the braves gathered around laughed at his discomfort.

"Are the rest of you not worried about it?" he yelled, waving a hand at the group. "How am I supposed to wrestle when I might touch places I should not?"

This only drew more laughter.

Willow said, "Rushing Bull, I am used to that during practice. It does not bother me. However, if you tried to—"

"Willow!"

She whipped her head around at Soaring Falcon's voice. "What do you want? I am busy and only have so much time before I must go back to the twins."

Dark Horse lifted an eyebrow at the insolent way she spoke to Soaring Falcon.

The chief's obsidian eyes gleamed with anger. "Come with me right now!"

"But—"

"Now!"

He turned and walked away. Willow made a face at his back, which made the men smile. She grinned back at them before picking up her bow and quiver and following him.

"What is it?"

"You are coming along with your fighting," he responded.

"Not nearly enough. The men keep letting me win. How am I supposed to improve when they do not challenge me? I need something to work towards, not to be coddled."

He glanced at her. "You have to forgive them, Willow. They are not used to fighting with a woman. Our men are not trained to do so. Your men have been doing it for a long time, so they do not view you in the same way they do other women."

"I suppose."

"I have something for you to do," he said.

"Sentry duty?"

"No."

"Hunting?"

"No."

"Then what?"

Her irritated tone made him smile. "I would like you to train some of the younger boys."

"Me? Why not Dark Horse or Rushing Bull?"

"Because Dark Horse is going on a longer scouting run and Rushing Bull has his hands full tending to the day-to-day duties around here."

She groaned. "That means I have to work with Slither. Why do you need me when you have him?"

"You are the most exasperating female I have ever met!" Soaring Falcon said. "We have twenty-four young boys right now. Too many for Slither to train by himself."

"What about their uncles and grandfathers? Or even their fathers? They should be the ones training them."

Soaring Falcon stopped walking. "We have also lost soldiers, Willow. Some of these boys do not have anyone proficient to teach them because their male family members are dead." He gestured broadly. "In case you have not noticed, our tribe is much, much larger than yours. But, like yours, our number of men is lower than normal. We have more younger boys than girls right now, though. They need instruction. Will you help them?"

"Yes."

"Good. Come meet them and you can start with them tomorrow."

They reached the training field where targets had been set up. Slither spoke with a boy of around ten winters old, instructing him on the proper way to hold a lance. When he saw them, he paused what he was doing and jogged over.

"Are you here for a lesson?" He smiled sarcastically at Willow.

"I think you are the one who needs a lesson."

"Willow is going to help you train the boys." Soaring Falcon's tone brooked no argument.

Slither frowned. "Why? I am doing just fine."

Soaring Falcon said, "It will go faster with another person teaching them.

"Very well. Come. I will introduce you."

A smile spread across Soaring Falcon's face as Willow and Slither walked away.

Chapter Twenty-Three

Willow's days settled into a regular schedule. In the mornings, she took Lucien and Mia to Rippling Grass to nurse. Although she still longed to feed them herself, she was growing accustomed to watching other women provide food for her children. Rippling Grass's baby girl had passed when she'd only been a little over a month old.

As terrible as miscarrying her baby had been, Willow couldn't imagine how much it would've hurt if she'd lost the twins after only having them a month. She'd begun seeing that although some things had been taken from her, she was very blessed to still have her babies.

Rippling Grass was a sweet, talkative woman and Willow sensed that feeding and spending time with the twins was helping her through the loss of her own baby. Willow would stay and chat for a little while and then go to the training field.

At first, the boys had been skeptical of her abilities or shy, but she'd soon won them over. Training them was entertaining and rewarding. She and Slither taught them about sparring and target practice. They often divided the boys into teams and had them compete against each other.

Unlike some of the other Lakota men, Slither didn't hold back when he and Willow sparred. They enjoyed their fights and Willow was fast approaching her former skill level. Members of her Kiowa tribe came to visit, bringing her news from back home.

Several times during the day, she went to Rippling Grass' tipi to be with her children. They were growing rapidly, becoming chubby on the rich milk Rippling Grass and Sky Dancer provided them. Their eyes had indeed stayed blue and they both had Ames' smile.

While she kept busy during the day, at night once the twins were down, Willow was plagued by guilt over the way she'd treated Ames the day he'd left. He'd been right, both about her sulking and about no one else loving her the way he did. From the time they'd met, he'd accepted her for who and what she was, never trying to change her in any way.

She ached for him and missed working with him. His smile and laugh filled her dreams, taunting her and making her long for him even more. How could she have been so stupid to try to shut him out? Clearly, she hadn't been in her right mind, but she was now and she couldn't wait until he came home so she could apologize and beg for his forgiveness.

Even though the three travelers tried to be as quiet as possible, the Kiowa sentries heard them before they'd caught sight of them. The ox wagon they'd purchased had suffered a broken wheel a few days prior and the jerry-rigged conveyance was even noisier now.

Lightning Strike and another brave, Dagger, cautiously left their hiding spots, making their way through the foliage. Dagger was glad to have a reason to move. The muggy, late August weather had been lulling him to sleep.

Recognizing their friends, they burst from the woods onto the trail, laughing when the three men startled and assumed defensive stances. The dogs were happy to see their other family members and begged to be petted. The happy group made their way to camp, where they were greeted as enthusiastically as ever.

It was Ames' habit to look for Willow right away, and even though he knew that she wouldn't be there, he gazed in the direction of their tipi.

Firebrand laid a hand on his shoulder. "Go to your family, brother. We can take care of things here."

"Are you sure?"

"Yes. Go."

Ames grinned at him, grabbed his pack from the wagon, and strode to the rope horse corral. He caught one of Willow's horses and mounted up. As he cantered along under the hot summer sun, trepidation and excitement filled him.

Would he have to fight to make Willow talk to him or would she be happy to see him? Had she missed him as much as he had her? How big were the twins now? He hated that he'd missed three months of their lives, but he intended to make up for lost time. Ames put his horse into a faster gait, his impatience to reach his family growing with every passing minute.

"Pull back steadily and focus completely on your target. It is better to take your time and be accurate than to be hasty and miss an important shot," Willow said.

Eleven-year-old Little Frog lowered his bow and arrow as he looked up at her. His dark eyes were filled with doubt. "I am never going to be able to do this."

"I am going to tell you something that I have just relearned. If you let negativity keep a hold on you, you will never do anything well. There is nothing wrong with being upset or sad, but if you allow it to control you, you will miss out on all of the joy in life," she said. "There is too much to enjoy to be sad all the time."

"That's good advice, *mon amour.*"

A jolt of surprise shot up Willow's spine and her heartbeat leapt as the voice she'd been longing to hear for the last three months came from behind her. Little Frog's startled look reassured her that she hadn't imagined it.

Whirling around, she saw Ames standing a short distance away. He was sweaty and his clothes were dirty. Dark gold stubble covered his jaw and his shoulder-length hair hung limp, obviously in need of a good washing, but he'd never looked so good to her. His fabulous blue eyes shone with happiness, determination, and just a touch of uncertainty. She didn't blame him for being wary, but she wanted to put him at ease.

However, the only sound she could get past her lips right then was a cry of joy as she rushed to him. Ames dropped his pack and easily caught her when she jumped at him. He embraced her as she encircled his neck with her arms and wrapped her legs around him.

"Does this mean you're happy to see me?" he asked in French.

Willow couldn't speak around the lump in her throat so she pulled back and looked in his eyes for a moment before pressing her lips to his. Although she knew that such public displays of affection were usually frowned upon, she didn't care that their kiss of greeting was being witnessed by many people. His warm, supple mouth moved over hers and she held him tighter.

Ames didn't want to let her go as she kissed him with the passion that he remembered so well, but when he heard children's laughter, he relaxed his hold on her and eased her down to the ground.

"I've missed you so much," Willow said, resting her hands on his broad shoulders.

Speaking in French allowed them a measure of privacy since none of the Lakota gathered around spoke it.

"And I've missed you. You look well."

"Ames, I...let me introduce you and then we'll go see the twins," she said, looking around.

He understood that she wanted to talk in private. So, did he. However, he tamped down his impatience and greeted the youngsters and Slither, who grasped arms with him.

"I hope your journey was fruitful," he said.

"Definitely," Ames replied as he picked up his pack again. He'd already put his horse with the others. "You will see. It is good to see you. I am stealing my wife."

"I thought you might," Slither said with a wry smile.

As they walked away, Ames asked, "Where can I bathe? I am filthy and, as anxious as I am to see our little ones, I would rather be clean when I hold them again."

"They have gotten so big, Ames! They will be crawling soon. They are already trying," she said.

Her eyes were bright with happiness and her beautiful smile made his heart throb harder. His eyes traveled over her, and he found more gorgeous than ever. As with many things, Willow had her own ideas about fashion. She'd designed her short, sleeveless summer tunics with function in mind, but they also showed off her strong, toned arms and womanly shape.

He knew that if it wouldn't have caused a huge stir, she would've dressed just like the braves did in the summer; rarely wearing leggings or shirts. Indian women going topless wasn't unheard of. In fact, Ames had seen many Indian women do so in the summer since he'd first started traveling with his father. However, Willow walking around with bare legs would've been deemed very inappropriate by Indian standards.

His father had explained to him that it hadn't been until the Catholic missionaries had started converting Indians to Christianity that Indian women going half-nude had become an issue. François had laughed about it, telling Ames how scandalized he'd been the first time he'd seen an Indian woman bare from the waist up.

Ames forced his mind back to what Willow was saying instead of the image of how she would look wearing only a breechcloth on a hot summer day.

"Lucien's hair is a little wavy like yours, but it is darker than Mia's."

"I'm glad that I didn't miss them starting to crawl and I'm glad that I won't miss their first steps. I hope you won't object to me teaching Lucien how to hunt and repair weapons. I know grandfathers and uncles usually teach those things to the boys in many Indian cultures, but I ask you to indulge me in desiring to do it," he said.

Willow took his hand in hers. "There is very little I could ever deny you."

He smiled and squeezed her hand. "What would you deny me?"

She sobered. "I was so foolish to suggest that you marry another woman. I would deny you another wife. I don't want to share you."

"I'm glad you've come to your senses about that because I'll never take another wife." His intense gaze made her heart flutter. "You're the only woman I'll ever love or share sleeping robes with."

"I'm so glad."

Willow took him to a secluded spot where an oak tree hung partway over the large stream, providing shade. While he took clean clothes and soap from his pack, Willow undressed. She wanted Ames intensely and she was going to take advantage of the opportunity to have some private time with him.

Ames straightened and pulled in a deep breath at the sight of his naked wife. Her slim figure and high breasts ignited his hunger for her.

"I think I could use a bath, too."

Her saucy grin sent heat surging through him and he started to stir to life. Quickly, he shed his clothing, impatient to get into the water with her and make love to her.

Watching Ames undress, revealing his muscular body to her one piece of clothing at a time, made Willow ache for him. She stepped into the cool water, walking in up to her waist. Ames hurried into the stream and slapped water in her direction. She retaliated and they had a splashing war.

"You win," he said after a few minutes. "It is not a fair fight since I have only one hand." He held the bar of soap aloft. "Come here."

Willow swam over to him and stood up. Ames pulled her against his body with his free arm, pressing her against his hard chest and stomach. Lowering his head, he took her lips in a kiss that turned her insides to liquid and filled her with longing. His familiar taste and the way he held her excited Willow and she couldn't keep her hands off him.

Her hands roamed over his powerful shoulders and chest, down over his trim waist until she took his turgid member in her hand. He growled against her mouth and pressed his hips forward as she caressed him. Willow responded with a moan when he started soaping up her backside.

His big hands massaged and squeezed her firm bottom before moving up over her back and around to her front. Ames backed her into deeper water and proceeded to thoroughly wash her, missing no part of her body. By the time he was done, she was incredibly aroused and couldn't wait for him any longer.

"Make love to me now, Ames. I need you."

Ames was just as excited as she was and he couldn't wait any longer. After tossing the soap up on the bank, he lifted her up so she could lock her legs around his waist. The cool water against their passion-heated bodies added another sensual element to their lovemaking.

Willow wrapped her arms around Ames' neck and kissed him insistently, twining her tongue with his. She fisted her hands in his hair as he pushed her hips down so he could join their bodies. Her body adjusted to his gentle, erotic invasion and she closed her eyes in pleasure as they became one.

Ames held her close, kissing her neck and shoulders as he fought for control. Then with sure, expert movements, he moved her up and down in the water. He wanted to go slowly, to savor the experience, but the way Willow moved told him that she had other ideas. He knew how to give them both what they wanted.

Smiling, he slid his hand between them, finding her most sensitive place.

Willow gasped and arched her back as the first ripples of her climax began.

"Look at me," he commanded.

Opening her eyes, Willow was immediately trapped by his gaze as she shuddered against him in bliss. She whimpered and bit her bottom lip as she reached the crescendo. It held her in a powerful grip for several moments before she started coming down the slope.

Feeling her pulse around him was too much for Ames and his intention to draw things out fled. When Willow recovered a little, he began urging her to move again. Willow smiled as she repeatedly lifted and lowered her. His impatience and the way he felt excited her again.

They moved in tandem, increasing their tempo to a feverish pace. The water slapped against their bodies as they sought completion. Willow suddenly cried out and hugged Ames hard as she took her pleasure. Ames thrust against her several more times before he found his own release. He growled and bit her shoulder as ecstasy flooded his body.

Willow loved giving Ames pleasure and relished the fact that she affected him so strongly. Her body went slack in his arms and she rested her head on his shoulder.

"I love you so much and I'm so sorry about hurting you," she said. "I felt so lost and weak. I've always prided myself on being strong and I didn't know how to lean on you. I should've explained how I was feeling, but I didn't know how."

Ames drew back to look into her eyes. "Don't ever shut me out again. I'll never leave that way again, no matter how long it takes to work things out. I chastised myself about it the whole time I was gone. Never again will I go away with angry words lying between us. I couldn't take that again."

She smoothed back his wet hair. "I promise to never close my heart to you again. Maybe you won't understand this, but I also needed to get through everything somewhat on my own. If you'd been here, I would've kept relying on you and it would've allowed me to keep being weak. I needed to stand on my own two feet and face the situation so I could grow strong again."

Ames nodded. "I see what you mean. You're right and you're wrong. You seem to forget that I know you better than anyone. I would've supported you, but I wouldn't have let you be weak. I would've pushed you to get through it, to see all the blessings you still have in your life. You don't need to be smothered, you need to be challenged."

Willow shook her head. "I'm so stupid to have thought that you wouldn't understand. Can you forgive me for being such an idiot?"

Ames' smile filled her heart with love and light. "I already have. You know that I can never stay angry with you. You've bewitched me, remember?"

She laughed and hugged him. "I remember." Her eyebrows puckered as she met his gaze again. "Are you certain that you can handle the fact that I will never bear you more children?"

Ames tightened his arms around her. "Willow, we have our two babies to love and if we never have more, I'll truly be content with them. I promise."

Relief brought tears to her eyes. "All right. I believe you."

Ames kissed her softly and let her down. "I'll quickly finish my bath and then we can go see my adorable children."

Once he'd washed and dressed, he took Willow's hand and they set out for the Lakota camp. Smiling down at Willow, Ames tugged on her hand and started running. They laughed together as they raced towards their temporary home so he could be reunited with his babies.

The brightness of the August sun matched the light in their souls that day. Love and forgiveness had conquered anger and pride. It had been a painful lesson to learn, but it was one that they'd never forget.

Epilogue

Two weeks later, Willow and Ames watched Ten Thunders' adoption ceremony. Ames held Mia, who babbled at him nonstop. He whispered to her, trying to quiet her, but he wasn't successful. She had quickly become enamored with Ames and rarely cried when he was around.

Willow smiled as Mia went after Ames' nose and he dodged her chubby little hand. Lucien got a hold on her braid and tugged it hard. She disentangled Lucien's hand and kissed it.

Returning their attention to the ceremony, they chuckled at Ten Thunders. He stood proudly, grinning ear-to-ear as Cricket announced that Ten Thunders was now his brother and officially Kiowa. He bowed down slightly so that Cricket could put the special amulet he'd made around the brave's neck.

Then Green Leaf and Moonbeam stepped forward to also claim Ten Thunders as their family member. Once all of Jacqui's puppies had been weaned, he'd permanently moved into Green Leaf's tipi, no more a nomad, sleeping here and there. It filled him with pride that he had people to call his own and that he would fulfil such an important need within the tribe.

Although it was a small set up, Ten Thunders would be able to repair guns, make arrowheads, and help make jewelry until they could bring back iron next year. This would be a huge boon to their tribe in that they would have superior weapons and valuable products to trade with the neighboring tribes. As the amulet settled against his chest, Ten Thunders had a sense of belonging that he hadn't experienced in a long time.

He and Cricket grinned at each other as they grasped arms at the conclusion of the ceremony. A true brotherhood had formed between them, a bond as strong as the iron that Ten Thunders would one day work with. The only dark spot in Ten Thunders' life was finding out that Three Deer had become betrothed while he'd been away that summer.

But he was putting it behind him because his night with the tavern girl in Grand Forks had shown him that he wasn't in love with Three Deer. If he had been, he'd have been able to refuse the girl's advances. Therefore, it was better that Three Deer had found someone who loved her the way she deserved to be. In the meantime, Cricket would keep praying for him to find his special mate, and Ten Thunders had complete faith in his new brother.

Sleek Doe nudged Growling Wolf's arm. "We have an odd tribe, do we not?"

Growling Wolf answered her smile with his own. "Yes. We have a French fur trapper who has talked us into celebrating Christmas, a man who has been taken captive three times, and Lakota kin."

Sleek Doe took his hand. "And do not forget that we decorate a Christmas tree."

Growling Wolf's grin grew. "And a Christmas play."

"Ames is too charming to resist," Sleek Doe said looking across the clearing to where he stood with Willow and the twins. "As Willow found out."

The elderly chief squeezed her hand a little. "He could not resist her, either. The same way I could not resist my mate all those years ago."

When she looked into Growling Wolf's eyes, Sleek Doe saw only the handsome young brave she'd fallen in love with. "It does not seem so long ago." She dropped her gaze then. "Please do not go away."

Growling Wolf couldn't stand the sadness in her voice and shook her hand a little to coax her into looking at him again. "I think this old man has a few more winters in him yet."

Her beautiful smile still had the power to steal his breath. "I will show you later that we are still young at heart, husband."

His eyes gleamed. "I will not let you forget you said that."

They laughed together as they moved to where the celebratory meal had been set up.

Ames watched Willow sing Lucien to sleep that night. Rippling Grass, Hummingbird, and Spider had come with them for Ten Thunders' ceremony and they were staying in Willow's old tipi, which had been moved close to theirs. Seeing her with their babies was so moving and he loved all of them more with each passing day. They'd seen more than their share of tragedy that past winter. Although it had left scars on their hearts, they also had incredible joy in the form of two adorable children and in each other.

Willow laid Lucien down next to his sister and smiled down at them. She loved watching them and playing with them. They'd also started showing an interest in solid foods and she happily mashed up fruits and vegetables for them, thrilled that she could help feed them now.

It would be several more months before they could be weaned, but Willow was in no hurry for that to happen. She enjoyed her friendship with Rippling Grass and the young widow was often a guest at her and Ames' tipi. They also ate with Sky Dancer and Dark Horse and played games in the evenings.

Back in prime condition, Willow had served on sentry duty a few times at the Lakota camp, but she still enjoyed training the boys. They were a constant source of amusement and helping them master valuable skills gave her a sense of purpose.

She and Soaring Falcon still butted heads, but not quite as bitterly. Secretly, Willow enjoyed their heated exchanges, but she never let on. Soaring Falcon came to see the twins often and she couldn't refuse to let them get to know their great-grandfather.

Willow found it a little daunting that she'd suddenly gained a bunch of aunts, uncles, and cousins.

This further kinship between the two tribes had led Sky Dancer to tease Dark Horse that she wouldn't have had to marry him if they'd known that Willow was Soaring Falcon's granddaughter. This had earned her scowls from both her husband and Willow, which had made Ames laugh.

Willow made sure that Mia and Lucien were truly asleep before going to lay beside Ames on their sleeping pallet. They'd rolled the sides of the tipi up a little to allow the cooler night air to circulate through the dwelling.

"I cannot believe that the summer will be over soon," she said as she rolled over to lay her head on his bare chest.

Ames kissed her forehead and stroked her hair. "I know. This time last year, I was still on my way to you."

His sigh made her raise her head to look at him. "What is it?"

"We will be leaving as soon as the weather breaks in the spring. We are going to trade along the way to The Green Bay so that we do not have so much to slow us down when we come back. It will make the trip East quicker, but it will take us longer to get back," he said.

"If you leave in what you call April, how soon until you will return?"

Ames calculated, allowing for any unforeseen circumstances. "If we pull out of here by the first week in April, we could possibly be back by early July."

"But that depends on the weather."

"Of course. I am wondering if obtaining iron is worth the risk right now," Ames said.

"What do you mean? What risk?"

Ames told her of the increasingly volatile relationships between the other people of the continent and his concern that they might lead people to their camps. "What do you think about it?"

Willow played with his chest hair. "If you think it is too dangerous right now, then I would not chance it. You can get us guns, ammunition, and everything else we need in Grand Forks."

The moonlight coming in the smoke flap illuminated his face enough that she could see his smile. "I was hoping that you would say that. It reinforces what I was thinking. We can keep assessing the situation and decide what to do later. Besides, I do not think I can bear to be away from you and the twins so long."

Willow kissed him. "I feel the same way. Perhaps when they are a little older, it will not be so hard."

They looked at each other for a moment before they both shook with silent laughter.

"*Mon amour*, it will only get harder and harder to be parted from my family, but perhaps in a few years, you could go with me," Ames said.

"I would love to," Willow said. "Then we will both miss them."

"True, but we will make the trip as quickly as possible. But, we are getting ahead of ourselves. We must just enjoy the present." He pulled her down so he could kiss her. "And right now, I want to see how quiet you can be while we make love."

"Are you daring me?"

"Yes."

Willow let him roll her over and looked up at him as he settled on top of her. Stroking his stubble-covered jaw, she said, "I will never try to keep you out of my heart again. I still feel so foolish and guilty about what happened."

Ames said, "So do I. I will never go away with bitter words between us."

"Thank you for loving me so much. I know that no other man could ever love me the way you do."

His expression grew intense. "Do not ever forget that. Ever."

"And no woman will ever love you as much as I do. You captured my heart with your blue eyes and your smile." She grabbed the back of his hair and pulled it. "If I ever catch you with another woman, I will kill both of you."

Although he didn't doubt that, her possessive statement made him smile. "I will never touch another woman. Now shut up and let me love you."

Lightning flashed in the overcast night sky in early November that year. Snow fell heavily on an odd figure in the central fire clearing of the Kiowa village.

"I have heard about it, but I have never seen thunder snow before," Ten Thunders said as he and Cricket sat together under a couple of heavy buffalo robes. "It is beautiful."

Cricket had been praying when the storm had started and the next thing he'd known, Ten Thunders had shown up, crowding his way under the covering.

"I have seen it twice before," Cricket replied.

Thunder growled overhead and Ten Thunders grinned. "That is one."

"Two. We just heard one."

"Oh. Right. Two. Do you think there will be ten?"

Cricket laughed. "I do not know. Would you like me to ask Bison?"

Ten Thunders nudged him with an elbow. "No, but I would like you to ask him for something else."

Cricket laughed. "Let me guess; for a pretty girl."

"Yes, but not right now." His smile dimmed. "I would like you to pray for my white father, that he is well and that I might see him again someday."

"Very well. What is your father's name?"

"Christopher Blake. Maybe if you pray during the thunder snow, your prayer will be even more powerful than usual," Ten Thunders suggested.

The sky lit up, turning the night to day and the wind blew snow into their faces.

"I think Bison just told me no," Ten Thunders remarked wiping moisture from his cheeks.

Cricket grinned as he did the same. "No, I do not think so. Bow your head."

Ten Thunders dropped his chin to his chest as he usually did. Looking over at his brother, Cricket smiled. It always amused him how much confidence Ten Thunders had in his prayers. It both humbled him and made Cricket proud that someone believed in him so much.

Others in the tribe did, but he thought that perhaps Ten Thunders and Moonbeam had the most confidence in him of all. As though he'd conjured her, their sister scared them when she suddenly appeared.

"Moonbeam! What are you doing?" Cricket asked as she burrowed her way under the robes to sit on his lap. "Ow! Watch where you are sitting! This is not proper at all!"

"Hush!" she said, drawing the robes overtop of them again. "I want to hear the thunder snow."

"Cricket is going to pray for me," Ten Thunders told her, unperturbed by her intrusion. "So you have to be quiet."

"All right. Go ahead."

Cricket sighed. "I am not used to praying with someone sitting on me."

"I bet you would not mind Hummingbird sitting in your lap."

Ten Thunders burst out laughing at her remark and Cricket shoved him. He retaliated and Moonbeam scrambled out into the snow. Cricket gained his feet and scooped up some snow. Moonbeam did the same and the three of them had a snowball fight while the thunder snow fell.

They tired as the storm ended and the winter moon shone down on them. Moonbeam stopped and pointed at it. "Does it seem bigger than usual?"

Her brothers came to stand by her and looked at the pale, silver disc in the inky sky.

Ten Thunders nodded. "Yes. What do you think, Cricket?"

Gazing up at the heavenly body that did indeed seem unusually large, Cricket's shoulders prickled with goosebumps and he shivered. "Yes, it is bigger and there is a ring around it."

Moonbeam gasped. "I see it! What does it mean?"

"I do not know," Cricket said and then straightened suddenly.

Moonbeam looked up at him. "Bison is here?"

Ten Thunders looked around, but he didn't see anything of course. Looking at Cricket, he saw that his brother was staring blankly at the moon now. Moonbeam had also noticed.

"What do we do?" she asked. "He could be here for hours. We cannot let him just stand there like that."

Ten Thunders retrieved their abandoned robes and spread one on the ground. "Mighty Bison, let us make him comfortable without disturbing him," he whispered.

Slowly, they drew Cricket down to the robe and then sat down by him. Moonbeam and Ten Thunders drew the other robes overtop of the three of them without obscuring Cricket's view of the moon. Then they fell completely silent and there the three siblings sat while the winter moon told its secrets to a young Kiowa medicine man.

The End

Thank you for reading *Winter Moon.* If you enjoyed this book, you can find excerpts from the others in the series by visiting https://www.facebook.com/PahaSapaBookSeries/. You can also find FREE excerpts from my Chance City Series at https://www.facebook.com/Chance-City-Book-Series-Free-Chapters-352892035583433/

About the Author

Robin Deeter fell in love with the written word the day she picked up "The Black Stallion" by Walter Farley, and that love affair continues to this day. In high school, she realized she could do more than read good stories; she could learn to write them, too. She went on to hone her craft with the Creative Writing Program through Full Sail University.

But her first love was entertaining, so she tried her hand at singing and acting. But Motown and Nashville didn't call, and Hollywood and Broadway ignored her. So, she concentrated her creative juices on writing to entertain others. And she's been writing ever since.

In between writing her historical western and contemporary romance novels, she still pursues her love of music and theatrics with local performances. She currently writes two book series; the Chance City Series and the Paha Sapa Saga. She's also involved in several other multi-author series and has more novel ideas that she's exploring.

If you can't find her writing or performing locally in Pennsylvania, where she resides, you'll catch her sporting the Black and Gold and cheering on her Pittsburgh Steelers. You can find her books on her website www.robindeeter.com. You can also connect with her on Facebook at https://www.facebook.com/authorrobindeeter, and join her exclusive reader group, Deeter Divas at: https://www.facebook.com/groups/DeeterDivas/

This novel is a work of fiction. Names, characters, places, and incidents are either products of the author's imagination or are used fictitiously. Any resemblance to actual events, locales, business establishments, or persons, living or dead, is entirely coincidental.

Dear Reader,

The main reason I write is to entertain my readers, and I hope that you enjoyed *Winter Moon, The Paha Sapa Saga, Book Two*. If you like my work, please share it with others. I would also greatly appreciate it if you would take a few moments to leave a review. They really do matter and I always listen to my readers. Stay tuned for more books in this series and, as always, thank you for reading!

Robin

Made in the USA
Middletown, DE
27 July 2020